Praise for *The Caddie Wh*

"I found myself enchanted by the marvelous purity and smooth narrative swings of *The Caddie Who Knew Ben Hogan,* and must admit to a measure of envy for readers who come to these pages with an enduring passion for the game, the same sweet passion that Coyne's novel seems to have reawakened in me."

—Bob Shacochis, winner of the 1986 National Book Award
for *Easy in the Islands*

"This novel achieves something remarkable: . . . the two fictional marathon golf contests . . . are presented with such narrative skill, such compelling detail, and such evident love of the game, that they are transfixing. John Coyne has managed to employ golf as a lens through which aspects of Midwestern daily life in the 1940s, of thwarted love, of social class, are revealed with stark and unsettling clarity."

—Norman Rush, winner of the National Book Award for *Mating*

"I knew Ben Hogan on the golf course and off. John Coyne has captured the spirit of the man as well as the player himself."

—Jules Alexander, photographer for *The Hogan Mystique*

"A must-read not ju   bout the
game of life."   ssociation

"John Coyne know   who loves
golf—and many   on from a
free-throw—will   drawn into
this fine story."   *g with God*

DATE DUE

THE CADDIE WHO KNEW BEN HOGAN

JOHN COYNE

THOMAS DUNNE BOOKS

ST. MARTIN'S GRIFFIN ⚐ NEW YORK

THOMAS DUNNE BOOKS.
An imprint of St. Martin's Press.

www.thomasdunnebooks.com
www.stmartins.com

Library of Congress Cataloging-in-Publication Data

Coyne, John.
    The caddie who knew Ben Hogan / John Coyne.
        p. cm.
    ISBN-13: 978-0-312-37125-8
    ISBN-10: 0-312-37125-X
    1. Hogan, Ben, 1912–1997.—Fiction.   2. Golf stories.   3. Caddies.—
Fiction.   I. Title.

PS3553.O96 C33 2006
713'.54—dc22

                                                    2006040164

First St. Martin's Griffin Edition: May 2007

10   9   8   7   6   5   4   3   2   1

For my brothers, Tom and Jim . . .
legendary caddies at Midlothian Country Club

ACKNOWLEDGMENTS

On any given day on any given golf course in America, there is a good chance some golfer is telling a Ben Hogan story. Tales of Hogan have been told and retold, passed along from fathers to sons, from one player to another, as they all marvel at and remember a man who defined everything that was great and good about professional golf in the twentieth century.

Jack Nicklaus summed it up when he said, "Nobody was like Hogan." Jimmy Demaret, Hogan's friend on the early PGA tour, believed that what set Hogan apart from the other pros was his determination to win, his intense concentration on the course, and his incredible shotmaking skills. In two decades of tournament play Hogan won sixty-four times, including nine major championships. He dominated the world of golf in the way Tiger Woods dominates it today. But Hogan was more than a great golfer; he was, in the words of James Dodson, one of his biographers, "one of golf's most enigmatic legends."

During his long career, Hogan presented different faces to his family and friends, the PGA competition, and the public. One way he often played with his identity was to jokingly introduce himself as Henny Bogan.

Coming of age as a caddie in the Midwest when Hogan was in his prime, I made him my hero and followed his career in the same way other kids religiously tracked baseball players' batting averages.

Over the years, I've read all the Hogan books, beginning with the one he wrote himself, *Power Golf,* first published in 1948. Most recently I read *Ben Hogan: An American Life,* by James Dodson, and *Afternoons with Mr. Hogan,* by Jody Vasquez, both published in 2004. Between these hardbacks are Hogan's most important instructional book, *Five Lessons,* written with Herbert Warren Wind (1957); Gene Gregston's *Hogan: The Man Who Played for Glory* (1978); *The Hogan Mystique,* by Martin Davis, et al. (1994); *Hogan* by Curt Sampson (1996); *Ben Hogan's "Secret": A Fictionalized Biography,* by Bob Thomas (1997); Mike Towle's *I Remember Ben Hogan* (2000); and *Ben Hogan: The Man Behind the Mystique,* edited by Martin Davis (2002).

All of these books have proven invaluable in my research for this novel. As a novelist, I wanted to write about the real Hogan in a fictional setting, staying true to the man's personality while creating an entertaining and suspenseful story. I hope that I have been successful.

In the course of my writing, a number of friends were kind enough to read drafts of the manuscript and contribute suggestions and clarifications. I am deeply appreciative of their help and would like to especially thank my old college buddy Michael McNulty, as well as Nancy Reeves, both of Tulsa, Oklahoma. Many thanks also to the great golf photographer and Hogan aficionado Jules Alexander. At the United States Golf Association, where they keep alive the history of Hogan and all great golfers, amateurs as well as professionals, Patty Moran and Rand Jerris filled in many missing historical facts on Hogan and his era.

Most important, however, was my brother, Tom Coyne, also a former caddie, who read and fact-checked the manuscript and interviewed on my behalf a good friend of ours, PGA professional Tony Holquin, who played with Hogan in the 1940s and had his own distinguished PGA career as tour player and teaching professional at Midlothian Country Club and Balmoral Woods Country Club, both in Illinois.

For their editing of the manuscript, I'd like to thank my friend and literary agent, John Silbersack; my editor at St. Martin's Press/Thomas Dunne Books, Peter Wolverton, and Peter's talented editorial assistant, Katie Gilligan; and, as always, my wife and "in-house editor," Judy Coyne, who for my sake took a deep dive into a sport she has tried—and failed—to enjoy.

People are always wondering who's better, Hogan or Nicklaus. Well, I've seen Jack Nicklaus watch Ben practice, but I've never seen Ben watch anyone else practice. What's that tell you?

—Tommy Bolt,
1958 U.S. Open Champion

The Caddie Who
Knew Ben Hogan

1

MEMORIES ARE MAGIC. OUR LIVES COME BACK TO US WITH THE edges smoothed out, those long-ago days all sunny and bright with southern breezes and sapphire skies, and we hardly notice the dark and threatening clouds that frame the picture.

I state that now—at the very beginning of my afternoon talk—as a cautionary comment. I have been kindly asked by your anniversary committee chairman, Dr. Hughes—and thank you, Doug, for inviting me—to recall when the Chicago Open was played at this course, an anniversary you can surely be proud of. I once heard a pro say his club had no history because Ben Hogan never played there. By that standard, your club is rich in history, for Ben Hogan played here in the summer of 1946.

Yesterday, when I first arrived, I walked out onto the first tee and was thrilled to see your golf course again, so much more majestic and manicured than I recalled from my caddie days. I congratulate you on your success in keeping this grand clubhouse, indeed all the grounds, the tennis courts, the lawns and fields, in such wonderful condition. You honor your past by preserving it with such loving care.

My new book is entitled *Ben Hogan's Lesson*. But it's not a fan's memoir. Nor is it an academic treatise, even though I was a college professor and I have done a great deal of research on the history of golf. This book is my attempt to tell the truth of what occurred in '46 at this historic Chicago Open, filled as it was with tension and drama, brilliant golf, and a terrible tragedy.

When I reviewed the program for this weekend, I realized something: Of all of us, I am the only one who was actually at the club that year. Dr. Hughes, and you can correct me, Doug, began caddying a year later. True, I was only fourteen in 1946, but it was an important time in my life. A few months earlier my father had been killed serving with the army in Europe, and I felt adrift in the world. It was Hogan who got me back on course. What he taught me became the touchstone for how I would live my life.

And that is the story I will tell you this afternoon.

My tale begins, however, not with Hogan, but with someone you've probably never heard of: Matt Richardson, a name not mentioned, I see, in the program of anniversary events, even though he played an important part in Ben Hogan's time at this country club.

Matt came from Gatesburg, Illinois. He was nineteen or twenty, a tall, gangly, handsome guy with thick blond hair, cut short in the style of the day, bright blue eyes, and the shy and serious manner of a small-town boy from southern Illinois. A high school graduate, he had been drafted in '44, and after V-E Day he was discharged and played briefly on the winter tour before coming here to the country club early that spring to become our assistant pro.

Everyone at the club adored Matt: young girls, wives, mothers, men and women, and caddies like myself.

Matt had this incredible ability to lift our spirits. He'd say hello and you'd feel as if you were the most important person in his life. And he didn't do it on purpose, to manipulate you. He never wanted anything from anyone. That was his gift, and his great charm.

He also had another rare gift: a velvety, natural swing. Anyone who follows golf knows there are two kinds of players: shotmakers and ballstrikers. In his day, Ben Hogan was both. And so was Matt Richardson. He hit a golf ball in ways none of us had ever seen, with a long, loose, perfectly cadenced stroke.

The balls Matt hit flew off the club face and rose effortlessly into the sky. One thought at first they might never return, and then, far up against the sky, the small white ball would appear to pause and drift slowly downward, ever so slowly, riding the breeze to land with the gentleness of a gesture, the softness of an open hand of greeting.

The year Matt arrived at your club Ben Hogan and sixty other touring professionals came to play in the Chicago Open. And one more person came—a girl named Sarah DuPree.

Sarah was the only child of Dr. Henry DuPree, president of the club, and that June she returned from Smith College to her parents' stone and stucco mansion—which I see is still there today, across from the tenth fairway.

Sarah grew up alongside the course, but she never paid attention to golf until that summer. I saw her the first time she came out to play, after six o'clock on a warm Sunday evening in early June. She drove her convertible over from her parents' house, under the shadows of those ancient American elms that once graced the main entrance, and parked in the lot below the pro shop. She lifted a baby blue golf bag from the car and swung it onto her shoulder as if she were a caddie herself, then walked up the shady gravel path to the first tee as if she had been playing all her life.

She was wearing gray FootJoy shoes, a gray pleated skirt, and a white blouse. In her bag were Patty Berg signature woods and a new set of women's irons by Wilson. In front of the pro shop, she raised her chin and glanced around, her blond, cornsilk hair swinging in the sunlight. At that moment she was the most beautiful woman I'd ever seen.

I was a half-dozen yards away, waiting on the caddie bench with Matt's bag. Like other local pros, Matt had to qualify for the Open, and we had started to play a quick nine holes late in the day when the course was empty in preparation for the tournament.

Watching Sarah, I knew she didn't know where to go or what to do, and I vaulted the iron railing on which we stacked our players' bags and walked around the back edge of the tee box as if I were on my way to do something important.

"Hi!" she called as I passed.

I slowed, trying to appear as if I hadn't actually been aware of her.

"Do you know where I can learn golfing?"

I smiled at her terminology and asked, "Are you looking for a game or a lesson?"

She frowned; apparently this was too tough a question. "I want to hit golf balls. My dad said I should practice golfing."

I gestured toward the range beyond the ninth green. "You can hit balls down there."

She shielded her eyes against the sun and stared toward where I was pointing, but it was clear she had no idea what I was talking about.

"You have practice balls?" I asked, knowing she didn't.

She shook her head.

"You can get some from the assistant pro." I nodded toward the pro shop.

As I spoke, Matt came out the door of the pro shop located under the men's locker room and up the steps, moving so fast his metal spikes on the concrete sounded as if he were tap dancing.

"That's him," I said. But as I came to learn, she knew exactly who Matt was.

He started toward me, his spikes crunching on the gravel, and then he looked up and saw Sarah DuPree. He slowed, and one of his famous smiles developed on his face.

"She wants to hit balls," I announced.

He didn't take his eyes off Sarah, and I saw she was smiling back, all of her earlier nervousness vanished.

I started to say something more and stopped. The two of them had dismissed me.

"Hi," Matt said. "May I help you with something?"

He took another step closer and she disappeared in his shadow.

"I want to learn golfing," Sarah answered softly.

"I can't give you a lesson now," he answered apologetically. "I've got a game." He glanced at me, as if I were responsible for this problem.

"Oh, I'm sorry. I guess I should've made an appointment." She seemed almost embarrassed to discover Matt wasn't necessarily at her beck and call.

"It's okay." He smiled quickly. "Listen, this is what we'll do. I'll get you a shag boy and some practice balls and you go down to the range and hit a few." He nodded toward me. "Jack and I . . . we'll play a quick nine, and when I finish up I'll come over and work with you." Matt turned to me. "Get a kid, Jack."

He smiled again at Sarah, letting his full attention sweep over her like a summer breeze. I ran off to get the practice balls, and by the time I lined up Kenny Burke's kid brother to be the shag boy, Matt and Sarah were standing together at the top of the eighteenth green.

She was perched on one foot, pelicanlike, with her long, tanned bare arms crossed at her waist and her head tilted back so she could look up at him. Already I knew, though I am sure I wouldn't have known how to put it into words, that she was standing too close to him, too close for the assistant pro and the daughter of the club president.

On the tee, I propped Matt's bag on its wide round bottom. From the deep zipped pockets I pulled out everything he needed to play: some tees, his glove, a couple of MacGregor balls. I took the leather hood off his driver and leaned against it while Matt and Sarah kept talking as if they had all the time in the world.

Finally he sent her toward the practice range and hurried over to me, ready to tee off. I tossed him a ball and handed him the driver. He was moving quickly as if he owned the tee, owned the golf course, owned all of us, and in many ways that summer, Matt Richardson did.

. . .

I loved to watch Matt hit his woods. And I wasn't the only one. Club members would pause in the middle of their own games to watch him tee off and marvel at the power he could generate from what we called his butter-greased swing.

As always, the ball exploded off his club face and rode the soft wind to disappear beyond the sloping fairway and run a dozen yards farther, leaving him a short iron to the green.

Swinging Matt's bag onto my shoulder, I was down off the tee before he caught up and handed me his driver.

"Wow, some girl, huh? You been hiding her from me, Jackson?" He clipped the back of my head with his open palm, still grinning, happy with himself, happy at having pounded a 260-yard drive down the center of the fairway on the par-4 first hole.

"You know her old man is Dr. DuPree?" I said and stepped away so he couldn't clip my head again.

"So . . . ?"

"Dr. DuPree isn't going to let his daughter hang out with the hired help."

"I'm the golf pro!"

"You're an assistant pro."

"I'm the best player in Chicago."

"That doesn't mean squat to DuPree."

We had reached his ball, and Matt took in the lie and then reached into the bag and pulled out the 9-iron.

"Not enough," I told him.

He was standing behind the ball, staring up at the green and swinging the club loosely in his hand, as if he were a gunslinger looking for trouble.

Although we didn't term it that at the time, his preshot routine was to stand directly behind the ball and stare down the target line, visualizing how he wanted the ball to play. While he studied the shot, he took two or three easy practice swings to find his rhythm. It was his way of getting his focus and relieving any tension.

Only after he had decided on the ball's flight would he step up and play the shot. He never took any practice swings without a purpose, and in this way he predated Tiger Woods's preshot routine. Tiger, I read recently, says his routine is to take a couple of practice swings just to reinforce the mechanics of the swing he wants to make, to restore in his muscle memory the results of having hit hundreds of practice balls.

We, of course, were playing years before Nicklaus and Tiger, and for that matter Arnold Palmer, but Matt had their same rage to win, and now I had challenged him about the club selection and he was going to prove me wrong.

It was a lesson I had learned early about Matt: He always took a challenge without thinking about the consequences. It made him an exciting player to watch, but some days out on the course, he drove himself right into trouble. He wasn't like some pros you see on television today who find themselves in contention and the air starts leaking out of their game, one hole at a time. Not Matt. He'd just self-destruct all at once, as if a hand grenade had blown up on the fairway.

"I'll knock down the flag," he told me, addressing the ball. He set his right foot first, then his left, and took another quick glance at the green, a final look down at the ball. Then a long pause as he refocused his attention on the task at hand. It was a routine I knew by heart.

His swing was as casual as his stride, and he cut a thick wedge of turf from the fairway playing the shot. I dropped his bag and walked ten yards up to retrieve the divot as I watched the ball in flight. I knew when he hit the 9 that he didn't have enough club.

It was a pretty iron. We watched it float against the blue sky of the late afternoon.

"Dead perfect!" he declared.

"Not enough," I answered. The ball caught the front lip of the bunker and bounced into the sand.

Behind me Matt swore and thumped the flange of the iron against the turf.

Walking back, I tossed him another ball and said, "Hit the eight and let it work toward the flag; you know how the green slopes." I pulled the club from the bag.

Matt took the 8 without objecting, but I knew he was hoping I was wrong. He set up to play the ball to the right of the flag and hit the iron with the same pure sweet motion, and it landed ten to twelve feet beyond the hole but with enough spin that it took the natural slope and came down toward the cup, disappearing from sight beyond the lip of the bunker. My guess was that the ball would be less than three feet from the pin.

Matt tossed me the iron, grinning as he did, and swearing at me, too. He was pleased by the shot, and also, I let myself think, pleased that I knew his game and would be caddying for him in the Open.

He made the short putt, and he kept up his good mood as we walked over to the par-3 number two. I swung the bag off my shoulder and he stepped up to the tee, pulling on his glove as he looked at me.

"Okay, what do I play?" he asked.

"There's wind." I nodded toward the patch of tall oaks circling the club's small reservoir to the left of the hole. From the tee, we could see the treetops swaying in the late-afternoon breeze, and we both knew that while we couldn't feel it, down by the green the wind was strong enough to blow a long iron a dozen yards off line.

"Hit a soft five," I said.

"Give me the six."

"Not enough club."

"I'm going to hit it in low and let it run," he explained.

I pulled the 5-iron from the bag. "Hit the five," I repeated.

He took the club and, grinning, said confidently, "You may know how to club me, Jackson, but you don't know how to charm women."

"It's not her you have to charm," I told him.

"Old Man DuPree doesn't know who he's dealing with."

I didn't need to say it again. Matt was an assistant pro, making fifty dollars a week. My big sister, Kathy, who waitressed at the club, had it right: No matter how often a member smiles at you, you're still just the hired help.

Matt nodded toward the distant flag stick. "Go pull the stick, Jack. I'm going to knock this sucker in."

And he almost did.

He let the iron work with the wind and the ball landed short of the green, on the left-side apron, and rolled up to within four feet of the flagstick.

I was off the tee while the ball was still in the air. I could hear Matt behind me. I heard the swish of his trousers as he walked, his footsteps heavy on the hard turf, and then I heard him exclaim in a voice that was both amused and startled, "Oh, my God!"

I glanced around and he nodded toward the practice range on the far side of the first fairway. There was Sarah DuPree. She was alone on the tee, hitting balls out to Kenny Burke's little brother—but she wasn't so much hitting as flailing at them with the most god-awful swing one could imagine. It was mortifying. I was offended by her, as anyone might have been who loved the game.

"Isn't she something!" Matt exclaimed. "Here!" He handed me the 5-iron. "Go pick up my ball and take the clubs back to the shop." Already he was cutting across the rough, heading for the girl.

"Hey! You've got to practice!"

"Later," he said without looking back.

"Later will be dark."

"Tomorrow morning. Be here by six; we'll play before breakfast." His voice faded into the warm evening as he reached the first fairway and went toward Dr. DuPree's daughter like a clothesline drive, low and hard and bullet-straight.

At the clubhouse, I went to the back of the pro shop and cleaned the few irons Matt had used, dumping the heads into a bucket of sudsy water; wiped the clubs dry; and stacked his bag in his locker at the rear of the shop. Then I walked out to the starter's tent at the side of the first tee, where the players coming off the eighteenth green could pause in the shade, sit down, and fill out their cards before their scores were posted on the large white sheets.

The scores were still up from the day's play, and it was Matt's job to take them down and call the *Chicago Tribune* so the next day members who had won the weekend events could read their names in small print in the sports pages.

But he hadn't called the *Trib*. He was still out on the practice tee with Sarah DuPree, though now *he* was hitting balls to Kenny Burke's little brother.

Matt was showing off, hitting soft wedges, high floaters that drifted out to the caddie. Burke's brother had set down the shag bag, and Matt was dropping his chips within inches of the target. Some landed close enough to bounce into the open bag.

He was trying to impress Sarah, but the truth was she didn't know how great Matt's short game was. She didn't know there weren't a hundred pros in the country who could make a golf ball dance that way.

I sat up on the back of a bench and watched Matt hit the wedges. It was a special, quiet time of the day when the course heaved out the heat of the afternoon and a cool breeze for evening picked up to fan the members sitting on the open terrace.

Half a dozen members had come out to enjoy the view and to watch Matt. The only sounds were an occasional brief burst of laughter from one of the women, the click of glass touching metal tables, and the soft thumping of a screen door as my sister, Kathy, waiting tables on the terrace, came and went from the bar.

Spotting me down on the bench, Kathy gestured that I should be heading home. I nodded but didn't move. Since our dad died, she was always watching out for me, checking to see where I was and what I was doing. It was annoying at times, but also kind of nice, knowing she was around the club in case I needed her.

As I sat in the shadows of the starter's tent, more members arrived for the customary Sunday evening dinner, the women in heels and bright short-sleeved dresses, the men in vivid sports jackets and white shoes, all of which, aren't we happy to see today, have gone forever out of style.

Remembering times like this, hearing again the laughter and the tinkling of glasses after the nightmare of the war we had survived and won, we all thought—I certainly did—that everything was going to be all right for all of us and for all time.

2

I WAS STILL SITTING ON THE BENCH WHEN BEHIND ME I HEARD A rush of footsteps on the gravel path. I glanced around to see Dr. DuPree coming toward me through the rapidly fading light. He was a square block of man, with the same sort of raw-looking flesh you might have found on a slab of beef downtown in the old Chicago Union stockyards. His thin silvery hair was slicked straight back on his round head, and there was a film of sweat on his cheeks.

"Is my daughter on the range, Jack?" he demanded, panting from his rushing.

"Yes, sir." I was on my feet. "She's taking a lesson."

"Get her. Her mother's waiting supper." He bit into his lower lip, which he always did on the course when he misplayed a shot.

I was off and running to deliver his message before he could bark another order. Still, from behind he shouted after me, "And tell her if she wants golf lessons, take them from the pro, not that kid."

I kept running, cutting between the eighteenth and ninth greens on a narrow strip of apron, then jogged another hundred yards to Matt and Sarah. Neither one was hitting balls. Matt was standing casually, his wedge braced against his thigh. Sarah was gazing up at him like he was the sun and moon and everything else.

But there wasn't any sun or moon. There was just the two of them silhouetted against a stretch of poplar trees that edged the left side of the range. The lesson had gotten them beyond introductions and the small talk of golf instruction—how Sarah needed to keep her head down and her left arm straight and shift her weight and make a good turn on her follow-through. By now they were on to personal histories, and she was quizzing him, I'm sure, about where he was from and what he wanted to do with his life, and did he, by any chance, have a girlfriend back in his hometown.

"Oh, God!" Sarah exclaimed when I delivered her father's message. "Already!" Her eyes went dark and her wide lips slipped into a pout. Hurriedly she began to gather up her clubs, but Matt stopped her and turned to me.

"Take her bag up to the shop, Jack, and clean her clubs." He looked at her and asked, "Is that okay, Sarah?"

When he said her name his voice softened, and I caught a glimpse of sweet surprise on her face. I guess this was the first time he had addressed her that way, for her face flushed and she nodded, thrilled to hear him speak her name.

They walked off together, moving slowly up to the clubhouse as if they didn't want their walk to end. They crossed the eighteenth fairway and circled the green, walking by the screened porch of the summer dining hall and the open terrace filled with members and their guests.

Everyone could see them, though it was all natural and innocent enough, the young assistant pro finishing up a lesson with a member's daughter. It was always good to see young people learning the game, so the members might think, if they thought about it at all.

I suspect some of the members' wives noticed them and drew other conclusions, as women will.

Still, if you put all of that aside, what you saw in the fading sunlight was the lovely tableau of two young, good-looking kids walking together in deep conversation, the sun framing them in profiles, casting their shadows in long, thin finger shapes down the length of the golf course's green and manicured final fairway.

Matt called in the scores to the *Trib,* and we locked up the pro shop and went upstairs through the men's locker room. Matt always said good night there and headed up to his room on the third floor of the clubhouse, and I'd go home, walking across the empty course.

That night when we locked up, Matt asked if I wanted a ride home. He felt like going for a drive, he said.

I was always ready for a car ride, especially since Matt sometimes let me drive on the back roads.

"Where does Sarah live?" he asked as soon as he turned his Chevy out onto the country club drive.

"You don't know their house?" As a kid you always assumed adults knew everything, but Matt didn't know where Dr. and Mrs. DuPree lived, just as he didn't know it was impossible for him to date their daughter.

The DuPree home was 280 yards down the right side of the tenth fairway, on what once we called Cottage Row Drive for those of you here today who are new to the club. The house has a giant boulder as an accent mark on the front lawn. I pointed it out to Matt as we went slowly down the road, and told him what members lived in the other mansions that had been built at the turn of the century when the country club was founded by rich Chicagoans. He didn't seem at all interested. It was something I was beginning to learn about Matt: Wealth didn't impress him.

At the time Cottage Row Drive ended at Jim Thompson's mansion behind the tenth green, though I see the drive has now been extended so it goes all the way out to the highway, and there are new homes along the length of the eleventh hole.

But on that long-ago evening we stopped at the Thompsons' drive and turned around. As we came back toward the clubhouse, Matt pulled a folded piece of paper from his pocket and said, "Jack, when we get to the DuPrees', run this note up and drop it off. There's one of those pots—'urns,' Sarah called them—on the terrace by the glass doors. Drop the note into it."

"Drop your own goddamn note into the pot," I told him.

He whacked me on the arm and said beseechingly, "Come on, Jack!"

"Do it yourself." I gestured toward the house. "There's no one home. They're having dinner at the club."

"Seeing some caddie doesn't attract anyone's attention. People know me." He grinned like it was all a game.

"I'm not some caddie!"

It was a second before he answered slowly, "I know you're not *some* caddie. But you are someone I can trust."

I knew he meant it. I reached over and grabbed the note, then jumped from the car and ran up the drive to the terrace. I dropped the folded piece of paper inside the urn and ran down-hill to the Chevy.

He shifted into first, gunned the engine, and we were gone.

We were almost to my house before I told Matt why I was so sure Sarah's old man wasn't going to let his daughter date him. I had caddied for Dr. DuPree dozens of times since I started looping at the club when I was twelve. I had heard him bragging to the other members how he had sent his daughter back East to Smith College. You marry the people you meet in college, he always said, and the best people go to Ivy League colleges.

At the driveway of our farm, Matt cut the Chevy's engine and looked at me. "Sarah said maybe we should keep our dating between ourselves," he admitted.

I shrugged and kept staring ahead, down the drive to where it circled the big oak in front of the double doors of the red barn. The cows were in the small pen beside the barn, already milked by Mom and let out for the night.

"You think I'm not good enough to date a member's daughter?" he asked.

"It ain't what *I* think," I told him. I said I thought he was the best damn player I'd ever seen. "But you got to know, Matt, playing scratch golf doesn't mean squat to rich people, not when they're away from the club."

"There's where you're wrong, Jackson." Matt reached over and jerked down the bill of my cap. "Wait till the Open. Wait till I beat Hogan and Nelson and Snead and all those other goddam pros."

He was okay. I heard the sureness in his voice, felt the warmth in his big smile. As always, he made me feel better.

Outside the Chevy, I could see my mom coming up from the cow barn. She was carrying two pails of steaming warm milk and struggling with the weight. "Gotta go," I told him.

"I'm counting on you, Jack. I need you if I'm going to win," he called after me.

I grinned and flashed Churchill's victory gesture, thrilled that I was important to him, that I would be caddying in the Chicago Open, and I ran down the farm drive to help my mom carry the milk pails up to the house.

3

DO YOU REMEMBER THE MOVIE *THE GO-BETWEEN*, ABOUT A BOY who carries love notes between the aristocrat Julie Christie and the farmer Alan Bates? In June I became Matt's and Sarah's go-between, ferrying notes from the clubhouse to her home, dropping slips of paper into the large urn on the terrace, or seeking Sarah out in the clubhouse or by the pool and handing her a folded note as if it were a message from her parents.

Then one afternoon, a few weeks after they first met, I was crossing the parking lot, heading for the pro shop, when Sarah came driving by and stopped her convertible to wave me over.

"Jack, would you give this to Matt, please?" Handing me a note, she smiled sweetly, whispered, "Thank you," and sped off. As I walked up the shaded path between the parking lot and the starter's tent, I flipped it open. Her message was simple and clever. All it said was: 7/10.

Matt glanced at the note, then folded it away without comment. I went over to the table where the players sat to sign their scorecards and busied myself with straightening the pencils. Out of the corner of my eye, I caught Matt glance again at the note and smile.

I asked him if we were playing later.

"Sure, why not!" He was on his feet and stretching, eager for the afternoon of work to be over. "Hey, Jackson," he said, "I need you to do me a favor."

He picked up a scorecard and stared at it, then carefully, as if he were putting down his score, marked a 7 for the tenth hole.

"Here, drop this off in that urn thing." He handed me the scorecard.

"Now?"

"Yep, now."

I was, as kids now might say, "out of there," crossing the front of the clubhouse, walking toward the tenth tee, then along the right rough of the fairway toward the DuPrees' house.

At the time, there was a small rock wall marking the out-of-bounds, which I hopped over, crossed the narrow tarmac drive, and stopped in the shade of the elms fronting the lawn to make my plan. I'd go ring the doorbell first in case anyone spotted me from inside the house, and if the maid answered, or Mrs. DuPree, I'd give her the card and say it was for Sarah, a note about her golf lesson. If no one was home, I'd drop the note in the urn.

I jogged up the driveway and onto the front terrace, rang the bell, and listened to the chime echoing through the big house. I waited another minute, then walked to the urn and flipped the scorecard into it. I was about to make my getaway when Sarah's mother stopped me.

"Jack!"

She had the voice of a nun, a voice that could pin a student against the back wall of a classroom.

I turned and found her watching me. She had obviously been sunbathing by the pool behind the house. She was wearing a swimsuit, with a loose robe pulled around her small, slight frame, and an elaborate hat, I later learned, meant to protect her bleached-blond hair. In one hand she carried a tall drink and a lit cigarette.

"What are you doing, Jack?" she asked, smiling, but also gazing at me steadily.

I shrugged, and mumbled I had a message for Sarah about her golf lesson.

Mrs. DuPree eyed me a bit longer, then stepped over to the urn, reached down, and pulled the scorecard from the dark hole.

"Is this the note you were giving Sarah?" she asked quietly, turning the scorecard in her fingers.

"Yes, ma'am."

"What does it mean?"

I shrugged.

"Who gave it to you?" When I hesitated, she asked, "Matt?"

I nodded and she tucked the note into her pocket and tightened the robe around her waist, doing it all with one hand while she held her drink and cigarette in the other.

"Thank you, Jack. I'll tell her." I turned to go, but she said my name again. "Jack . . ." She paused, tapping the long ash of her cigarette into a row of flowers that edged the red brick terrace. Then she continued, "Jack, my husband and I would be most appreciative of your help." She looked down at me, raising her pencil-thin eyebrows. Her eyes were glassy from an afternoon of drinking. "Is my daughter bothering that golf pro?"

I nervously tugged my cap, mumbling how I didn't know anything.

"Don't lie to me, Jack. You know everything about *all* the members. Is my daughter hanging around that young pro?"

"She's taking lessons," I answered, as if trying to be helpful.

Mrs. DuPree tossed the lit cigarette into the flowerbed and exhaled a storm cloud, saying in the hard, edgy voice of heavy smokers, "If you know what is good for you, Jack, you'll make sure Dr. DuPree knows when the two of them are sneaking off."

Then she pointed toward the urn with an accusing forefinger.

"And don't let me catch you on this terrace again leaving his little notes for my daughter!"

With that, she crossed the brick terrace, opened a French door, and disappeared into the house.

I waited until the glass doors clicked shut, then I ran down the lawn, hopped the stone fence, and headed away from the DuPree house, back to the first tee as fast as I could.

When Matt went out to play later, he said he wanted to start on the back side, and we hadn't even reached his fairway drive on ten when I spotted Sarah waiting for us up by the green. I asked him what time it was and he said it was a little after seven.

On the tenth hole we had decided Matt should always drive on the right side of the fairway because the ground there was higher and drained first, and a ball hitting that patch of fairway, some 260 yards from the tee, would get a good bounce off the hard ground, and could run another 20 yards.

The trouble about ten, however, was the overhanging branches of a giant elm tree guarding the green, blocking any second shots coming in from the right side.

Now Doug tells me the old tree is gone, victim of the American elm disease that ravaged this course and all of the Midwest in the early 1960s, and the hole today is much more accessible from the right side. That's good, I guess—but the giant elm did make ten a difficult and interesting hole.

In the 1940s, when the cup was cut on the upper level of the two-tier green, Matt would play his second shot over the top of the hanging branches, letting it flop down and hold. And this was years before Phil Mickelson made his lob wedges famous on television.

Here's how Matt did it.

Early in the spring, when Matt first came to the club, he spent a lot of time on those cold, rainy days of May in the back of the pro shop, working on his sand wedge, giving it a sixty-degree angle before anyone else had thought of manufacturing a club with so much loft. Then he welded metal to the base of the club so it had a wider flange and would slip smoothly under the ball when he played the shot. When using the wedge, Matt opened his stance, spread his feet shoulder-wide, and played the ball forward. As he played the shot, he brought his arms and club back together and took a full turn. On the downswing he led with his legs and kept the face of the wedge open. With this setup, and this club, the ball would shoot almost straight up, carry over the high branches, and drop down vertically. The shot was a thing of beauty.

I'm not sure if many of you know, but the sand-wedge we had in the 1940s, the forerunner of the pitching, sand, and lob, all those fancy hybrid wedges we have today, was invented by a man named Eugenio Saraceni. I can see from your faces that many of you are not familiar with the name. You think it sounds like someone who'd play the violin, not golf.

Well, Eugenio Saraceni, the son of an Italian immigrant in Westchester County, New York, thought so as well, and he changed his name when he saw it in the newspaper for the first time, after he made a hole-in-one during a caddie tournament. Gene Sarazen, Eugenio Saraceni thought, sounded more like a golfer.

Gene Sarazen won the New Orleans Open, the U.S. Open, and the PGA Championship when he was only twenty. A year later, in 1923, he won the PGA again. But for a decade he didn't win another major, and it was because he couldn't get out of bunkers.

Then Gene happens to go flying with Howard Hughes—remember him? You've all seen the movie about Hughes, I'm sure. Sarazen saw how the tail fins of Hughes's plane operated on takeoff, and got the idea that if he could lower the sole of his niblick—what we then called a 9-iron—it would give him more loft. He soldered a thick flange on the back of the club and angled it so the flange hit the sand first, allowing the front of the club to bounce upward.

What Matt did was to take Sarazen's idea about the wedge and give himself more loft, create, really, the first lob wedge. The rest, as they say, is history.

Matt made his shot with his makeshift lob wedge, and Sarah cheered. He tipped his hat to her and grinned, then tossed me his club. As I recall, it was the first time I was jealous of her, and how she had suddenly captured all of Matt's attention that summer.

Sarah tagged after us as we played eleven and twelve onto the long par-5 thirteenth, which was across the two-lane country road from our farm.

Does the thirteenth still have the low mound crossing the fairway a hundred yards off the tee? In my day the mound was the width of the fairway and had the initials of this club cut into the side. We called thirteen the signature hole not for its beauty but for those initials. I see from your faces it is no longer there. For those of you who don't know, that sort of obstruction comes from the early days, when American clubs were imitating Scottish links.

It was part of the penal school of golf architecture, where novel approaches were tried on courses. This mound crossing thirteen had no purpose except to stop the drives of players who couldn't hit a ball at least a hundred yards. There were other geometric designs on this course in those years. I remember a coffin-shaped bunker on nine. Is it still there? And, as I recall, a bunker on four shaped like a heart, for Sir Walter Scott's novel *The Heart of Midlothian*. These unique bunkers came over from Scotland with the pros who immigrated to America during the early twentieth century to teach us how to play, and on their days off designed the first golf courses in the United States.

The mound, of course, was no trouble for Matt. He hit a high draw that worked its way down the right side of the fairway and landed safe. I took off after it, circling the right side of the signature mound, but when I turned around to say something to Matt about his drive, I saw he and Sarah had gone the other way, around the left side of the mound, and were walking with their heads bent together in conversation on the far side of the fairway and away from me.

That annoyed me unreasonably, and I charged ahead to his drive and waited until they finally ambled up to his ball.

"Go for it," I told Matt when he arrived.

He took in the lie and glanced up at the corner of the dogleg. He could make the green if he caught the ball flush and landed it between the two front bunkers framing the small green.

"Okay," he said, taking the challenge and also, I'm sure, trying to show off to Sarah.

He still had his driver and the ball was sitting up, and I moved the bag away while he stood behind the ball, swinging the club loosely, looking at the ball, tracking its flight around the edge of the dogleg.

Matt would hit another draw, fly it past the corner, and bend it enough to land in front of the green and run up the narrow entrance onto the putting surface.

We didn't have any of those fusion drivers at the time with movable weights and 10.5 degrees of loft, or even a hybrid recovery club to hit out of a tight lie. Matt just carefully fit his small driver head behind the ball, touching the ground softly so as not to disturb it, and to make sure he could get the full face of the wood on the ball. Sarah moved away and stood behind me as if she needed to protect herself from his swing.

Matt slowly coiled his long fingers around the grip, worked them into his interlocking grip, and planted his right foot and then his left, giving himself a slightly closed stance to help the draw. Everything got real quiet out there at the far corner of the course. Behind me, Sarah took quick, soft little breaths. I could hear Matt's heavy golf shoes moving slightly, gripping the hard ground as he maneuvered the driver into position.

Matt didn't change his rhythm or tempo playing the 1-wood from the tight lie. All he did was widen his stance and, with his smooth, sweet swing, hit the fairway ball as cleanly and powerfully as if he were driving off a long tee.

The shot shaped itself around the end of the dogleg, carried to within thirty yards of the green, landed hard, and ran straight up the slot between the two bunkers guarding the entrance. From where we stood, I saw Matt had less than a thirty-foot putt for an eagle.

"How's that one, Jackson?" Matt tossed off, tapping down the turf he had torn up, and handed me the driver. He kept smiling as Sarah applauded the shot and beamed at Matt.

"Okay, let's eagle this one," I declared, swinging his bag onto my shoulder and striding toward the green, but neither of them was paying any attention to me. I glanced around and saw Matt was holding Sarah's hand as they sauntered down the fairway. It was as if they were out for a walk in the park and Matt wasn't playing golf at all.

Matt missed the eagle putt, knocking the ball 6 inches by the hole. He tapped in for a birdie and I replaced the flagstick, and then he told me I could head home. He took his bag off my shoulder and said it was late, and he knew I had farm chores to do. He'd carry his bag the final holes, he said, as if he were doing me a favor.

I protested, saying it was okay, I could do my chores later, but Matt wanted me out of the way so he'd be alone with Sarah. And as they left the thirteenth green and headed for fourteen, walking along the dark path that cut through a thick stand of trees, I saw them stop to kiss, thinking they were hidden from prying eyes.

It was all very romantic, and it annoyed me no end. I stalked off and went down to the end of the metal fence, to the far edge of the property where there was a small gully. I crawled under the wire and crossed the road and walked home.

Mom was at the kitchen sink, as she always was. She hung out in the kitchen, I often thought, as much as I hung out at the pro shop. I pulled a few bills and change from my pocket, eight dollars for two rounds of carrying double, and dropped into a chair.

I never said much at home about what went on at the club. Mom wasn't interested in gossip about members. "They're not worrying about me," she said once, dismissing them all. She resented them in the same way most people resent the rich.

Kathy and I, however, were always talking about members, sharing stories from the club. There wasn't much we didn't know—Mrs. DuPree was right about that—but for some reason I didn't tell my sister about Matt and Sarah, or how I had become their go-between.

Mom set a plate of warmed-up dinner onto the table without a word, as if she were a waitress in a highway diner, pausing only long enough to sweep my earnings off the table. She shoved the few bills into her apron pocket and went back to the sink.

She had not been this way during the war. But then, only months after Germany surrendered, two army officers and Father Fuegner from Saint Christopher's Church came out to the farm to tell her Dad had been killed in a jeep accident. After that it seemed as if all the interest she had in the world went out of her. Dad was thirty-nine, too old to be in any war, Mom said. She kept saying he only enlisted to help America and wasn't he doing enough already, raising food for the soldiers?

From the kitchen windows where I ate my supper, I could see most of the farmyard: a slice of the red barn and the small pasture where we let out the cows after the evening milking. I remembered one time when I was three or four and I had somehow crawled under the fence and walked into the barnyard with a dozen cows. I was looking for my father, not realizing I was in danger of being trampled.

All I could recall afterward was trying to weave my way between the cows' legs and how one of them dropped her head and nudged me with a wet muzzle as if I were a calf. She was gentle but strong, and she pushed me right over. Terrified, I began to cry—and then my dad came along and saved me, sweeping me up into his arms and out of harms way.

Now my dad was gone—but I had Matt. In the spring, before Sarah came home from college, we had become a team. Every afternoon after school, I'd rush to the club to caddie for him before heading home to do the evening chores. And on weekends, I'd spend the whole of Saturday and Sunday at the golf course. By learning to club him, caddying for him in practice rounds and in pro-am events around Chicago, I helped Matt Richardson become the best golfer in the state.

What any good caddie knows is the moods of his player and also what club in the bag can always be trusted. Shagging balls for Matt and caddying for him, I learned his moods, and I learned what type of shot he could always make, even when the pressure was on.

Matt was learning my moods as well, I might add. He had become a brother to me, listening to my stories from school and telling me his tales about growing up in southern Illinois. Being on his own at the club, I think he enjoyed this role as my older brother.

Best of all for me was that I could talk to him about what I was feeling, and how sad I was that my dad had been killed. I didn't want to tell Mom and Kathy anything about my feelings. I didn't want them worrying. At fourteen, I guess, I thought I had to be the man in the family. Not with Matt. I could tell him anything and he'd listen and listen, as if he had all the time in the world for me.

And we did have some great times together, playing alone and late on the empty course on those warm early summer evenings. Often when Matt and I would be coming up eighteen a handful of members would wander off the terrace and amble down to the edge of the green, standing there with drinks in their hands to watch us finish up the final hole of our practice round.

Carrying Matt's bag, I would never go ahead and forecaddie on eighteen. I'd walk with him to the championship tee that was then, as it is today, deep in that cluster of evergreens. From the tee Matt would work his ball right to left, keeping it in the fairway, which as I am sure you are all well aware is so necessary on this finishing hole with its deep bunkers on both sides. Not that the bunkers came into play for Matt, even from the back tees.

Matt always hit a couple of drives during his practice round, and he always pounded them. The balls would sail out into the evening, rising on the crest of the setting sun. That's when the members would step off the terrace and walk over. In their bright green or yellow or pink sports jackets, they looked like tropical birds parading across the lush lawn.

Matt and I would hear them standing on the apron, their voices and soft laughter carrying easily in the warm air. They'd have already had a couple of drinks and were enjoying themselves and the pleasure of acting as if they were at a tournament, this gang of guys encouraging their young club pro. Several of them would set down their tall drinks in the grass to applaud, and shout out to Matt to "stick it in there stiff."

The members weren't usually rowdy on the course, but on those evenings they felt good about themselves, felt good, too, I am certain now as I recall the time, about America and the American way of life and how we had defeated the Germans and the Japanese and were the greatest power in the world. We were in the middle of the American Century and everything seemed right with the world.

On one particular evening early in the summer, as I recall, the hole was cut in the lower righthand corner and tucked behind the right-side bunker. The green slopes and, as those of you who play here all know, the grass grows toward the setting sun.

On that evening long ago both of Matt's drives were to the left side of the fairway, leaving him a clear shot to the flag. He had less than ninety yards, and he could hit a knockdown eight but it was the wrong shot for a lot of reasons, not to mention the members standing beyond the green. It would be what they would do: play it safe by hitting a pitch-and-run, keeping the ball low to make sure they didn't make too many mistakes.

"What's it look like?" Matt asked, slipping his driver into the bag.

"You've got one shot," I told him. "You hit the pitching wedge over the flag with enough spin to come back to the cup."

"Or I hit it low and let it run to the hole."

Matt loved those run-up shots, and the truth was, they made sense on eighteen. I noticed, in the years since I caddied here, you've changed the contour and enlarged the greens on this course. But what we had in those days were the original greens, postage-stamp-size and heavily bunkered, with a narrow entrance to the putting surface. Matt had learned, as all the pros did in those days, to run the ball up to the hole. And he was damn good at pitching with his 7- and 8-irons.

"It's the wedge," I said. "Work the ball off the ledge. Play it a couple yards to the left of the stick and the ball will feed to the hole."

Remembering back, I am surprised I was so cocky. I never had the game my good friend Doc Hughes had, and I'm sure Doug will be happy to tell you how he always beat me when we played against each other in high school matches. I never could outplay the good doctor, but Doug will admit I was a hell of a caddie. I loved looping more than I loved to play.

Matt knew that. More importantly, he knew I knew his game, and he grabbed the club and played the shot as I had instructed.

He hit a perfect wedge. The high arching ball caught the slope as I had told him it would, spun back, and rolled a dozen feet down to the flag, hit it flush and dropped into the cup as if it had eyes. It was the only time he ever eagled eighteen.

There was stunned silence from the cluster of members and then they erupted into cheers, thrilled by the sight, and thrilled to realize this amazing player was their own young assistant pro.

I didn't give Matt the chance to play his second drive. I scooped up the other ball and we kept walking toward the green. Matt was enough of a pro to know he had to leave his fans wanting more. The members were still applauding when we reached the green, and Matt tipped his cap as if he had beaten Ben Hogan in the Chicago Open instead of just playing a quick nine holes late on a summer evening.

4

THE WEEK AFTER MRS. DUPREE CAUGHT ME TRYING TO SNEAK A note to Sarah, Dr. DuPree came into the pro shop and asked me to caddie for him at a Monday pro-member event at Medinah Country Club. That was fine with me—I was always looking for an extra loop, especially one that would take me to another course.

In this Monday event Dr. DuPree and two other members played with Jimmy Walkup, our head pro, against members and pros from other clubs in Greater Chicago. During the round, DuPree didn't say anything about Matt or Sarah, but when he was giving me a ride home he began to talk about how his daughter had taken up the game.

"I just hope she hasn't been bothering the staff," he said, "or making too many demands on the pro, or Matt, or anyone." I didn't say anything, and he kept talking, glancing over and grinning as he said, "If she gets in your way in the pro shop, Jack, I

want you to let me know. Don't make a big deal of it," he instructed, "just let me know." He winked at me as we sped along,
driving by the entrance of the club and heading for my home. I
didn't think he would know where I lived, but that wasn't Dr.
DuPree's way. He always learned, I came to realize, whatever he
needed to know.

He spun into the gravel driveway of our farmhouse and
stopped. He sat and glanced around, taking in the apple orchards,
the chicken coop and pigpen, the other small buildings surrounding the main big, red barn.

"A lot of work running a farm," he remarked.

"Yes, sir," I said, and pushed down on the handle, thanking
him for the ride home, but also guessing he had more to say to
me, stuff I didn't want to hear.

"How's your mom doing?" he asked next. "Is everything going okay?" He kept smiling. "If she needs anything, you let me
know. Okay? Or if your sister needs anything."

I nodded nervously, and thanked him again for the ride. He
told me to wait. He hadn't paid me, he said, and slid his hand into
his pants pocket.

It was the fashion of the day for men to carry money in a
money clip. Dr. DuPree's clip was silver, engraved with this country club's seal, and thick with large bills.

He peeled off two twenties and handed them to me. It was a
ridiculous amount of money to pay a caddie in '46. We only
made $1.50 for eighteen holes single. Before I could say anything,
he repeated that if my mom or sister wanted anything to just let
him know and he kept smiling in the overly friendly way he had
that made me nervous. As a caddie I'd learned that whenever a
member was being particularly nice, it meant he wanted something, so I waited for him to tell me what it was.

Then he added in a low and confidential voice, as if he were a car salesman, "Let me know if my daughter is hanging around Matt, if you see them going off together."

He winked again as if it wasn't any big thing, but I knew it was. And what did happen between Matt and Sarah that summer would indeed change all of our lives.

Now on that note, perhaps, we might take a short break. I see Doug nodding in agreement. You know, when you get to be our age, you can't be too long between rest stops, so to speak, so let's all stretch our legs, get a little fresh air, and start again in ten minutes.

Jack Handley stepped away from the podium and heard brief, scattered applause and a quick shuffling of the folding metal chairs as everyone stirred and stood. A few people spoke, then more, and there were brief moments of laughter. Gradually the room full of members changed from an audience to a crowd of friends. Someone pushed open the double-wide French doors to the terrace, and a surge of fresh air swept into the parlor rooms that had been arranged into a makeshift lecture hall.

Jack was surprised to feel the soft coolness on his face. He hadn't realized how warm he'd been, there at the front of the room. Looking up, he saw Doug gesturing toward the terrace, and he nodded that he would join him. But first he wanted to rearrange his notes so he was ready to begin again. He was straightening them in his folder when he felt the woman's presence beside him. He looked up, and at the sight of her, his eyes widened.

"Sarah!"

She shook her head and smiled apologetically.

Of course not, he realized. This woman was only in her twenties.

"My grandmother," she said. "Sarah DuPree was my grandmother, on my father's side."

He smiled, embarrassed, and reached his hand across the lectern to shake hers. "So nice to meet you. And you are?"

"Sarah, too . . . I'm named after her . . . Sarah Burke. My husband is Jeff Burke, the club president. Jeff said he met you yesterday." She glanced around, as if to locate her husband in the room, which now had only a scattering of people. Everyone had walked out onto the open, sunny terrace, their voices rising in the out-of-doors.

Jack nodded. He had met the man briefly, when Doug was showing him around the clubhouse. Burke looked too young to be the club president, he thought, and too presumptuous.

"And your grandmother?"

"Nana passed away seven years ago. She would have loved all of this," young Sarah continued, smiling again. "All this talk of the Open and Ben Hogan."

She was just like her grandmother, Jack thought. He couldn't take his eyes off her. It was as if he were young again. But all he said was, "Really?"

"Oh, yes! The Hogan visit was a big event in her life. She talked about it often toward the end. Nana was living with us, before going into the hospice, and I heard a lot about that summer, how Ben Hogan came to the club."

"Did she tell you about Matt Richardson?"

"Not directly, and not by name. She did tell me she had a 'beau,' as she put it, when she was my age who taught her how to play. I was going through a rocky college romance at the time and I dropped out of school for a semester to get my head straight. I was living at home. The two of us spent a lot of time together. My grandmother was a great listener, and I could talk to her in ways that I couldn't with my mother. She was wonderful with matters of the heart."

Sarah paused and looked across the room and out through the French doors. Jack watched her face as she found the person she was looking for.

On the terrace, Jeff Burke tossed back his head and exhaled a cloud of cigarette smoke, and Sarah said rather wistfully, "She told me I should do whatever foolish things I wanted when I was young. Then, no matter what happened later, I would always know that once I had lived at the edge of my feelings. Don't you think that's wonderful advice?"

"Did you do that, Sarah? Did you follow your heart?" he asked.

He realized at once the question was inappropriate, but the sudden intensity of their conversation reminded him of what happens at times when strangers meet, the intimacy of chance encounters.

Sarah cocked her head, in a gesture just like her grandmother's. The softness of her brown eyes disappeared and he saw she could also be steely.

"There's still time," he added before she could respond.

She smiled briefly, brightly, and for just a second she looked as young as she was. Then the smile was gone and her face became carefully composed.

"Thank you for coming today. It's meant a great deal to my husband, and I'm sure to everyone else. I shouldn't monopolize your time."

"We'll talk later," he suggested, giving her an exit.

"I hope so." She fluttered her fingers in goodbye and, turning, walked purposefully out to the terrace where her husband was dominating a conversation.

Watching her, Jack did not hear Doug's quiet approach and was startled when his friend said, "Sarah is quite an unhappy young woman. She's my patient, and I care a great deal about her."

"*Do we know why she's so unhappy, besides the obvious reason: that she's married to an ass?*"

"*Sarah doesn't know who she is.*"

Jack glanced at his old friend. "*Is that why you asked me to come back today, Doug? To tell them what happened to Matt and Sarah back there in 'forty-six?*"

"*Perhaps,*" *the doctor said.* "*Perhaps.*"

5

IN EARLY JULY, ON ONE OF THOSE LAZY MONDAY AFTERNOONS when the course was closed, and having played golf that morning on Caddie Day, I was hanging out at the first tee when I heard a car coming down the road from the main gate. Glancing around, I saw a gleaming black Cadillac pull slowly into the empty parking lot. Like all caddies, I knew the members' cars, and this was not one of them.

A woman stepped out from the passenger's side. I didn't recognize her, but I saw she wasn't dressed to play. Then a man got out of the driver's side and he, too, was dressed in street clothes. I couldn't make out his face, but I watched as he carefully removed his jacket, as if it meant a great deal to him, and handed it to the woman, who deftly folded it inside out and placed it on the back seat of the Cadillac.

Next he opened the trunk and brought out a flat white linen golf cap. He put it on and instantly I recognized him. His profile was famous from the sports pages, from the Movietone newsreels I had seen at the Towne Theatre, from the dozens of golf magazines I read all summer long in the pro shop. The breath went out of me.

He reached into the trunk of the big car and lifted out his golf bag and swung it onto his shoulder with the ease and sureness of someone who had once been a bag rat himself.

Before the strap touched his shoulder, I was off the bench and charging down the slope. There was no way I was going to let Ben Hogan carry his own golf clubs at the course where I was a caddie.

Can any of you understand how famous Ben Hogan was in 1946? Some of you may have seen *Follow the Sun,* the movie that was made of his life. I'm told there will be a special showing tomorrow morning. The movie's not very good, but nevertheless it is the first film ever made about the life of a professional golfer, and that says something about Hogan's impact on the golf world and beyond.

Let me explain how great a player he was. Hogan served in the Army Air Force during the war and was discharged in 1945. In 1949 he had a near-fatal car accident. But in those three and a half years in between, he won thirty-eight tournaments. No player before or since has so dominated the game.

This was the era when woods were made of persimmon, and shafts of steel. There was no such thing as Big Bertha drivers or graphite irons. No one said a driver had a 460cc titanium head or a 10.5 loft. We couldn't imagine 11-degree woods, weight cartridges to control the ball trajectory, or sixty-four-degree lob wedges. Players had names like Sir Walter, Slammin' Sammy,

Porky Oliver, and Lighthorse Harry Cooper. Hogan had the most nicknames: Bantam Ben, the Wee Ice Man, the Little Texan, the Century Club Sharpshooter, and, always, the Hawk. The name fit his personality. Unlike, say, Tiger Woods, with his easy smile filling the TV screen, Hogan was silent on the course and distant with fans. He played a brooding, methodical game. Still, the great PGA player Tommy Bolt would say Hogan knew more about golf than any other five pros. Hogan, all the pros would say, played the same game they did, but stood apart from them. I could tell Hogan stories all day, but let me just share just one, told by Jimmy Demaret.

Demaret was leaving Oak Hill in Rochester hours after a round and when he flipped on his car lights, he spotted someone hitting balls on the practice tee. He could tell by the silhouette it was Hogan, so he walked out to the dark tee and asked, "Ben, have you been out here practicing since you played?"

"Yes," said Hogan.

"What the hell are you trying to prove?" said Jimmy. "You shot sixty-four today and birdied ten holes!"

Hogan stared at Demaret, then said with complete conviction, "Jimmy, there's no reason in the world why a man can't birdie every hole."

That was Ben Hogan.

I arrived at the Cadillac at full speed, and tumbled over myself skidding to a stop on the gravel. Valerie Hogan looked startled, then relaxed and smiled shyly. Ben, I recall, turned quickly from the car and froze me with those famous slate-blue eyes.

He was small, not much taller than five-eight, and he weighed less than 140. Back then, people said he resembled the movie star George Raft, who played gangsters in the 1930s and 1940s. With his face half-hidden in the shade of his white linen cap, there was something sinister about the man, I'll admit.

"Mr. Hogan, can I carry your bag, sir?" I blurted out.

Hogan held me with those fierce eyes and I felt instant panic.

"I'm not Ben Hogan," he said, "I'm Henny Bogan."

"Oh, Ben, don't tease the boy," Valerie whispered.

Hogan smiled, the familiar, gap-toothed grin I had seen in photos where he was holding up the winner's trophy. He swung his bag off his shoulder and gave it to me, asking, "Are you big enough for it, son?" His voice was clear and sharp, and although he'd grown up in Fort Worth, there was no trace of a Texas drawl.

I heaved the bag up on my back and staggered some from its weight—or perhaps from the importance of its being Ben Hogan's. It was the first time I had carried a *real* player's bag, and every caddie knows what an honor that is.

Hogan reached into the huge trunk and lifted out his gray golf shoes, and continued to talk. "Mrs. Hogan and I were guests at a Western Golf Association dinner last night, and before we leave the Midwest for Texas, I thought I might play a practice round on your course for the Open next month. Is Jimmy around?" He was asking for our home pro, who was also from Fort Worth.

"No, sir," I said.

"Do you think he'd mind if I played a few holes?" Hogan slammed the trunk closed and sized me up again with his slate-blue eyes.

"No, sir," I said, then added, by way of explanation, "you're Ben Hogan!"

Both Hogans laughed, and then Ben did something that displayed a gentleness people rarely saw. He reached over and rubbed the top of my head, asking, "What's your name, sonny?"

"Jack, sir. Jack Handley."

"Well, what do you think, Jack, can you handle my bag? We'll play a quick round."

"Yes, sir! Sure!" I couldn't stop grinning. We were moving out of the parking lot and up the shady path.

"Is your clubhouse open, Jack?" Valerie asked. She had a very soft voice, and each word came out in a whisper. I could hear Texas in her voice.

"Not officially open, ma'am, but Mr. Vicars, the manager, he's in his office."

"Will you be all right, honey?" Hogan's voice softened when he spoke to his wife.

"Of course." She fluttered her hands dismissively as if this was no bother, his going off to play. "I have letters to write."

We came out of the tree-lined path and into the sunlight. I pointed Mrs. Hogan toward the terrace. "The door's open, ma'am. You can get in there," I said.

"I'll see Mrs. Hogan to the clubhouse." Ben took her hand protectively. He nodded toward the first-tee box. "Wait for me there, Jack."

They say few other touring pros spent more time with their wives than Ben Hogan. He wasn't one for hanging out in the locker room or clubhouse bars with other golfers. Players from his time remember Hogan as always being with his wife; he'd go window-shopping with her instead of playing cards with the other pros. It was as if the two of them had decided early in their marriage that they didn't need anyone else. They were happy being alone together.

It wasn't ten minutes before Ben came back to the tee, wearing his golf shoes and ready to play. Unlike some PGA pros today—Duffy

Waldorf or Jesper Parnevik—who dress like circus clowns, Hogan wore three colors on the course: gray, white, and blue.

That Monday afternoon he was wearing a gray Pima cotton shirt and the flat white cap from Cavanaugh, a shop on Park Avenue in New York where he bought all his golf caps, and gray, neatly pressed gabardine trousers. It was his shoes, however, that most impressed me. I later learned he had them custom-made in London with a special extra thirteenth spike to give himself more traction when he swung.

Coming toward the tee, he was already staring down the length of the first hole, taking it all in, deciding where he would place his drive.

When he played a tournament, Hogan always said he lingered longer on the first tee than any other hole on the course. It was his method of getting ready to play. He would take three or four practice swings without even teeing up the ball. What he was doing was organizing himself. Hogan believed the first drive was the most important one of the round. He thought more about it, he said, than any other he'd play.

"How far is that right bunker, Jack?" Hogan asked, stepping over to me and his golf bag.

"Two-twenty-five." I tried to match the sharpness of his question with a confidence of my own.

Hogan pulled the head cover off his driver and glanced at me before replying, "More like two-fifteen."

"There's a hollow before the bunker," I said. "You can't see the slope from here. It looks closer, but it's two-twenty-five."

He smiled, amused, I guess, by my detailed explanation.

"Do you play, Jack?"

"Yes, sir."

"Play today?"

"Yes, sir, it's Caddie Day."

Ben nodded, as if he needed to be told when caddies could play on a private course. He leaned over to tee up the ball and sweep the grass smooth around it with his fingertips. Then he stepped back, feeling the club in his hands as he stared ahead.

"What did you shoot?" he asked without looking at me.

"Seventy-nine. I birdied eighteen."

Now he glanced over. There was no smile. He was impressed.

"Where do I play this?" he asked next, still looking at me.

I had a certain feeling, and perhaps it was simply the arrogance of teenage years, that he was speaking to me as a player, not just a caddie.

"You're hitting everything with a fade," I said, knowing his game from the magazine articles I had read. "Aim to the edge of the left-side bunker." I pointed down the fairway. "The hole feeds to the right, and you'll have a short iron to the green." I kept talking. How to play this course was something I knew. "The hole is cut on the left side, up on a ridge," I told him. "You've got a wide-open second shot."

"How do you know I hit everything with a fade?" Hogan asked.

"I read about your duck hook."

He smiled and looked again down the first hole. Anyone who knows anything about Ben Hogan knows how he struggled with a demoralizing hook in the early years of his career. The hook was the result of his caddie days at Glen Garden in Fort Worth. When Hogan was a kid, caddies bet money on who could drive the ball farther, and Hogan, determined to win those caddie yard contests, learned to hit a massive duck hook that served him well on the hard dry ground of Texas because a ball hit with a hook overspin would run forever.

To help Hogan out, Ted Longworth, the pro at Glen Garden, gave Hogan a distance grip, turning Hogan's left hand over the top of the shaft and moving his right hand underneath the club. It was a great grip for distance, but a disaster on the PGA Tour, where players needed to control their shots and keep the ball on the short grass.

When Hogan turned pro, another tour player, Henry Picard, helped him get rid of the duck hook by correcting his grip, and Harry Cooper, whom the pros called "Pipeline" because of how straight he was off the tee, noticed at the 1937 New Orleans Open how Hogan was letting go of the club with his left hand at the top of the backswing and then regripping it, closing the face.

I've seen a lot of great players in my day, everyone from Snead to Arnie to Nicklaus. And players today like Mickelson, Sergio, and, of course, Tiger. We know how far they hit the ball. But none of these great professionals, and I tell you this with the clearest of recollections, could hit a ball as well as Hogan with his old persimmon driver.

With the possible exception of Matt Richardson.

6

I DIDN'T MENTION MATT TO HOGAN UNTIL WE REACHED THE FIFTH hole. On that July Monday afternoon practice round, his drive landed on the rise and in the middle of the fairway, giving him a clear view of the green. If my memory serves, number five has two large bunkers on each side, clamping the green. I see a few heads nodding, so my recall must be holding true.

For Hogan it was an open shot, and since it was downhill, I knew, as Hogan knew, the second shot would play a half-club shorter. My guess, reaching his drive, was that he had a 7-iron left, as the flag was cut close to the front edge and to the left. Since, as I mentioned, Hogan liked to hit the ball from left to right, it was a tight shot.

I was resting my hand on the club he should play, ready to pluck it from the bag, when Hogan came up beside me. He didn't reach for a club, but stood staring down at the green as he lit a cigarette. Out of the corner of his eye he must have caught sight of me tugging at the 7-iron. He just shook his head and pulled the 8 from the bag.

"Not enough club," I told him.

My comment made him smile. With the toe of the 8-iron he pointed to a patch of bare turf a few feet from where his ball had landed.

"What do you call this?" he asked, nodding at the bare ground.

"Hardpan."

He tested the ground with the toe of the 8-iron. "I've got to pick the ball off this lie with a big sweeping swing, otherwise the chances are I'll hit it thin. And this over here?" He gestured with the club to where his ball had landed on a patch of clover.

"The grass, you mean?"

"Not grass. Clover." With the toe of the blade, he pawed the patch. "Clover is oily," Hogan said. "You can't make solid contact. The ball is going to skid and float, and there's no backspin." He pointed toward the green. "See the level spot, short and to the right of the bunker? I'll knock it down onto that patch and let it run up."

"It's a slow green," I told him, trying to regain some authority.

"What's behind the green?"

"Thick grass, that's all."

"That's all!" Hogan smiled again. "If I fly this shot onto the putting surface it could run through the green and I'm in trouble. If I'm short, I'm fine. I'll chip up and get my par. What matters in golf, Jack, is always the next shot, not the one you just hit."

I pulled the bag away to give him room to play the shot and announced, "I like going for the green."

"That's because you don't play for money," Hogan answered. "In 1938, down in St. Petersburg, I hit the flags twice, on eleven and sixteen, and my ball bounced away. I was hitting everything too close and it was costing me birdies. So I learned to play for the flattest part of the green nearest the hole and leave myself up-hill putts."

He tossed away his Chesterfield and refocused his attention on the next shot: the short waggle to set himself and the smooth, flat, swift swing. He laced the 8-iron to the front edge, where it hit softly on the flat patch of fairway and kicked forward, then ran to within 6 feet of the flag.

"Nice," I said, dropping the bag to retrieve the divot. "You kept it below the hole. Still, it's a fast putt," I went on recklessly. I carried the divot back and stamped it into place.

"Why? You just told me this was a slow green." Hogan bent over and picked up his cigarette.

"These are bentgrass greens." I nodded toward the horizon. "Bentgrass grows toward the setting sun. Any good caddie knows that."

I swung his bag onto my shoulder.

"And you're a good caddie?"

"I'm number one."

"How 'bout looping for me in the Open?"

In the 1940s, you may know, there were few caddies following the tour. Pros picked up kids wherever they played.

"I can't," I said, not having the courage to look at Hogan.

"Why's that?"

"I'm caddying for Matt. Matt Richardson."

"Who's Matt Richardson?"

"Matt's our assistant pro."

"He'll have to qualify, right?"

"He will."

Hogan smiled at my confidence.

"He plays this course like a fiddle," I told Hogan.

Matt had shot 65 more than once since arriving at the club, I told Hogan, and once he had gone around in 64.

Hogan seemed unconcerned about what Matt had shot on those early morning practice rounds, and it surprised me. Matt's scores were all we talked around the club. When we reached the green, Hogan marked his ball and tossed it to me to clean as he studied the grass, the slope of the green, moving around behind the hole and kneeling to look at the putt from the other side.

I pulled the flag and handed him the ball as he walked around me, and as he did, almost as an aside, he said, "Any fella can shoot sixty-five on any given day, Jack. Come later this August, your pro will have to do it four days straight." Having made that point, Hogan addressed the putt and drilled the six-footer in the center of the cup. Then he walked off to the next tee, leaving me to retrieve the ball and replace the flag. I had to jog after him to catch up.

We had gone on to the sixth tee, the par-4 that runs along the small creek. It's a simple enough par-4, not particularly distinguished, nor difficult. It isn't a hole where many players score birdies or get into serious trouble, but there is the out-of-bounds to the left that troubles players who hook, as some of you in the audience must know.

Hogan stood on the tee in that wonderful measured way he had, taking in the hole, judging it, making his own evaluation. Jimmy Demaret wrote about how Hogan always planned his shot before swinging, how other players got to calling him the surveyor because it seemed he looked over the fairway with a telescopic eye.

Hogan was taking so much time on the tee, I was about to explain where the green was, since it was then, as I am sure it is today, a blind shot, and what mattered was the right-side bunker, which was out about 270. I didn't think Hogan could carry it. The fairway was wide, and all he had to worry about was keeping the ball away from that bunker. He stood there and slowly, carefully smoked another of those endless Chesterfields.

His arms were crossed as he took in long, slow drags, and then he suddenly picked up on the exchange we had had on the last green. "You're right about caddying for your pro, Jack." He pulled the driver from the bag and handed me the cover. "What's important in life is loyalty. A few years back, before the war, when I couldn't buy a good round, another pro, Henry Picard, helped me out when he didn't have to do a damn thing.

"Mrs. Hogan and I were in Fort Worth at the Blackstone Hotel at the time, standing in the lobby, and I was telling Valerie I had to quit the tour because we didn't have the money for me to keep playing. Henry Picard was walking through the lobby and heard me talking to Val and asked me what the trouble was. I told him we were flat broke.

"And I'll never forget this, Jack. Without hesitating, Henry told me to go out and play and if I needed any money down the road to let him know. You can make it out there, he said, and he was about the first person on the tour who thought I could.

"I never needed to call him for money, but his offer meant the world to me. I won a little money in Sacramento and then Picard asked me to play in Pennsylvania, at the Hershey Four-Ball. Only a handful of the best players were invited. I wasn't one of the best, but Henry asked me anyway. I won one thousand one hundred dollars. It was my first win on tour and my real beginning as a pro golfer."

Hogan stopped speaking but kept staring down the fairway. Slowly, thoughtfully, he took one drag after another on his cigarette, but I could sense he wasn't thinking about the shot. He was thinking of a time when no one thought Ben Hogan could make it as a player and Henry Picard had come along and made all the difference in his life.

Hogan looked at me again. "You bring him home, Jack. You bring your player home, that's your job."

And then Hogan stepped between the markers, threw down his cigarette, and laced a drive some 280 yards, farther than I had ever seen anyone hit it on the sixth hole, farther than Matt could drive, even on his best day.

7

BUT THAT MONDAY AFTERNOON I HAD OTHER THINGS TO WORRY about besides who I would caddie for in the Open. My stomach had been churning all summer about Dr. DuPree and what he wanted me to do. So when Hogan, walking up to his drive on six, asked me offhandedly what this club's members were like, I blurted out what was troubling me.

I'm not sure what caused me to confide in Ben Hogan. Maybe it was because he, too, had once been a caddie. I was telling the great Ben Hogan my problem when I had not said a word to my mom or my sister, let alone to Matt. I was telling Hogan, I guess, because Hogan was like a god then, and I couldn't imagine holding anything back from him.

After I spilled out my story, Hogan fell silent. He might have been absorbing what I'd just told him, or he could have been plotting his next shot.

His drive had cleared the bunker on the right side of the fairway, leaving him a soft 7- or hard 8-iron into a well-bunkered green. The shape of the green looked like a kid's balloon squeezed by the bunkers. As I recall number six, there's a slight mound behind the green. Is it still the case?

The hole location was tucked into the right corner, making it a difficult shot unless you played it to the middle, which is what I suggested to Hogan.

"Two putts from there," I told him.

I'm not sure Hogan was even paying attention to me on the two putts strategy because what he asked me next was the distance between the corner of the right bunker and the hole. I guessed what he was thinking was to drop a high short iron into the tight corner.

Maybe five yards, I said, and told him there was no more than twenty feet from the edge of the bunker to the apron and the small bluff behind the flag. I studied the trees behind the hole. A tall stand of poplars stood motionless in the warm afternoon. Those of you who play know how swirly the wind can get at that corner of the course, much as it does on the back side at Augusta.

I might mention here I've always thought your country club is just as lovely as Augusta. And perhaps there is no better place to view the beauty of this course than from the rise in the middle of the sixth fairway, where you have a full panorama of the landscape with the sprawling colonial clubhouse in the far distance, beyond the creek, high on its own terrace and brilliantly white in the bright afternoon sunlight, dominating the scene of sculptured fairways shaped as they are as if two open hands with fingers spread wide apart are pressed down hard onto the earth itself. It is one of the great country club vistas, in my opinion, in America.

. . .

Hogan seemed to not be aware of the beauty around him. He pulled the 8-iron from the bag and prepared himself to play. I had already become mesmerized by his routine, the way he stood behind the ball, staring down the fairway toward the flagstick and the flag limp against the bamboo shaft. Many people think this was the secret of his success, his unique ability to block out everything but the task ahead. He would reduce his entire universe to playing one shot.

Today, touring pros have trainers and teachers and sports psychologists helping them get in the zone, but years ago, before any of this was fashionable, or even known to be important, Hogan figured out how to play tournament golf. The key for him was "the waggle," taught to him in '32 by a wonderful pro named Johnny Revolta.

Revolta won a few tournaments himself, but he wasn't long off the tee, so it was his short game that he depended on, and he used the waggle for his short game.

The waggle, as you all know, and have seen endlessly on television, is the way a pro, or any player, settles in to make a shot, the way all of us who play the game get comfortable over a ball.

Hogan took the idea of the waggle and used it on all his shots, setting up with a different waggle for whatever club he had in his hand.

Hogan's waggle wasn't a mindless flipping of his club, or random body movements. He had a series of systematic motions to what he called "the bridge between stillness and execution."

Hogan was also pulling from his memory, from the thousands of such high 8-irons played to a small green with tight pin placements, the shot he wanted to make. He fit his waggle to the shot.

He set himself, worked the waggle until he was comfortable. He glanced down the fairway once again. He was a human computer absorbing into his data bank everything he needed to know to play the shot. The 8-iron was hit high and soft and floated toward the green.

There was no break in Hogan's rhythm. He swung in one effortless, smooth motion. Remember what W. B. Yeats wrote in his wonderful poem "Among School Children": "O body swayed to music, O brightening glance, How can we know the dancer from the dance?"

It was a perfect shot. Perfect in the sense it didn't drop into the hole on the fly; then we would have all thought he was just lucky. It was perfect in its execution, perfect in flight—a thing of beauty—just the correct distance, the correct reaction on the green. The ball hit a yard beyond the hole, then spun back and came to a stop within 6 inches of the cup. Hogan couldn't have given himself better placement if he had walked down the hill and planted the ball on the green.

"Wow!" I breathed.

Hogan laughed and I took back the 8-iron, wiped the club face clean with a damp white cloth, and slid the club into the bag. Then we walked down the hill toward the green, which was already in shadows from the long line of trees running the length of the fence, a green barrier against the two-lane country road that edged the course.

"You know," Hogan said softly, finally responding to my poured-out confession of my fears about Dr. DuPree, "when I was growing up in Texas, we didn't have much money, but I've always remembered something my mother used to tell me. She said never to forget, no matter what, that I was as good as anybody else in the world. I think all I've ever done in life is try to live up to what she thought." He briefly rested his arm around my thin shoulders and gave me a squeeze. "You're as good as any of these members, Jack. Don't ever forget it."

I couldn't answer. I just trudged along with my head down, balancing his big bag on my lower back and thinking about what he had said, when he reached over and gently rubbed the cap on top of my head. "All right, Jack?"

I nodded, but I wasn't sure I was all right, and I think Hogan knew that as well.

8

WHEN WE REACHED THE NINTH TEE, I SAW MATT ON THE PRAC-
tice range, which ran parallel to the ninth fairway, but in the op-
posite direction. Matt was hitting balls out of the shade of the
trees, and behind him, sitting on a folding chair, was Sarah. He
had no shag boy and later, I knew, they'd walk out together and
pick up the dozens of balls.

Hogan's drive on nine carried the hill and rolled to within
twenty yards of the service road that cuts across the fairway. Walking toward it, I spotted Hogan glancing over at Matt. He watched
Matt hit a driver the length of the practice area. It was a drive
over 270 yards.

But Hogan didn't watch the flight of the balls, nor where they
landed. He just focused on how Matt swung the wood.

I didn't say anything, but when I reached Hogan's ball and set
the bag down beside it, Hogan came up and asked, "Is that your
man?"

"Yep!"

Hogan glanced over as Matt hit another drive, watching him with those hawkish eyes as if he were drilling the image into his mind. Matt's drive came blazing out of the dark corner of the practice tee and flew high and long and down the length of the range.

"He can hit the ball a ton," I said.

Hogan nodded and turned to his next shot, glancing at the lie and up at the left-to-right sloping green, then, without comment, he pulled the 7-iron from the bag. He was halfway through his routine when he spoke softly, tossing off the comment as if it didn't matter if I were listening or not.

"There's no such thing as one good shot in tournament golf, Jack. All your shots have to be good—and for seventy-two holes. As Bobby Jones told me when I first came out on tour, there's golf, Bobby said, and there's tournament golf." Hogan fell silent, refocused his attention on the ball, waggled, paused, and swung.

Hogan's quick, tight swing wiped the iron through the air and cut away the turf. The ball flew to the top edge of the target and, as it came down, faded toward the center of the green. I knew from the flight it had been hit high enough, and with enough cut backspin, the ball would hold the green and work itself down toward the flag.

He held his finish, then reached out with the 7-iron, slid the blade under a thin wedge of divot, and replaced the patch of green. As he stepped on it, he handed me the club and said, "You know, I think the greatest pleasure in this game—and I can't think of anything that matches it, really—is watching a well-hit shot. You know you've hit the ball flush when this wonderful feeling comes off the club face, along the shaft and into your hands and up your arms and straight into your heart. There's nothing quite like it because you don't hit a perfect shot every time or every day."

And then he glanced over at Matt standing in the shade of the giant poplars and added with a small smile, "Unless you're Matt Richardson."

I slid Hogan's 7-iron into the bag, grinning myself, pleased by Hogan's kidding.

"That's his girl?" Hogan asked.

"Yep."

We were both striding across the service road. Neither of us was looking over at Matt and Sarah, but from the corner of my eye I could see Matt had paused in his practicing. He was staring at us, leaning against the long-shafted 1-wood with his legs crossed as if he were just catching his breath from all the pounding, pausing before teeing up another ball. He watched as we went up the rise to the green, where I saw Hogan had drilled the 7-iron to within four feet of the hole, and I knew Matt, too, had seen the 7-iron, and had recognized it was Hogan. Anyone who knew golf in the 1940s and 1950s knew Hogan's famous profile.

I couldn't see Matt's face in the dark shadow of his cap, but I knew the look he'd have, a mix of awe and puzzlement as he tried to sort out why Ben Hogan was walking down the ninth fairway and what the hell was I doing caddying for him.

I dropped Hogan's bag at the top of the green and walked down to attend the flag. Hogan had already repaired the green where his high 7-iron had left a ball mark.

I pulled the flag and stepped away from the cup, moving to the right so my shadow wouldn't fall across Hogan's line of sight.

I glanced up at the clubhouse, bathed in the afternoon light with the sun sweeping across the long façade. There on the terrace was Valerie Hogan. She was sitting far enough back on the veranda to be out of the sunlight, but still she had seen us coming up the fairway, finishing the front nine.

Hogan didn't take much time with his putts. He crouched behind the four footer, which would, I saw when I pulled the flag, break two inches to the right.

It was a fast green; I knew from having played it earlier in the day. When I didn't say anything, Hogan asked me what I thought, and when I told him he got up, settled himself over the ball, and made a smooth, soft stroke. The ball clinked into the center of the cup.

I've read in later years that it got so Hogan couldn't pull the trigger on short putts. Hale Irwin remembers the 1960 U.S. Open at Cherry Hills, when Hogan froze so long over a three-foot putt on the fourth green Irwin thought a pigeon might land on him. The truth, I learned a few years ago, was that the optic nerve in Hogan's left eye had been damaged in the '49 accident, when his car was hit by that Greyhound bus. My guess is the injury was the reason his putting style changed so dramatically. His impaired vision was not helped as he aged, yet he refused to wear glasses while playing.

The blurriness meant he couldn't relax over the ball. He even took tranquilizers to calm himself down and tried hypnosis, but nothing worked. He could no longer read the line and he had lost all confidence in his stroke.

Hogan plucked the ball from the cup and said he wanted to speak to Mrs. Hogan before starting on the back side. Then he looked past me and nodded toward the practice tee.

"Why don't you go see if your pro wants to play nine? You can handle double, can't you, Jack?"

He tapped the bill of my cap and, smiling, walked up to where his wife was sitting. As he got closer, he took off his soft cap as if he were a gentleman caller.

.   .   .

I left Hogan's bag on the apron and ran down to the range. Matt hadn't gone back to hitting woods, but had watched Hogan make his putt, watched me run toward him.

As I reached them, Sarah asked, "Is that him?"

I nodded, and said to Matt, "He wants you to play the back side with him."

Matt glanced at Sarah, who said at once, "You've got to play, Matt. We can talk another time."

"I'll carry double," I told Matt, picking up his bag.

"Come with us," Matt said to Sarah.

She shook her head and nodded toward the clubhouse. "I'll wait for you."

"Mrs. Hogan is on the terrace," I added, swinging Matt's bag onto my shoulder, trying to hurry Matt along.

Up at the clubhouse, Hogan was still talking to his wife, but he was stepping away, moving toward the tenth tee.

"Hey, Matt," I said, "we gotta go."

Matt and I headed for the tenth and Sarah went up the slope to the terrace. Hogan was back on the course, and once again Valerie sat waiting, her hands clasped in the lap of her summer dress, her brown leather purse beside the metal chair, her eyes closed against the soft summer sun of the late afternoon.

Let's pause here for another short break before we reach the heart of my tale—the nine holes when Matt went up against Ben Hogan in what, for me, was perhaps the greatest golf match ever played at this country club.

9

WHEN JACK HANDLEY RETURNED FROM THE MEN'S ROOM THE terrace was crowded with members, more than he had seen at his afternoon lecture, and he guessed some had skipped the first part of his talk to play golf. He couldn't blame them, and he wondered if there might be time in the morning to play a few holes before Doug drove him to O'Hare.

Doug had suggested they play when he first arrived, but he had begged off. Instead, he borrowed his friend's BMW and drove by himself to see his family's old farm, which was now a McMansion in an upscale subdivision.

He knew the farm was gone; he'd just never seen the new house and now he took a good look, pulling into the main circle drive as if he'd gotten lost and was just turning around.

In the distance he saw the chicken coop had been converted into a bathhouse for a swimming pool. The orchard had been leveled, except for a few apple trees, and there were Adirondack chairs on the sweeping front lawn and a screened gazebo beyond the barn where his mother had kept the pigs. The barnyard had become a flower garden, and the small field where they put out the cows at night was a tennis court. He stared hard at the house and lawns, trying to pull back to mind the image of what had once been his home.

He wanted to walk down the tarmac drive for a closer look, but he didn't know what he might say to the owner. He couldn't have explained, even to himself, what he wanted. The farm was history, and so was his family. His mother was gone, having died as she had spent her life, passing away from a stroke while working at the kitchen sink. Kathy, his sister, was gone, too, dying young of cancer and leaving behind a family who had never known anything about her life on the farm, her teenage job as a club waitress, or even their grandfather, the one who had died in the war.

Jack was the only one left alive who could remember a time before the country road was widened and the farm sold off to the developer who had created these cul-de-sacs and playgrounds and grossly huge homes.

As he sat in the car, his memories of the farm came back in disjointed flashes, fragments of dialogue, tiny recollections. He saw an image of his father moving across the barnyard, pushing a wheelbarrow, bent forward, laboring under the weight of the heavy load.

And as he remembered, he saw again his father's face, the smile that always came quickly to his eyes and mouth whenever Jack rushed into the barnyard to track him down. Jack was carrying a message from his mother, perhaps, or sometimes he just paused in his play because he wanted to be with his dad. And his father was always eager to set down the load of work and sweep the boy up, lifting him effortlessly into his arms with his strong arms.

Jack had never imagined such joy could be so brief, that when he lost his dad to the war, he would lose so much of his happiness. He understood now that in the summer of '46 he hadn't just been caddying. He had *gone looking for someone to fill the emptiness he had not even realized he held deeply in his heart.*

Jack felt a warm softness on his cheeks and realized he was crying. He wiped his eyes and blew his nose, and when he looked up again he saw a boy standing a dozen feet from the car.

"Hey, hi!" Jack called out, embarrassed, blinking his eyes to dry his tears. He guessed the boy was about fourteen, the age he'd been when he caddied for Hogan.

"Hey, you okay?" the boy asked, peering out from under the bill of a golf cap. He was tall and skinny in his shorts and sneakers without socks. His bare arms and face were deeply tanned, and the shoulders of his white T-shirt were worn brown from the leather straps of golf bags.

"Oh, I'm fine. Thank you. Got some dust in my eye." Jack nodded toward the house. "I lived there once. When all of this was farmland."

"A farm?" The boy looked down the driveway. "This is the Haley-Beil residence. I live here! My father's the caretaker. A farm?" The boy glanced around, then grinned and asked, "You messin' with me?"

Jack smiled. The boy's slang reminded him of his grandchildren. Half the time he had no idea what kids were saying to him.

"It was a long time ago," Jack replied, "long before you were born." Then he spotted the caddie badge on the boy's hat.

"Been looping?"

The kid nodded, and now he was staring at the BMW and said, "That's Doc Hughes's car!"

"That's right. Dr. Hughes is a friend. I've come for the Open celebration. Doug and I . . . we were both caddies here at the club. It was a long time ago."

"Doc Hughes was a caddie?" The boy pushed the golf cap up off his forehead. "No way!"

"One of the best." Jack kept smiling, feeling good about this happen-

stance meeting. He asked quickly, "You know about the Open celebration?"

"Sure! A lot of old guys have been playing here all week." Glancing at Jack, he looked sheepish and said softly, "Sorry."

"Hey, you're right! We're a bunch of old guys, no question about it."

"Did you play in the Open?" the kid asked, suddenly curious.

Jack shook his head. "Oh, no, I didn't play. But I caddied in the Open."

"You for real?" the boy exclaimed. Now he was impressed.

Jack nodded, staring out at the land again and trying to pull back more memories. "I'm giving a talk tomorrow about Ben Hogan." When the caddie didn't react, Jack asked, "You know who Ben Hogan was, right?"

"Sure," he said, shrugging. "A pro. A good player." He said it without much interest. "My pop has one of his golf books."

"Power Golf?"

"Yeah, I think so. My pop says he was 'bout as good as Tiger."

"A lot of us think he was better," Jack replied, sounding defensive. He searched for the right way to explain Hogan's appeal to so many people. "He was like a movie star. You know, someone you see on the big screen who is larger than life. People didn't know Hogan, and it made him mysterious."

"You knew Hogan?" The boy's attention picked up.

"In a limited way, yes."

Jack pulled a copy of his book from his briefcase and handed it out the window to the boy, saying, "The whole story is in here."

The boy flipped through the pages and looked at the cover, stared at the photograph of Ben Hogan on the first tee. He was gazing away from the camera, staring down the fairway. Behind him in the fuzzy out-of-focus background of the black-and-white photo was the façade of the colonial clubhouse.

"It's our club!" the boy exclaimed.

"Yep."

"Hogan?" the boy asked, looking at Jack.

"Yep."

"It must have been something, I mean, caddying for him." He handed the book back to Jack.

"It was. I caddied for him and Matt Richardson in a practice round before the Open. Do you know who Matt Richardson is?"

The boy slowly nodded. "Doesn't he hold the course record or something?"

"Yes, he still does. He played a match against Hogan and I looped for both of them."

"For real?"

"For real." Jack smiled once more, then nodded goodbye, saying, "I better get back to the club or Doc Hughes is going to think I stole his car. It's nice meeting you, son. Stop by the clubhouse tomorrow and say hello. I'll show you the photographs they have on display and get you a copy of this book."

The boy nodded quickly and grinned, then said, waving good-bye, "Peace out."

"Peace out, yourself," Jack answered and backed the BMW slowly out of the driveway.

10

HOGAN WAS STANDING ON THE TENTH TEE OF HIS PRACTICE round when I brought Matt to meet him. Hogan immediately put out his hand and said, "Jack tells me you're one helluva player. Hello, I'm Ben Hogan."

"Mr. Hogan, it's an honor, sir." Matt was grinning and blushing. He gestured toward me and said, "Jack has a vivid imagination. Too many comic books, right, Jack?" he said nervously.

Hogan responded that I was a well-seasoned caddie who knew his way around the course. I was straining to hear every word as I took the bags off my shoulders.

Standing with both of the thick barrel bags leaning against me, I saw the differences between the men played out in their clubs. Hogan's all matched, and he had bright hoods on all his woods. None of Matt's matched, and he had only three woods— a driver, a brassie, and a spoon—and a set of Armour Silver Scot irons he had picked up in Florida when he was in the army. His two wedges, both of which he had worked on in the pro shop, had the look of being handmade.

Matt also carried a left-handed club, an old pitching niblick with a Tennessee hickory shaft. It was the first club Matt ever owned, given to him by a member at Gatesburg Country Club when he was a caddie. He carried the club for sentimental reasons, he said, and also to use when he couldn't play out of trouble with one of his right-handed clubs. Matt had been born a left-hander, and at first he'd play golf that way. But soon he realized there were no great left-handed golfers, nor could he find many left-handed clubs before the war, so he switched to right-handed clubs. Ben Hogan was also born left-handed. It was all that, I came to realize, that Matt Richardson and Ben Hogan had in common.

Now they were ready to play and Hogan said, "Hit away, Matt!"

"No, Mr. Hogan. It's your honors. I couldn't."

Hogan glanced down the fairway, taking it in, but I could see he was thinking of something else. He turned and said nicely to Matt as he made his point, "Matt, don't ever call anyone 'Mister' that you have to play against."

And then he looked at me and asked, "Where do I play it, Jack?"

"Right edge of the fairway bunker."

Hogan was gripping the wood, fitting his powerful hands into a Vardon grip on the leather. He was taking in the fairway as he always did, but he didn't move purposefully toward the ball as I had seen him do on the front side. Instead, still staring down the fairway, he spoke casually to Matt.

"You know, what I've learned playing golf is what's most important is taking time, hitting each shot as if it were the only one I'd make. I take the whole round, every one of my drives, fairway

woods, putts, all of them, and think of each shot as a drama, something you might see onstage, with a beginning, middle, and end."

I glanced over at Matt to see how he was taking this.

"I say that because when I was walking down nine, I watched
you whacking those drives out there without taking time between shots."

"Well, it was only practice," Matt answered, shifting his feet.

"If you're going to play the tour, fella, there's no such thing as
'only practice.'" Hogan dropped his wood and said next, "In fact,
how 'bout a little game to make the back side interesting?" He
said it pleasantly, as if it was just a friendly wager between friends.

"Sure, I guess." Matt glanced at me. I knew he didn't know
what to say.

"Five a hole, two presses?"

Matt let out a sigh and stared down the fairway. He never
played for more than a buck a nine.

"Five a hole is pretty steep, sir," he finally answered, not looking at Hogan.

"Oh, on the tour it's what we play for, but if it's too rich . . ."

"Sure, why not?" Matt shot back, taking the bait before I
could stop him.

Hogan nodded and stepped forward, addressed the ball, and
paused to set himself, first planting his right foot perpendicular to
the line of flight. Many say, by the way, when they talk about
Hogan's great golf secret, it was the placement of his legs, how he
locked his right leg, but I can assure you, it wasn't his secret.

Then the famous waggle to settle himself. Not moving his
shoulders or his hips, just his arms and legs. He glanced again
down the fairway, getting his rhythm, feeling for the tempo he
wanted in his hands and feet, and up and down the length of his
body, getting all of his limbs in sync. Then the coil.

There has never been a player with such a massive coil. He took the driver the length of his small body, a full wrist break at the top of the takeaway with the club head pointed straight down to the ground, and the slash, a whippy hiss in the still air as if a bullwhip was cracking across the tee. And then he struck the ball. *Shhhwhack!*

Hogan's swing mesmerized Matt. He wouldn't be the first golfer, nor the last, to be awed by Hogan's power. There had never been a player before him—or after—who swung a club as fast, as furiously, as fiercely as Ben Hogan. The long, graceful sweep of Sam Snead's swing, for example, was a good second slower than Hogan's.

Hogan's drive cleared the right edge of the bunker and went bounding down the fairway, leaving him nothing more than a 9-iron into the tenth green. For a second longer he watched his ball, checking to see if there was a falloff to the right side of the fairway, and then he bent over and plucked up his tee. It had bounced forward another three yards, a sure sign he had hit the drive dead straight.

Matt said something gracious about the drive, praising Hogan, one player to another, as he stepped between the markers and searched for a spot to tee up his ball.

"I didn't get all of it." Hogan slid his driver into the bag in the same way a medieval knight might plunge his sword into its sheath. I started to understand what was happening: This wouldn't be a friendly nine holes, a gentlemen's game. Hogan had a reason for asking me to invite the young home pro for a quick nine holes on that quiet Monday afternoon.

Matt teed up and stepped away. He was going through his own preshot routine. But it wasn't so much a preshot routine as Matt simply trying to calm himself after seeing Hogan's drive.

Matt must have taken a half-dozen easy swings, standing behind his ball, before he took a deep breath and stepped between the markers.

He set his right foot, then his left, in a manner like Hogan and he, too, took a quick glance down the fairway. I knew where he was aiming, which wasn't over the right edge of the bunker, where I'd directed Hogan.

Remember how I mentioned earlier, before the break, how Matt had started to hit big sweeping hooks, starting the ball out over the right rough and letting it work toward the short grass? About 260 yards out, he was able to catch a hard piece of high ground, and his drive would bounce hard off the patch and run further down the right edge, leaving him a wedge to the flag.

Now on the tenth tee, with Hogan standing away and dragging on another Chesterfield in the slow, careful way he had, Matt set up to hit his sweeping hook. He placed his left foot forward an inch or two into a draw stance and aimed toward the two oaks bordering the out-of-bounds and the drive.

I held my breath, knowing from experience that when Matt was anxious his swing got so fast he might whack the ball over the trees and onto the front lawn of one of the mansions beyond Cottage Row Drive.

But on the tenth tee he took his time and hit a perfect drive. The ball flew straight for the deep right rough and began to work toward the fairway, catching the hard surface of the high ground and bouncing forward, running like a rabbit down the right edge.

Hogan nodded and said, "Good shot," which was about as much praise as any player ever got from Ben. For example, at the 1965 PGA Championship at Laurel Valley, Palmer's club in Ligonier, Pennsylvania—the last time, by the way, Hogan ever played in that championship—Hogan was paired with George Knudson, who made a hole-in-one on a 238-yard par-3 and the gallery went wild, but all Hogan said was, "Nice shot."

I knew Hogan hadn't seen just how good Matt's drive really was, but Matt and I did. We both knew Matt's ball was a good fifty yards beyond Hogan's. Matt had outdriven Hogan, and there weren't many pros who could make that claim.

We crested the ridge, and Hogan got his first real look at the two drives.

"Why did you tell me to hit over the edge of the bunker, Jack?" he asked. "The right side's the shot."

"You hate the hook, Mr. Hogan, and if you hit the fade, the ball's going to scoot into the rough. It's safer on the left side, and you've got what you like, a clear approach." I kept talking fast, justifying myself. But it wasn't any use. Hogan didn't like to be outgunned off the tee.

Once I read a story told by George Archer, who played in the Masters one year with Hogan and Palmer. There were some twenty thousand people following them, following Palmer mostly, who was then in his prime. On the third hole, Palmer hit a low screamer and the crowd went crazy, roaring over the length of it.

Hogan didn't say anything, Archer remembered. Hogan just took the cigarette out of his mouth and flung it onto the ground, furious at the applause Palmer had gotten, and he stepped up and hit a draw to the left of the fairway.

People applauded but it wasn't anything like the roar Palmer received. Archer hit a 3-wood, and when he got to his ball, he spotted another one at the same length, and the third ball eighty or so yards farther along the fairway.

Palmer and Hogan came by him, both walking fast and talking as they went past the other, shorter drive, with their caddies in stride with them, and when they reached the long ball, Hogan stopped and kept puffing on his cigarette as he looked up at the green. He never glanced down at the ball.

Finally, Palmer did bend over, realized it was Hogan's ball, not his, and walked back as the gallery went, "Wooooooo." So there was Palmer retreating like a dog with his tail between his legs, and old man Hogan, still the big gun on tour.

Hogan didn't ask me how to play his next shot. He stood quietly puffing on his cigarette and staring up at the green, which now in the afternoon had fallen into shadows. In its day, after three o'clock, the massive elm guarding the right side cast a pattern of shadows across the green and disguised the slopes and ridges.

When Hogan finished the cigarette, he didn't pull a club. Instead he left me with the bag standing beside his ball and walked the 130 yards to the green, walked to the flag, which was cut on the top tier, less than 5 yards from the back edge of the long, narrow, contoured green.

I glanced over at Matt, who was standing by his ball on the far right of the fairway. He wasn't studying his next shot. Matt was looking at Sarah's house, the big stucco Mediterranean mansion that, as always, appeared deserted in the middle of the summer day.

Hogan came back to his drive and pulled out the 9-iron. He didn't say a word, and I guessed he was still annoyed. He glanced once at the flag and played the shot.

He took as much time as Tom Watson would today. In other words: not long at all. Setting himself, glancing at the green, knowing just where he wanted to place the ball, he hit a soft 9 punch shot. The ball ballooned up slightly and dropped down less than two yards from the flag. It never bounced. It never ran.

In all my years of following golf, Tiger Woods is the only person I've ever seen hit a punch iron like the one Hogan played. Matt didn't react, but I could tell by the way his shoulders sagged that he was shocked at how perfectly Hogan had played the shot, how close he had worked the ball to the cup.

Hogan handed me the 9-iron and took his putter without a word. His face seemed to close down, to block out who I was, what I had said, and I went humbly away to replace the wedge of divot. Without breaking his stride, Hogan leaned over and plucked his cigarette off the grass, then headed for the green with his putter tucked up under his arm. He never looked over at Matt.

I grabbed the bags, swung them onto my shoulders, and started toward Matt in a quick trot, the irons rattling as I ran. Matt had already addressed the ball, but he was swinging too fast, I saw, so before he could set himself, I called out to stop him and he stepped away from the ball.

"What!" he said, annoyed at me for interrupting his routine.

"Hold it!" I said.

"What's the matter? I've got the right club."

I swung the bags off my shoulders. "Easy, easy." I was out of breath from rushing.

I pointed to the green. "Don was here this morning," I said. Don was the son of the greenskeeper. "He replaced the turf on the right apron and watered it. That whole right side is soaked. Hit a knockdown nine to the front and let it run up."

I didn't need to tell him how to play the shot, but I wanted to make sure he didn't rush it. I could see him calming down as I spoke. I looked up and saw Hogan standing in the shade of a cluster of trees, near the path leading to the next tee. He was leaning against his putter watching Matt.

In years to come, whenever I thought of Hogan I always remembered this image of him, there by the side of the tenth green. It was the classic Hogan pose: the white cap, the slouching shoulders, the legs casually crossed, the burning cigarette in one hand as he rests lightly against his putter and looks off.

There are many memorable images and photographs of Ben Hogan. Many of you may have seen the famous photo taken by *Life* photographer Hy Peskin of Hogan hitting the 1-iron onto eighteen at Merion at the 1950 U.S. Open, the major he won only months after the automobile accident.

This story about Hogan is worth mentioning, as it says an awful lot about the man. On eighteen that afternoon at Merion he needed a 4-wood to get the ball back to where the pin was, where he would have a birdie putt to win over George Fazio and Lloyd Mangrum, or a par to force a playoff.

The eighteenth at Merion was a par-4, over 460 yards. From the championship tee, the drive has to carry 210 yards just to reach the fairway. It also has to carry a ridge that hides the fairway, and be threaded through trees on both sides.

The hole location was on the right side, behind a bunker, so Hogan thought about cutting a 4-wood. But again, he worried about running over. He was also hitting into a tight green, less than fifteen feet deep; a green shaped like the top half of a barrel lying on its side, its axis at right angles to the line of play. Another problem he faced was that the right side was higher than the left. So if Hogan's ball lands short of the landing area, it stops. Land past it, and his ball goes over the green into grassy hollows. Remember what Hogan told me back on the fifth about hitting long and into trouble?

It was also a difficult shot because with either a long iron or a fairway wood, the only way to approach it is with a high, soft fade, but the contour of the fairway, sloping from right to left, means the ball is above his feet, a lie we all know normally produces a draw.

Now any one of us today would just hit a drive into the middle of the fairway, knock a metal wood into the swale short of the green, pitch up with our third shot, and play the hole as a par-5. Not Hogan, of course.

He took the 1-iron—the butter knife, as it was called—with the idea of just getting on the green. We all know the 1-iron is the hardest club in the bag to hit. In fact, today most manufacturers have even stopped making the club, and most pros have replaced the 1-iron with those hybrid rescue metal woods, giving themselves more club head speed because of the longer shaft.

At the time Hogan had none of those advantages of technology. Hogan would not normally even have had a 1-iron in his bag, but when he played a practice round, he realized there were no 7-iron shots at Merion, so he pulled the 7-iron to make room in his bag for the 1-iron. It was the only time he would use the 1-iron in the Open—on that final hole of the closing round.

Playing sixteen months after his terrible car accident, Hogan was in great pain, and coming up eighteen after playing thirty-six holes his legs began to give out and he thought he had lost the Open. He had three-putted three holes in a row and blown a three-shot lead to Mangrum and Fazio. All he wanted to do, he told reporters later, was finish and get off the course. The afternoon round had taken nearly six hours to play.

Hy Peskin, the *Life* photographer, was covering his first golf event and he was in the right spot at the right time. Back then, spectators could stand up close to players and when Hogan hit his drive off eighteen tee, Peskin followed behind him.

Hogan made a quick decision about hitting the iron and not a

wood. He took a deep drag on his cigarette, tossed it aside, and
pulled out the 1-iron. Stepping up to the ball, he settled himself,
glanced toward the green, and swung.

When he hit the 1-iron, over sixteen thousand fans lined both
sides of the fairway. It was the greatest single-day gallery in the
fifty-year history of the Open, and they squeezed the hole in a
tight figure eight circling the green below the white-columned
clubhouse.

The ball soared high into the clear late afternoon sky, and
Hogan held his strong finish as he followed the flight. For those
of you who haven't seen this black-and-white photograph, it
shows Hogan still taut and facing the target. His back is to the
camera. The photo captures him and the sixteen thousand spectators framing the hole. It was the pivotal shot of the Open and
proved to be the most important one for Hogan.

Hogan once remarked all he saw in the photo was his properly
balanced finish, the blacks and whites and grays of the gallery, and
himself. Nothing more. Others, of course, saw much more. They
saw a small and fierce man who had come back from a terrible
automobile accident to play and win again. They saw what Hem-
ingway defined as grace under pressure.

Matt played his 9-iron perfectly. The ball cleared the front
bunker and hit the soft green where it had been watered and
rolled up the slope and lipped the cup. It stopped three inches
past the hole.

"Great shot!" I exclaimed, but immediately I shut up, afraid
Hogan might hear me.

I had both bags on my shoulders and took the club from Matt
as we walked to the hole.

"Hogan's mad," Matt said. "I jammed my nine inside his. I can play him."

"You've played one hole," I told him.

"Yeah, watch me." With that he picked up his pace and stepped onto the green, saying quickly, "I'll mark my ball, Ben."

"No need." Hogan tossed me his ball to clean, then told Matt, "You're not in my way."

This was the first time I noticed how Hogan would get when he was annoyed, how his voice softened, not to a whisper, but a calmness without any modulation. There's a '40s movie starring Alan Ladd called *Whispering Smith*. Alan Ladd is a railway detective who has to chase down an old friend, and the closer he gets to killing him, the softer his voice becomes. That was Hogan.

I felt Hogan's coldness, and knew it was only because Matt was inside his ball on the tenth green.

Many of you have heard how Hogan never said anything to anyone he was playing with. Once he walked up to his playing partner at the start of their second round and said, "I'm sorry I didn't speak to you yesterday, but just so you're not surprised, I won't be saying anything today, either."

All of this was attributed to his great ability to concentrate, but there was something else going on with Hogan. I identified with him there on the tenth green, though it would take me some time, several more years of growing up, to fully understand his coldness, the way he closed out the world around him. Hogan couldn't afford to lose.

I've always believed Hogan and I were alike in one respect: We both lost our fathers. My dad died in the war; Hogan's father killed himself in their Texas home. Others have commented about Hogan and his father. Ben Crenshaw talks about how golf gave Hogan the solitude and peace he never found as a child. The golf professional turned writer Curt Sampson compares Hogan to Charles Dickens, the English novelist. Dickens used to visit his father in debtor's prison, just as Hogan visited his father in a sanatorium. Both, Sampson writes, turned the heartbreak of their early years into an unshakable determination to succeed.

On the tenth, when I saw Hogan close down, I realized what had changed: Hogan had seen he wasn't playing some twenty-year-old flash in the pan. He was playing a pro who might beat him.

I quick pulled the flagstick and, without much attention, Hogan drilled the three-foot putt. When he reached for his ball, he picked up Matt's, tossed it to him, and walked wordless toward the eleventh tee.

Matt glanced at me and grinned. This wasn't going to be a friendly round of golf, but then, for Hogan it never was. He said as much himself, commenting once that though he played golf with friends, it was never a friendly game.

11

WHEN MATT AND I ARRIVED AT THE ELEVENTH TEE, HOGAN pulled out his driver and handed me the cover.

"What do you say, Jack? Draw it off the top of the ridge?"

"No, sir," I answered. "The fairway narrows beyond the ridge, and you might catch the rough. Go for the left side and you'll end up in the Danakil."

"Danakil?" The strange name caught Hogan's attention. "What does it mean?"

It was the name I had given the low spot on eleven that always flooded after a heavy rain.

"The Danakil depression in Ethiopia is the lowest spot in Africa," Matt answered. "Jack read about it in one of his schoolbooks. He's got all the members calling this hole the Danakil."

Hogan smiled.

"Good for you, Jack. Stay in school and you'll learn things. I never finished high school. It's the only thing I never finished in my life and I'm not proud of quitting. Now, how do I play your Danakil?"

"Aim for the dip in the treeline." I pointed to the spot on the horizon. "And hit a clothesline."

"Yes, sir." Stepping to the ball, Hogan hit a screamer. It cleared the ridge by less than a man's height and disappeared in the glaring sun.

"Will that reach your Danakil?" Hogan asked, giving me his driver.

"You're beyond the Danakil, Mr. Hogan. You don't have anything but a half-wedge to reach the hole."

Matt stepped over to me and reached for his 1-wood.

"Hit the three-wood," I whispered.

Matt's hand hesitated.

"You're pumped up, Matt. You'll lose it right."

"No way! Hogan will have me by a hundred yards," he answered under his breath.

When Matt addressed the ball, I saw he wanted to kill it. He wanted to outdrive Hogan again. Seeing the tension in the muscles of his left arm, I knew what he'd do, what he always did when he went to kill the ball. He'd lose his tempo, hit from the top, cut across the line, and hit a sweeping slice—which is exactly what he did then, driving the ball over the tops of the maple trees lining the length of the out-of-bounds.

Before the ball was out of sight, I fished another one from the deep pocket of his bag, and when he looked over at me with both pain and embarrassment on his face, I tossed him a ball.

Behind him a small amused smile slipped on and off Hogan's face.

Matt slowed down on the second drive and hit a high soft hook that landed over the ridge and cascaded for another forty yards into the lowest spot on the course, less than 120 from the green. It was the only way for Matt to play eleven; we knew that from dozens of late-night practice rounds.

"Nice drive," Hogan said, moving off the tee. Then he grinned and added, "Next time you should listen to Jack."

Furious, Matt bent over and grabbed his tee.

Hogan fell into step beside Matt and glanced into his bag.

"You're playing Armour Silver Scots. You like them?" he asked.

"Yes, sir."

"I've been playing them for years," Hogan said. "They make them special for me in their plant in Dayton. I go to Ohio and work with the men who run the milling machines. We take the forged irons and work the metal until I like the look of it. With my irons, I have them move the sweet spot to the heel of the club. I prefer it there; I can work the ball better hitting it from the heel instead of the center of the face. Have you been to Dayton, Matt?"

"No, sir," Matt answered, smiling.

"You might want to go by the factory and pick out a set. If you play the tour, fella, you have to have the right equipment. Now, I tend to be a lot fussier than most. Byron, why, he goes to MacGregor and walks past the shelves of 2-irons and 5-irons and all the other clubs and puts together a set in ten or fifteen minutes. It usually takes me three or four days, but it's because I start with the blank forged clubs and mill them down myself. I want just the right feel and look, and that sweet spot in the heel."

"I'm not sure MacGregor is going to let me mess around with their forged irons," Matt answered, amused by the idea of picking out a set of clubs at the factory.

Hogan stopped walking. Matt did, too. Hogan, who was famous for never speaking on a golf course, was now talking, and for a couple of minutes I couldn't figure out why. But as I said to you earlier, caddies don't miss much.

"You have a solid swing," he began. "You might someday be a helluva player. But if you're going to play on tour, you're going to have to take yourself seriously. It looks like you can work the ball—at least some of the time—but you need to learn how to manage yourself, mentally and physically." He glanced to me and, softening his tone, added, "And you should listen to Jack. He was right about that three-wood."

With that, he took another long drag on his cigarette, blew out a cloud of smoke, and walked through it toward the ridge of the fairway. When we got there, I looked down and saw where the drives had landed. Matt's ball had rolled to the bottom of the Danakil. Hogan's had run through the depression and was fifty yards longer off the tee than Matt's drive.

Walking to Matt's ball, it dawned on me what Hogan was doing: as we like to say today, "he was playing with Matt's mind," getting Matt wondering about his clubs, questioning whether he had the right equipment, and not thinking about playing the next shot.

I reached Matt's ball and planted the bags beside it. In those days, the eleventh was the only target hole on the course: small, flat, elevated, and well bunkered, much like the eleventh at Shinnecock. It was a hard green to hold a second shot, and most members drove into the front slope and let the ball bounce up onto the putting surface.

When Matt stepped over he whispered, "Give me the sand wedge and don't tell me it's not enough club."

"It's not enough club."

"I hit a pitching wedge here two days ago and it flew the green, remember?"

"You'll hit it thin."

"Watch me."

"I will. And so will Hogan. He's going to know you're a pigeon, come the Open. Hey, don't listen to me. I'm just a caddie."

I grabbed the bags and walked halfway over to Hogan's ball, then paused while Matt played the iron. Even in flight, I saw it was short. The ball caught the front apron of the green and rolled back, gaining speed as it tumbled to the bottom of the hill. Matt finished his swing by banging the club into the ground.

"What did he hit, sand wedge?" Hogan asked when I reached him.

"Yep." I swung the bags off my shoulders.

"He didn't let you club him?"

"Nope."

Hogan fingered the short irons and pulled his sand wedge from the bag. I had noticed early in the round that he always pulled his own clubs. In events Hogan never wanted anyone touching his club. "How far back is the hole cut?" he asked.

"Maybe ten paces. The green's small, but it's holding. You've got sixty-five yards to the front edge. Hit it high enough and the ball will stay."

He paused behind the ball and thumped the ground and felt the hardness of the turf, then played the shot.

"Okay, Jack, let's see how good you are at judging yardage."

From where we were I couldn't see the ball land, but from its flight I knew it was beyond the pin, and if it hit too hard it might bounce into the long grass over the green.

I dropped the bags and sprinted forward to pick up the thin

divot, and Hogan pulled his putter out of the bag. When I ran back to him, he said quietly, as if he had been reading my mind, "It's within two feet of the cup, Jack. You really can read yardage." He seemed impressed.

Hogan took another drag on his cigarette. Twenty yards across the fairway Matt was standing with his arms folded, watching the two of us. It didn't bother Hogan that Matt was annoyed at having to wait.

"That fella doesn't belong on tour. He'd be smart to hold onto this club job and keep some money in his pocket."

"He's a great player, Mr. Hogan," I said quietly, defending Matt.

"We're all great players, Jack, but that's not going to help him win on the PGA tour," Hogan said and walked off.

"What the hell were you and Hogan talking about?" Matt asked when I arrived with his bag.

"You."

Matt grabbed the sand wedge from the bag, but he did it slowly and I knew he was wondering about what I had just said.

"Don't hit any dumb shot," I said.

I took a deep breath.

"Hit it to the flag," I told Matt. "The green's soft."

Hogan had already climbed the rise and was standing on the putting surface. Matt lobbed the ball into the sun, and it carried over the rise and disappeared. I watched for Hogan's reaction to the shot. He started to move forward and then stopped and signaled the ball had dropped.

"It's in?" I called out.

Hogan nodded and Matt handed me the wedge as he walked toward the green.

"Is that good enough for you, Jackson?"

"Hey!" I called after him. "Even a blind pig can find an acorn."

We reached the green together as Hogan plucked Matt's ball from the cup. He tossed it to him, saying, "Nicely done."

"Thanks." Matt grabbed the ball out of the air. "Well, you know, even a blind pig can find an acorn."

I kept from looking at Matt as Hogan made his birdie putt. I knew if I looked at Matt I would burst out laughing. That was the thing about Matt. He really didn't take golf that seriously, which was something I hadn't realized until that day when Hogan taught him what it meant to play with someone who did.

12

FROM THE TEE AT TWELVE I LOOKED ACROSS THE SMALL POND OF the par-3 and saw Dr. DuPree standing with Sarah in the shade up by the green. DuPree must have spotted us on the tenth, or Sarah had told him Hogan was playing. I glanced over at Matt. Hogan was talking to him, nodding toward the green as he asked, "Is that your girl?"

"Well, sort of," Matt mumbled. No one had ever referred to Sarah as his girl before.

Hogan didn't reply. He stepped around Matt and teed up his ball, patted the ground behind the ball with his right foot, and then came to where I was standing. He took the 6-iron from his bag and, playing the shot, he drove down hard, cut a thick wedge of turf, and hit the ball high and to the left of the flag stick

As the ball crossed the small pond, it worked toward the cup, fading gently, landed on the lower front half of the green, then spun toward the flag stick stopping less than a yard below the hole. Beside the green, Dr. DuPree and Sarah both applauded, and the sound of their clapping was muted and polite as it carried across the still water.

As Hogan walked over to where I was standing with both bags, he saw Matt reaching for the 6 and said to him, "If I were you, Matt, I'd hit the seven; you've got so much adrenaline running through you now, you're liable to hit the six as far as the Loop."

Matt didn't hit it downtown, but he jumped all over the 7-iron and launched the ball to the far left, where it careened off the top branches of the elms guarding the hole and dropped limply into the green side bunker.

"Is it the girl or her old man who made you jerk the club, Matt?" Hogan asked, and walked off before Matt could reply.

When you come off the twelfth tee, as those of you who play the course know, you have to circle the pond. Hogan took the right path and Matt went left. Sarah and Dr. DuPree were standing to the right of the green and there was no way Matt wanted to walk by them.

I didn't catch up with Matt until he reached the bunker. He had a good lie, I saw at once. The sand at the back edge of the bunker was thin and wet. He could chip it close for a par. Hogan's ball was less than a yard from the hole, an easy birdie.

Hogan had come up to the green on the other path and I watched as he stopped and shook hands with Dr. DuPree. He took off his white cap, greeting Sarah, and even from across the wide green I saw him beaming at her, his smile warm under his farmer's tan.

"Give me the wedge," Matt said.

"It's not a wedge. Look at that lie."

"I'm looking at it. I'm going to skim it off the sand."

I knew by his tone that he was still furious at himself for jerking the 7-iron.

"Calm down," I told him.

"What shot do you want to play?" he asked, calming some, but also annoyed at me for second-guessing him.

"Pick it clean with the nine. Let it run up," I told him. "Even if you hit a perfect wedge it won't hold the green. Use the nine. You're deadly with that club," I added, encouraging him. I handed him the 9-iron and told him to hit it stiff.

Matt took my advice, I think, because he had been so wrong about his club selection on the last hole, and here he was already down one skin. Not only was he losing money he didn't have, but he was losing on his own course.

Hogan had walked over to mark his ball and was standing clear of the flag stick when Matt chipped from the wet sand.

Matt hit a great shot. The ball came out low and fast and caught the ridge, which immediately cut down the speed as it ran along the edge, then across the flat top shelf. The ball curled to a stop within six inches of the hole.

Sarah let out a squeak and applauded, and Hogan glanced over at Matt and nodded approvingly.

I dropped both bags and raked the bunker, and when I grabbed the bags again, Hogan had made his birdie and he and Matt were walking off together, headed for the long par-5 thirteenth hole.

When I reached the tee, Matt was launched on a detailed description of the par-5, telling Hogan he needed to keep his drive to the right, aim for the bunker wedged into the fairway 240 yards out. He had to give himself enough room to maneuver a wood around the corner of the dogleg, Matt said. It was the way we always played the hole.

Hogan listened without saying anything. He had already teed up way to the left side of the markers and was working diligently on another cigarette as he stared at the wide-open fairway. There were no trees in the right rough, but in preparation for the Open the grass had been left to grow. All of us caddies lived in fear of members slicing into the weeds.

Hogan's ball was six inches from the left marker, so he had to stand outside the markers to drive, and I knew from where he had placed his tee, it was too far left, that he wasn't going to play a hook. He would drive down the left side and fade the ball into the center. A drive like that would give him a spoon to the green. But a lie on the left side, close to the trees, meant Hogan needed to get his second shot up fast to clear the corner. It wasn't the percentage shot, as all those golfers-cum-announcers declare today on television.

Speaking of television, I recall how Ken Venturi said Hogan told him once there were three ways to beat your opponent. Outwork him. Outthink him. And if those didn't work, then intimidate him. I got the feeling, standing on thirteen, Hogan was doing all three to Matt.

Hogan had been taught this lesson by Paul Runyan, whom the touring pros called "the Cyanide Kid." Runyan won the '38 PGA Championship. He couldn't outdrive Hogan; he couldn't outplay him tee to green; but using an old metal-spooned putter, Runyan kept himself in the match and won. It was a lesson Hogan never forgot, and one he mentioned often later in his life. What mattered in golf was the ability to finish off the other guy. And Hogan was doing that now to Matt Richardson.

Everything got real quiet as Hogan prepared to drive. I was holding my breath in anticipation of the sudden, fierce whip of the club. The ball coming off the face of the driver even sounded different from drives by other players. It was like the reverberation from a shotgun blast on a dry cold winter morning across an empty farm field.

When he hit the ball, both Matt and I flinched. It was a low drive that didn't climb but bore against the air, edging the left side of the fairway and riding the stretch of trees like a taut clothesline. Then, about 240 out, it slowly began to fade and come back to the center. It disappeared beyond the rise, but I knew—and so did Matt that Hogan's drive had gone over 270.

Hogan didn't even wait to see where he landed. He finished his high, perfect swing, stepped forward, and, with an easy swoop, picked up his tee and walked over to where I was standing and handed me his driver.

"Wow," I whispered.

"Wow, yourself," he answered back.

Matt took several easy practice swings. He wasn't rushing. I saw he had gotten very serious. Hogan's presence was making a difference. The truth was, most of the time Matt didn't care about winning. He played for the sheer joy of hitting the ball, which made him wonderful to watch, and wonderful to caddie for. Now he was serious. He stepped up and without any fooling around addressed the ball and swung.

The ball followed the edge of the right rough. I held my breath and waited for it to move left, to draw back into the fairway. I was afraid Matt had hit it too hard, but then, over 250 down the right side, it went left, caught the short grass, and ran.

Hogan didn't say anything striding off the tee. Going left, he circled the signature mound, and I walked right. Matt caught up with me when I circled the mound. Hogan was way off on the left side, striding alone toward his ball. Sarah and her father were ahead, walking together.

"I creamed it," Matt said, falling into stride with me.

"So did Hogan."

"He's too far left."

It did appear as if Hogan had stymied himself on the left side and had not given himself room to play his second shot. But when we reached the ridge of the fairway, bracketed by two bunkers, and saw the drives, we realized Matt's had not carried as far as we'd thought, and Hogan had outdriven him by a half-dozen yards. Hogan's ball also had faded into the middle of the fairway, leaving him enough room to work a second shot around the edge of the dogleg.

"Nice drive, Matt," Dr. DuPree said as we approached. In all his life DuPree had never driven past the bunkers on thirteen.

I set the bags down as Matt bent over and nervously did some housekeeping, brushing away loose grass and sticks around his ball.

When he stood up and came over to me and his bag, he asked quickly, "What do you think?"

I could tell by his voice he really wanted my opinion. I looked up at the corner of the dogleg, and through the trees to the green. From playing in the morning I knew the pin was tucked behind the right side bunker.

"Okay," I said. "Don't go for it. Hit a five over the trees and to the left side. It will leave you a clear wedge to the pin."

Matt pulled the 5-iron from the bag. "Enough club?" he asked.

"Hit it to the right of the last tree and you have a wedge left." I pulled the bags away. "You're playing match now, not stroke.

Hogan's got the tougher shot. Hit it stiff." I crossed the fairway, headed for where Hogan stood beside his drive. He glanced into the bag to see what iron Matt had played. Seeing it was the 5-iron, he didn't react or say anything. It was as if he had watched another poker player being dealt a card.

Matt didn't rush his shot. He swung easily. The ball went to the right of the last tree and landed clear of trouble.

Hogan took his spoon and tossed me the cover. He was going for the green. Matt had made his play and Hogan was going to outplay him, and it was my fault. It was, as I told Matt, match play and Hogan had been given an opening when Matt played safe.

When Hogan hit the ball off thirteen fairway it seemed indeed as if all the air was sucked out of the day. It was frightening and compelling, as if a dangerous animal had gotten loose on the course.

The ball carried the last tall tree in the straight line of old oaks and would've had the distance to reach the green if Hogan hadn't put too much into the 3-wood and pulled it. The ball landed safely but kicked forward and into the left green-side bunker.

You know there are all these comments on how Hogan never made a mistake, never hit a bad shot, but as Hale Irwin once observed, there are plenty of black-and-white photos showing Hogan hitting out of bunkers and from deep in the woods, so we know he didn't hit every shot dead solid perfect.

Hogan didn't say anything. He didn't swear. But I could feel, standing a few yards from him, how angry he was as he moved toward the green without a word.

When I reached Matt and his ball, he was ready to play.

"A wedge?" he asked.

"Take your time. Hit it smooth," I said.

That is just how Matt hit it, floating it high where the ball bounced once and skipped forward and disappeared into the cup.

Caught up in the action, I didn't really appreciate the drama of this match. But Dr. DuPree did. He applauded Matt's eagle, and when Matt plucked his own ball from the hole and stepped over to the apron, DuPree came right up to congratulate him as they waited for Hogan to finish the hole with a birdie. I could see Sarah was thrilled, too, not just at the match, but because her father was being nice to Matt.

It was after five o'clock when we stepped onto the fourteenth tee and I remember the sun was low on the horizon. The shadows had lengthened and it was pleasant on the back nine, as it always was in the late afternoon, the best time to be on the course.

When I think about golf, and why people play the silly game—and it is silly, as we all must admit—one big reason is the moments like the one I experienced on fourteen when the day had lost its heat and the three of us stood looking down the tight aisle of the hole to where it burst open into a wide, open, flat fairway.

Matt reached for his driver, and I whispered he should play the spoon. While he hesitated, I went on quickly, telling him to take the safe shot. He didn't need the length, I said. A good 3-wood would clear the fairway bunker and leave him a pitching wedge to the green.

I saw then that he wasn't looking down the fairway, but staring at the tops of the tall red maples at the crook of the dogleg, a hundred yards away. He wanted to cut the dogleg.

Matt grinned, watching me, waiting to see if I knew what he was thinking.

"You still got to hit the three," I said. "You can't get the ball up fast enough with your driver."

"I'm going to fade the driver," Matt said. He teed up his ball and stood behind it, taking a few long sweeping practice swings. I glanced over at Hogan, who was slowly puffing on his cigarette, seemingly totally uninterested in the interplay between Matt and me.

It got real quiet on the tee. I could hear the soft creak of Matt's leather shoes as he set his feet and the subtle *whoosh* of the club head cutting the air on his practice swings.

For the last month, Matt had been working on his fade, a shot he didn't have earlier in the summer. The truth is, when you think about this course, as those of you who play here obviously have, you see it's set up for players who hit natural draws. There is only one hole, the fourteenth where fading the ball is a big plus.

Hogan would say later in his career that a professional had to have all the shots to make it on tour, everything from the draw to the fade to the knockdown shots played into the wind. But few players have all the shots. Lee Trevino, for one, never won at Augusta because he couldn't get the ball up, and a high trajectory is what a player needs at the Masters.

That's why the same small cluster of professionals always win the major tournaments—they've mastered every kind of shot. But Matt hadn't yet mastered the fade, which Hogan always said was the only way to hit the ball.

So here was Matt, going to play his driver on the short par-4 dogleg fourteen. If he didn't fade the ball, it would carry the fairway and go into the trees separating fourteen from the thirteenth fairway.

The only reason Matt was hitting the 1-wood, of course, was because he wanted to outdrive Hogan. Then, just before Matt stepped forward to hit away, Hogan cleared his throat and spoke up.

13

FROM THE SHADOWY EDGE OF THE TEE, HOGAN ASKED IN HIS SOFT voice, "What do you plan on doing with the driver, Matt?"

Without looking at him, Matt gestured with the club, pointing toward the distant fairway, and explained how he would fade the ball beyond the bunker, let it catch the short grass and run to the green, which we couldn't see from the fourteenth tee.

Hogan let Matt explain and then remarked, "You've got a natural draw—why work against it?"

I couldn't figure out if Hogan was trying to help Matt, or he trying to get him to doubt his ability to fade the ball.

"I like the idea of being on the green in one," Matt answered. It was a cocky reply. But I knew Matt needed to challenge Hogan, to show while he might be one down, he was still in the match.

Cocky or not, Matt was taking a big chance. If his drive off fourteen didn't fade, he'd be in the trees. But not that afternoon.

His drive rode the wind past the bunkers and gradually, as neatly as a farewell wave, faded into the fairway, landed safely, and rolled out of sight. I wasn't sure he had reached the green, but he was close.

From ahead on the forecaddie Sarah and her father applauded, and Matt tipped his cap as he slipped his driver back into his bag. I moved the bags over to Hogan, who approached the markers. He asked me immediately where the hole was cut, and when I said it was on the top shelf he asked next, "To the right side or left?"

"In the middle; it's tight at the top, less than six yards across."

Hogan stared down the tight slot toward the fairway. Occasionally his eyes would dart to the tops of the red maples as he, too, measured the distance and the height and contemplated cutting the dogleg with a high, booming drive. Then he pulled his 3-wood and teed up the ball, motioning for Matt and me to move out of his line of sight. He was going over the top of the trees.

Hogan's cigarette still dangled loosely in his lips as he set up to play the shot, moving his left foot forward to hit the draw and playing the ball off the toe to give himself plenty of loft. Then, just before he swung, he flipped away the Chesterfield. I can still see the cigarette tumbling in slow motion toward the ground as Hogan swung.

While I certainly thought Hogan was the greatest player of the day, I wasn't sure he could pull off the shot. One thing I'd noticed, this long-ago Monday afternoon, was Hogan's ball didn't have much loft—certainly not the loft players since then, guys like Nicklaus and Watson, were able to achieve. Hogan had learned to play golf in Texas, and all Texas players grew up hitting low drives, "snake rapers" they called them, because of the winds and the hard-packed golf courses. Ben's ball on fourteen did start out low but rose quickly. Somehow he got the shot up high enough to clear the treetops.

The flight was dead-aimed at the green. If it didn't bounce badly, Hogan would be putting for an eagle.

Grabbing his tee, Hogan charged down the fairway, leaving Matt and me behind. Caddying double, I couldn't catch up with either player, but when I reached the forecaddie, Sarah and Dr. DuPree were waiting, and fell into step with me.

"Do you think Matt can beat him?" Sarah whispered hopefully.

I shrugged that I didn't know, but the truth was, I thought he just might. Why else did it feel so dangerous out there, with Hogan furious at Matt, and both of them banging drives farther than I had ever seen hit on this course?

When I reached the corner of the dogleg, I spotted Hogan's ball; it had run onto the lower edge of the green. He had driven the ball over 280 with the 3-wood. Matt, too, was in a great position for his second shot, less than thirty yards from the cup. He could either play a pitch-and-run, or a long wedge up to the flag with enough backspin to hold it on the top shelf.

When I caught up with Matt, standing beside his ball, he asked me under his breath what shot I thought he should play.

I lifted the wedge up a few inches in the bag and said, "Hit to the top tier, but short of the flag. You've got maybe five feet this side of the flag. Get enough spin on it and the ball will hold and the pressure is back on Hogan." It was simple enough match play strategy.

Matt shook his head. "I'll run it up." He pulled the 9-iron. "I'll hit into the bank and let it check below the hole. I don't want to fly the green."

I nodded and pulled the bags away so he could play, and as I did, I glanced over at Sarah. Though her face wasn't showing any concern, I saw she had crossed her fingers for good luck. I lowered my head to hide my grin—as if her praying for good luck would help a player beat Ben Hogan.

In spite of her crossed fingers, Matt hit the 9-iron thin and the ball landed too high on the ridge. It jumped and ran past the pin and off the green, through the apron and into the long grass.

I was moving to the green before the ball stopped rolling, but I could hear Matt swear under his breath and heard him pound the club against the turf. Now he had a delicate chip just to get close enough for par. The trouble was, he couldn't control the ball coming out of the thick rough.

Matt was still off the putting surface and still away, and Matt and I walked to the top of the green and studied the shot. The ball was deep in the long grass beyond the fringe.

"Wedge," Matt said, deciding on the club.

I pulled the sand wedge. "Pop it up," I told him, "nice and easy, okay?"

The ball did pop out, but got caught on the fringe and rolled only a few yards onto the green, leaving him four feet downhill for his par. The breath went out of him.

"Okay," I said at once, encouragingly, and handed Matt his putter. "Knock it in, save par."

All of Matt's earlier cockiness had disappeared.

I walked down the edge of the green with Hogan's bag and he pulled his putter. His ball was fifty feet below the hole, but he was putting for an eagle.

Through the drifting smoke of his cigarette, Hogan kept studying the line of the putt. When I came closer, he crouched behind the ball and nodded that I should join him, which he had never asked me to do before. When I did, leaning over his shoulder as if to read the line of the putt, he didn't ask me how to play the break, but said softly, "Jack, I'm going to give your fella a lesson he needs to learn. It's a lesson he needs to know if he wants to play on the tour. It will do him a lot better if he gets it from me today than to come out here next month and be embarrassed in front of your members."

"Yes, sir," I said, not sure what I was agreeing to.

Hogan finished his cigarette, then stood up and exhaling a cloud of smoke, said, "Tend the flag, Jack. When I hit the ball, pull it out."

Now, we always tended flags in the '40s. Any caddie would, as we didn't have those fancy flagsticks you see today with thin metal shafts that leave room enough for a ball to easily drop into the cup. In my caddying days the flags were thick bamboo poles and a ball could bounce off if it came in hot.

I went up to the hole, pulled down the flag so it wasn't flapping in the breeze, stood so my shadow wasn't across the line of the putt, then watched as Hogan set himself. At this time in his career Hogan gripped the putter with a reversed overlapping grip. All five fingers of his right hand were on the leather. He crouched over the ball with his knees bent and his feet close together. Almost all of his weight was on his left side, and his backstroke was short and strong. His right hand drove the putter.

Holding the flag, I couldn't see the ball at Hogan's feet, but when he stroked the long putt, I didn't wait until the ball crested the ridge. I pulled the flag and stepped away, watching as the ball ran to the hole. Hogan had the line but not the pace, and the ball ran out of steam before it reached the cup. He had a foot left for a birdie.

Matt picked up Hogan's ball and tossed it to him, then picked up the dime he had used to mark his ball and walked off the

green towards the fifteenth tee. Matt had lost another skin and
was two down with four holes to play.

Hogan, with the honors, was standing in the middle of the tee
box staring up at the par-3 number fifteen when I reached him.
Hogan pulled out his scorecard to check the yardage and stepped
over to where I had set down the bags by the tee markers. From
the markers it was 160 to the green, and I had decided already
Hogan had to hit a 6-iron.

The fifteenth hole had two wide, shallow bunkers in front of a
narrow green that was hard to land on and hold. It was better,
therefore, to be in the front bunkers than over the green, where
the rough was deep and thick.

I was thinking of telling Hogan to hit it deliberately in the
bunker and have a safe sand shot to the hole instead of playing to
the flag and having the ball catapult over the backside, when
Hogan placed his hand on his irons and asked, "You're thinking
it's a six?"

When I nodded, he reached down and pulled the 7 from the
bag. I looked up at him, surprised, and he just smiled and dropped
the ball onto the smooth tee to hit it off the grass.

TV watchers today are accustomed to being told exactly
which club a player uses on every shot, especially from the tee on
short par-3s. So it's hard to remember that in the '40s and '50s it
was considered poor manners to look in another player's bag and
see what he was playing, though pros weren't above sneaking a
look.

Some pros deliberately misnumbered their irons. Hogan
hadn't, but he didn't like irons that were too upright—they put a
right-to-left spin on his shots and cause the ball to hook, or as

they say today, to draw. What Hogan did was reshape his clubs, pounding the faces of his irons with a two-by-four so his 7 played more like a 6-iron.

Hitting off the turf, Hogan kept his hands ahead of the club head through impact and hit a low fade toward the left bunker. As it flew, I could see it didn't have the distance to carry the front bunker, but the ball moved right a half-dozen feet and landed in the middle of the narrow tongue between the two bunkers. It took one long bounce and hit the putting surface with enough spin to die within ten feet of the pin, cut on the right side of the elongated green.

"Great shot!" Dr. DuPree exclaimed, excited by the way Hogan had sculpted the 7-iron between the bunkers.

As Hogan walked off the tee, he said offhandedly, as if speaking just to me, "You were right, Jack. I hit the wrong club." He slid the iron into his bag.

Those of you who play know much about winning a match is understanding what the other player is thinking, and how he is reacting to your game. They tell the story about young amateur Francis Ouimet, who beat the great English pro Harry Vardon in 1913 when the U.S. Open was held at the Country Club at Brookline, Massachusetts. Ouimet was one shot in the lead going into fifteen during the playoff round when Harry Vardon pulled out a cigarette and lit it.

Vardon never smoked on the golf course. Ouimet knew that. Ouimet realized Vardon was afraid he might lose to this American kid, and Ouimet said later that seeing Vardon take out a cigarette to calm his nerves gave him tremendous confidence. So Ouimet went ahead and birdied seventeen, while Vardon hooked his drive into a dogleg bunker and bogied the hole.

When Hogan made this short remark about his shot, I looked

up, expecting to see something in Hogan's face—anger, maybe, or outright fear. But I saw nothing. He wasn't blanching—a sure sign, as Dr. Hughes will tell you, a player is in a panic.

No, but I was looking at the wrong player. It was Matt who was choking. He heard what Hogan had said, how he had struck the iron as well as any, and still it hit a good five yards short of the green.

Now Matt had to match Hogan, and he reached into the bag and pulled out his 7-iron. He was going to be all over this 7-iron, I knew, and when he didn't swing within himself, as we've seen, he was a wild man. I pulled the 6 from the bag and stepped between the markers as he teed up his ball.

"Hit the six," I said.

Matt stared at me like a deer caught in headlights.

Now, no caddie should interfere when a player has made his decision, especially in a situation like this when tensions were running high. Oh, you see players and caddies on tour, going back and forth discussing what to play, but once the player has made up his mind, there's no second-guessing by the caddie.

"Hit the six and don't press it," I whispered. "You're going to be all over the seven." I edged the club closer and damn near yanked the 7-iron from his hands.

"We've been hitting the seven all summer," Matt said. He kept looking up the green as if he were missing something important about the hole.

"Hit an easy draw and aim for the right edge. You'll just carry the bunkers, land on the apron, and hold the green."

His face was worked into a puzzle, frowning and squinting, his eyes narrowed against the sun. He looked as helpless as any kid might be from a small town caught up in the big time. I had this sudden flash of realization that Matt was way over his head trying to play against Hogan. Who was he kidding? Who were we all kidding? Matt was going to embarrass himself. He was going to embarrass the members. He was just another one of those local hotshots who put together a couple of great subpar rounds and think they're good enough to play against the best players in the world.

"Hit the six," I whispered again, seeing he was wavering. When he was nervous he always did the same thing, which was to rub his lips with his tongue as if he had just tasted something bitter. Matt *always* wet his lips when he got nervous, and I wondered, too, if Hogan had already figured that out.

I thought he might still play the 7, but then he took the 6 and said almost as if he were asking permission, "Okay, I'll play the draw."

"Nice and easy," I ordered and stepped away.

He hit it high and soft, and because he didn't force the shot he was able to work the ball. It cleared the bunker, landed on the apron, bounced softly onto the green, and stopped eight feet beyond the hole. He had a downhill putt for his birdie.

Hogan didn't wait for the ball to land. With Matt's swing he went striding ahead. Matt stepped over to me coming off the tee and gave me his 6-iron. As he did, he said under his breath, "Thanks."

And then he reached over and tapped the bill of my golf cap as he often did when he was trying to be nice to me, and for just a moment it was like old times again, before Sarah DuPree came home from college and decided to learn how to play golf.

14

Hogan missed his putt on fifteen. Perhaps he rushed it. Perhaps he missed it on purpose. He didn't take a lot of time.

Not that it was an easy one, some ten feet and mostly straight in. He didn't ask me to help read the line. He just went up and slammed it, much the way John Daly putts today.

I think Matt was stunned when Hogan missed. Hogan hadn't done much wrong since we started the back side, and Matt would have had to admit he was only in the match because of a few lucky shots. Now Matt had a chance to win a skin.

I was standing on the apron, holding the flag and watching Matt look over his putt. He studied the break from both sides, and when he crouched behind the ball, he glanced my way, signaled me to help him read the line.

It was an eight-footer, and it looked as if it should break several inches from left to right, but in the morning I had had a similar putt and it hadn't broken at all, which I told Matt. I also told him he should play inside the left side of the cup in case it broke. What was important, I reminded him, was to strike the ball. As all of us know, most golfers putting downhill have a tendency to baby the shot and the ball won't hold its line. Think of hitting the putt 6 inches beyond the cup, I reminded him.

Matt hit a beautiful putt with all the smooth grace he was capable of. When the ball reached the cup it was moving fast, but it struck in the center, jumped, and dropped. Matt had won a hole and was only one down.

On the sixteenth I gave Hogan and Matt their drivers and walked ahead to the forecaddie on the long par-4. Dr. DuPree and Sarah followed after me.

"He's holding his own," DuPree said, joining me in the shade of the trees dividing fifteen from sixteen. It was another tight tee shot.

That was, of course, the style of all the old golf courses: holes hewn out of forests. Augusta was originally a Civil War indigo plantation converted into a horticultural nursery. What Bobby Jones did in Augusta, and what the designers all did back in the 1890s, was build courses that grew naturally out of the terrain. They had to, since they didn't have the heavy earth-moving equipment necessary to build a golf course in bare, brown land. A golfer had to keep the ball in play on these old, tight courses, and as any good caddie knows not to look away from his player once he's stepped onto the tee, I was watching Matt at the same time I was listening to Dr. DuPree going on and on about how great Matt was playing.

"If he can beat Hogan, he can beat any of these touring pros," DuPree declared, as if the thought had just come to him.

"Hogan hits the ball farther than Matt," Sarah added softly, thinking distance was all that mattered in golf.

I kept my eyes on Matt. Even from 100 yards away I saw him take a deep breath as he stared down the fairway, picking the spot where he wanted to place his drive. He walked up to the ball, placing his right foot, then his left, then gripped and regripped the driver as he glanced once, twice, and finally a third time down the long fairway. He paused and concentrated, focused his attention, and swung.

The ball came straight over our heads, as I knew it would. We had decided the perfect drive for Matt on sixteen was to hit as close as he could to the trees on the right side, for once the ball cleared the narrow opening and burst into the wide fairway it would catch the breeze that always blew from right to left across this hole. The breeze would push the ball into the center of the fairway and onto the short grass beyond the right-side bunker, 250 yards from the tee box. As the ball flew over my head, I spun around and watched it draw back into the fairway and land safely.

"Christ, what a shot!" Dr. DuPree whispered. It never ceased to amuse me how members were humbled by great golfers. It has always been that way. They tell the story that whenever Tommy Armour, a prewar champ, walked into 21 in New York, the wealthiest people in America would stand up from their meals and cheer the man who could hit a mid-iron better than any one of them. And he wasn't the only pro to enthrall Wall Street. Back in 1900, when Harry Vardon showed up in New York City to play in the new U.S. Open and give an exhibition for the Spalding gutty ball, his signature Vardon Flyer, the Stock Exchange closed for the day so brokers could watch him play.

I made sure I knew where Matt's ball was and turned to watch Hogan tee off. I had come to know Hogan's movements, the way he pulled himself together to drive. It was a script, an act played out on every tee: the look down the fairway followed by the lengthy cigarette drag, the cigarette flicked away as he prepared to play. No motion was wasted. Everything about Hogan was surgical. He was the safecracker, the diamond cutter. He took your breath away.

Hogan's drive came out of the dark cluster of trees behind the tee and flew past us like a white bullet. We spun around to follow the blur of the ball's flight.

His drive was to the left side, to the wide-open flat stretch of rough between the sixteenth and seventh fairways. I could see by the flight that the ball wouldn't carry as far as Matt's, and that it might end up in the long grass where the fairway narrowed 240 yards out from the tee.

"He's in the rough!" Dr. DuPree said, but it sounded more like a wish than a fact.

"Maybe." I picked up the bags.

"He can't reach the green from the rough," DuPree declared, following after me.

"Maybe," I said, speeding up to distance myself from him.

Matt's ball was in the middle of the fairway, and I saw that Hogan's was sitting up in the short fringe grass. He had escaped the deep rough by less than a yard and he had, at most, a 6-iron to the green. Matt would play a 7-iron, as he had been playing that same shot all summer long. It was a shot, as pros say today, he had "grooved."

Hogan's second shot was more difficult. The ball was sitting up, and that meant he'd have to be careful. It could come out heavy and not carry to the green if he got too much grass between the ball and the club face. For once, I had no clever suggestion on how to play his next shot.

Not that he asked.

He came striding up and without any hesitation reached into his bag and pulled out the 7. My guess was he had decided the ball would come out hot with plenty of overspin, and he was protecting himself by playing a shorter iron.

But it wasn't the shot Hogan had in mind. He hit a soft cut that worked from left to right and came up short, took two healthy bounces, and spun to a stop a dozen feet beyond the flag, which was cut in the dead center of the tight, flat green.

"What a shot!" Dr. DuPree exclaimed. "Perfect!" He walked right over to Hogan, grinning and all excited, and said, "I would have thought you'd hit a hard eight." He pointed to the thick fringe. "Given the grass. But you pulled the right club, that's for sure!"

Beaming, he kept on babbling. I don't think I ever felt more embarrassed by anyone's enthusiasm. It wasn't the way to behave around Ben Hogan.

Hogan looked at Dr. DuPree as if he had never seen the man before, and then he did a surprising thing there in the middle of the sixteenth hole.

He stepped to his bag and opened the deep pocket full of balls and dug out a dozen. He tossed them into the thick fringe, then pulled the 9-iron. It wasn't enough club to reach the green, but Hogan turned in the toe and, playing the shot off his right foot, hit a hard, low ball onto the putting surface.

He came back to me, shoved the 9-iron into the bag, pulled the 8, and used it to drive the second ball onto the green, 160 yards away. He finished off the irons, including the 1, making adjustments with each club, choking up on the long irons and working the ball into the green with slight fades so the ball coming onto the putting surface would hold on the small green.

He walked over to the bag and took out the spoon and, tossing me the cover, hit a high, soft fade with the 3-wood and landed the ball on the putting surface. Next, he hit the brassie, and finally the driver. The dozen balls he had played from the rough were scattered like snowflakes on the flat surface of sixteen green.

Then, without a word to DuPree, he pulled his putter from the bag and walked off.

Dr. DuPree stood dumbly there, as if he had been hit between the eyes with one of Hogan's woods. I left him and hurried over to Matt.

"What the hell was that all about?" Matt asked as I arrived.

"DuPree annoyed Hogan," I whispered, as Sarah was standing near us. "Let's go. Hit the seven," I said, getting Matt to focus on his own game.

"You sure?"

"You've been hitting the seven all summer." I took the club from the bag. "Don't jump on it."

As I stepped out of the way, I saw that Sarah was now standing only a few yards from Matt.

She didn't come near him; she didn't want to interfere with his game. But she couldn't keep away from Matt, either. What I found touching was that she wasn't impressed by Ben Hogan, or the incredible display of skill he had just demonstrated. As the old song from my generation goes, she only had eyes for Matt.

Matt hit the 7 and in spite of my warning, he jumped all over it and pulled the ball left, missing the green by several yards. The ball hit where the players walked to the next tee and the ground is hard and the grass beaten down, and it bounced high and flew beyond the green.

"I should have hit the eight," he said, glaring at me as if it were all my fault.

He banged the club against the ground, and I grabbed the iron from him and kept walking, saying over my shoulder, "I told you it was an easy seven."

When I reached the green, Hogan had corralled the golf balls into a tight white pile. Here we had Matt, who couldn't hit the green with a 7-iron, while Hogan had peppered the putting surface with every club in his bag.

Matt stared at his ball, buried in the coarse grass. The rough behind the green, left to grow for the Open, now resembled the gorse you see pros playing from at the British Open. Matt would have to chop the ball out of that cabbage.

Hogan marked his ball. I was feeling guilty about Matt's erratic play. It was slowing down Hogan, though Hogan did have a reputation himself for playing slow.

One time at a U.S. Open, Hogan was approached just before he teed off by Joe Dey, then executive director of the United States Golf Association, who informed Hogan he had played pretty slow the day before and if it happened again, he'd be penalized.

Hogan just turned those steely eyes of his on Dey and said in his equally steely voice, "Joe, if you want to put two on me, do it now so I know what number I have to shoot."

Then Hogan went out and played his own game at his own pace, and Joe Dey never penalized him. That was Hogan. Everyone was intimidated by him in one way or another.

"Wedge?" Matt asked when I reached him.

I pulled the sand wedge and added what was our expression for that summer: "Even a blind pig can find an acorn."

Matt didn't find an acorn. He flubbed the ball coming out of the grass, leaving a long, thirty-foot putt he hit two feet beyond the hole. Hogan missed his birdie putt but tapped in to win the hole with an easy par. Matt was down two skins with two holes to play.

15

AT THE SEVENTEENTH TEE, HOGAN HAD A PROPOSITION FOR Matt. "How about we double our bet?"

Before Matt could reply, Hogan went on, "Tell you what. Here's another idea. Let's forget about the money bet. Jack says he's planning to caddie for you in the Open. What if we change the wager. If you win these two holes, Jack caddies for you. If you lose these two holes, Jack caddies for me." Hogan never looked at me. He kept his eyes fixed on Matt, as if he were back in Fort Worth dealing cards at the Eighth Avenue garage, the job he had in the early days before the war when he went broke trying to make the tour.

I held my breath, dreading Matt's answer. But I knew damn well what he'd say. Not only had he just lost the sixteenth hole, he'd been totally humiliated when Hogan hit the green with every stick in the bag but his putter. Hogan, I realized, hadn't actually been upset by Dr. DuPree's silly remark—he had only used it as an opportunity to intimidate Matt with a brilliant display of shotmaking.

I tried to catch Matt's eye, to warn him, but Matt jumped right in.

"Sure, why not?" He acted as if he knew he'd recoup on these last two holes—and maybe he would. The truth was, Matt did have a secret about how to play seventeen, a secret Hogan had no way of knowing.

Hogan had the honors, and when I came up to him with his bag, he asked, "Is there water up by the green, Jack?" Hogan could see a dip in front of the green that might mean a creek, as it does at the eleventh at Merion.

I shook my head. Not water, I told him. Trees were the hazard on this hole. They wedged the green on the left and right sides. Besides the trees, there were two deep bunkers creating a narrow opening. But none of that mattered, unless you didn't start by hitting a long drive.

Hogan hit his drive a ton off of seventeen. The ball carried the only bunker and ran another ten yards on the smooth, sloping fairway. He had less than a 3-iron to the green—a doable second shot.

Then Matt stepped up to the tee, grinned at me, and pulled the 2-iron from his bag. Early in the summer, he had hit a driver wide on seventeen and it had caught the service road that ran parallel to the fairway, between seventeen and the back of number four green. The service road was nothing more than hard, bare ground, and Matt realized if he could land his drive just beyond the rise, the ball would bounce down the truck tracks, leaving him a short club to the green.

As soon as Matt set himself to play, aiming right of the fairway bunker, I saw Hogan look toward where he was driving. I knew he could see the narrow truck tracks in the long rough. What he didn't know, and couldn't see from the tee because it was blocked by the right lip of the bunker, was the bare spot Matt was aiming for. Matt drove off with the 2-iron, and the ball came out high with a slight draw. It easily cleared the bunker, took one high bounce, and disappeared from sight.

Hogan said nothing. At the crack of Matt's iron, he was off the tee, lighting a cigarette as he walked. If he was mad about how Matt had inside information, he was determined not to show it.

In the early days of the PGA, players didn't always strive for such self-control. There was, for example, Lefty Stackhouse, a young pro from Seguin, Texas, who was once playing with Hogan in a local tournament. Duck-hooking his drive into a rosebush, Stackhouse got so furious at himself he raked his right hand across a bush until his flesh bled from the thorns. Then, staring down at his left hand, he shouted, "And you too!" and whipped his other hand across the bush until it bled.

And there was Tommy Bolt, so short-tempered other pros called him Thunder. Jimmy Demaret once said Bolt's putter had more flying time than most United Airlines pilots.

But Hogan was all about control. He kept his temper and, I noticed, he never changed his pace of play. He didn't rush shots under pressure. He didn't rush himself between shots, which probably reduced the pressure.

Matt had all that still to learn. Coming off the tee on seventeen, he charged after his drive to see where it had landed, his long stride chewing up the ground. Following him, Sarah and her father couldn't keep up as he stomped through the rough chasing his drive.

I stayed with Hogan, matching him stride for stride as he walked straight for his ball. From where we were in the center of the fairway, we could see he had a perfect lie with a long iron to the green.

When he reached his ball Hogan stopped, folded his arms, and stared toward the green with those cold eyes. I watched him sideways as if he might turn on me.

Hogan placed his hand softly on his irons and then turned to me. "Was that your idea?" he asked.

"We've been hitting the shot all summer," I said. "Matt gets another fifty yards from the roll off that hard ground."

Hogan nodded, then pulled the 4-iron from his bag and stepped toward his ball, saying, "The trouble is come the Open there'll be spectators lining the fairway. Your fella won't be able to play his shot."

I glanced again to where Matt had hit the ball and thought then what an idiot I had been to think there wouldn't be spectators down the length of the fairway. But the truth was, I had never caddied for a pro in a PGA tournament. I didn't know half the things I needed to know.

Seeing my reaction, Hogan tried to make me feel better. "Matt should have known that, Jack. It's not your job to think about where the gallery will be walking."

With that, he took another long drag on his cigarette but for once didn't flip the Chesterfield away. Instead he stepped up and played the iron with the cigarette still in his mouth. I've looked at hundreds of photos of Ben on the course, and there's only a couple where he's still smoking as he swings the club.

In '53 at his only British Open, there's a picture of him practicing at Carnoustie with a cigarette wedged between his teeth. And the photographer Jules Alexander has shown me a photo of Hogan smoking at Westchester in the '70s. Jules pointed out a series of three images in which Hogan made consecutive swings without removing the cigarette from his lips. With each shot the ash on the cigarette grew longer but never fell off, that's how smooth Ben Hogan could swing a golf club.

Of course, Hogan wasn't the only pro from those early years who smoked as he played. The guy who was famous for it was Lloyd Mangrum, who swung as effortlessly as Fred Astaire danced. He was also good looking, so he made it all look romantic. Women fans followed him around the course, and some of them followed him off the course as well.

Hogan hit a hard 4-iron into the tight seventeenth green, striking the ball with the special *thwack* only he could produce. His shot drove into the wind like a silver bullet, landing hard twenty yards short of the apron and bouncing up onto the green. But then it kept rolling across the flat surface and into the thick fringe beyond the hole.

Seeing how far his ball ran, Hogan said, "They must have missed watering this fairway."

"They watered the back nine this morning," I answered carefully. "But you've got to hit it just right to stay on this green." I didn't tell him why.

Hogan thrust the iron back into the bag. His eyes were squinting against the cigarette smoke, but a slow smile crept across his face. "You didn't think I'd miss it, did you?" he asked.

"No, sir." I started to laugh.

"When I hit two or three perfect shots in a round, Jack, I know I'm having a good day. It's what you do with the bad shots that makes the difference in a tournament." He nodded toward Matt. "Your fella there. He thinks hitting a patch of hard ground and getting another thirty yards is the answer." Then he asked, "Do you play poker, Jack?"

"Sure, but only when it rains. Mostly we shoot craps behind the handball court." I spoke nervously, wondering why he asked, since he needed no explanation of the sociology of caddies and caddie yards.

"Well, I grew up dealing cards in poker games, and a lot of my success out here on the golf course comes from what I learned watching people play cards. When you play poker, what's important is not the hand you're dealt. What's important are the hands the other fellas are dealt, and the mistakes they make playing those cards. The same is true in golf. You don't win tournaments. Other players lose them. You just have to figure out how to be the last player to lose."

I crossed the fairway to where Matt had hit his drive, and immediately he reached into his bag and pulled out the 9. He didn't consult me, but I knew what he was going to do. That summer we had noticed the underground sprinklers up by the green had a small leak in the pipes, so a flat patch of fairway ten yards short of the green was always soft. The piece of ground, maybe a dozen yards in circumference, was lush and green, like a birthmark on the face of the fairway. Hitting the spot would take the hard bounce off the shot and allow the ball to hold the putting surface.

Matt hit the shot perfectly. It landed in the thick green, took the soft bounce, and spun to within inches of the flag. He could make the putt and win the hole.

Ahead of us on the fairway I saw Hogan notice where the ball hit and how it had reacted. He paused at the spot, studying it, then he kept walking to where his ball had scooted over the green.

When I came up with his clubs, he said nothing. But he hadn't missed how Matt had played the hole. It was local knowledge, as golfers like to say, and now it was Hogan's.

Hogan's ball coming out of the greenside fringe lipped the cup, and he had to settle for a par. Matt made his birdie putt to win the hole, and as we walked off the seventeenth green, I began to think maybe I would be caddying for Matt in the Open after all. What I also realized was that I no longer knew if that was what I really wanted.

16

THE EIGHTEENTH, AS YOU PLAYERS ARE WELL AWARE, IS NOT A tough finishing hole, nothing like Bay Hill, for example, or most of the courses on the PGA tour, which are set up for those dramatic TV climaxes late on Sunday afternoons. Still, it is a beautiful hole, crowned by this majestic clubhouse. We caddies always called the eighteenth fairway "the run for the roses."

Sarah and her father followed me to the forecaddie. Both were beaming because of Matt's birdie on seventeen.

"He's playing great!" Dr. DuPree exclaimed. "Right, Jack?"

"Playing great," I agreed. Matt was teeing up, and I sneaked a glance at Sarah. She was such a golf novice I wondered if she understood how amazing it was that Matt had Hogan one down going into eighteen. Did she have any idea what it might be like being married to a touring player and following the sun with all the other wives? I doubted it. Her face was full of romance, and if she were back at Smith College, she would probably be daydreaming in class, writing *Mrs. Matthew Richardson* in the margins of her notebooks.

"He can do it—he can beat him," the doctor whispered under his breath, as if he had made an important discovery. I wasn't so sure he was right, but somehow Dr. DuPree made it all seem worrisome for him if Matt did beat Hogan.

Matt's drive came over us, flying high and working from right to left. Without turning, I knew where the ball would land on the fairway: close to the middle and bouncing left for another ten yards. Matt would have a soft wedge to the green.

Up on the tee, Hogan approached the drive, glancing down the fairway once, glancing again, and then his fierce swing. The ball came out of the shadows of the tee low and hard, and even before it crossed the creek, I realized he had hit one of his infamous duck hooks. The ball cleared the first bunker on the left side and dug down into the rough, disappearing like a scared rabbit in the long grass. I kept my eye on it the whole way, knowing if I lost the spot, I would never find his ball. And for a caddie, there's no bigger failure.

It was the first time in the round that Hogan had missed the fairway. But he didn't seem upset as he came up and handed me his driver.

"How did you like the hook, Jack?" he asked, bending to see his ball. After several months of dry weather, the thick grass had dried out and looked like nothing more than hay.

"You *wanted* to drive it in here?" I asked incredulously.

"Something like that." He grinned at me. "This is my practice round, Jack, remember. Now how do you think I should play out of this cabbage?"

I shook my head and stared at the ball buried in the rough. At best Hogan could get back on the fairway by playing the ball sideways with a wedge. Then he would hope to hit his third shot close to the flag.

"What did I tell you on the front nine?" Hogan said. "It's always the next shot that counts."

"You don't have a next shot!" I blurted out.

Hogan laughed and reached for his pitching wedge.

The safe shot, as I said, was to the right, to get onto the fairway. But Hogan didn't do that. Instead he closed the face of the wedge, set his hands forward, and took a wide stance. He was going for the green, an impossible shot. Even if he could chop the ball out of the rough, he had to clear a wide bunker that framed the green.

"Just hack it out," I said quickly, shaking my head at the deep lie he had found. "Get it on the fairway. You can't get it onto the green."

"No?" Hogan grinned, then addressed the ball, and tore at the buried lie. He must have cut out a foot of long, thick rough and the ball popped up, carrying almost to the green. Another half yard and it would have hit the putting surface and run up to the hole, but it didn't quite carry far enough and the ball landed in the left side bunker in a flat, fried-egg lie.

Hogan shook off the long grass caught on the club face and handed the wedge to me.

"Safe," I said, trying to be positive.

Ignoring me, Hogan tramped out of the rough toward the bunker, and I rushed over to Matt, as if escaping from an icy wind.

Matt didn't hit a great second shot into the eighteenth. All summer long he had been hitting wedges from the fairway into the big green, and regardless of where the flag was cut, he would stick it within six feet of the hole. This time he hit the ball too far over the top of the flag and it caught a bad bounce, scooting off without holding, and left him a thirty-five-foot putt, downhill and sidehill to the cup.

Matt didn't swear when he saw where he put the wedge. Sarah and her father were standing too close for that. But he did shove the flange of the wedge into the ground, and as fast I could I grabbed it out of his hand. I didn't give him his putter, either. I didn't want him bending its shaft as he walked up to the green. Also, I didn't want Hogan seeing how quickly Matt lost his temper.

I took off again, headed for Hogan, who was already greenside looking at his lie. Most of you here know the bunker, and those who don't, why, if you just turn your heads and look through those open French doors you'll see it—the flat one to the right of the green. It's not intimidating—more like the waste area you'd find on one of Pete Dye's courses, say, the TPC at Sawgrass. But what all of you players know is the sand in these two greenside bunkers is deeper and of a softer texture, a different grade than what we find on the rest of the course. I knew because I knew Ed, the greenskeeper at the time. He wasn't one of those fellows you employ today, those fancy agronomy B.S.s from colleges like Penn State and Michigan State. No, Ed was just a local farmer who hired half of his relatives to cut grass and water fairways and keep the golf course looking like a golf course.

What he had done with the bunkers on nine and eighteen was to make sure the sand was as golden as anything you might see in the Bahamas. Matt knew that. I knew that. But as Ben Hogan stood there, staring at his pancake lie and trying to decide if he should pick it clean or blast out, he didn't know that.

Hogan stared at the lie for a little longer and then he asked me how he should play the shot.

Now remember, Hogan had only been in the bunker once

before—back on thirteen when he had played a wedge off hard, wet sand. I told him to use the sand wedge, the sand was very fine, I said, and he would have to allow for it. I pointed to where he should aim, which was short of the flag by 10 feet, and way left. The ball would take that slope, I told him.

Hogan shook his head.

"There are too many variables with the wedge," he said and pulled the 9-iron from the bag. Then he told me to tend the flag, as if I were a kid who didn't know his way around a golf course, which, of course, he had just proved.

It was late, almost seven, and the shadows were long across the green. I stepped carefully around the flag, so my shadow wouldn't fall across Hogan's line. I tested the pole, made sure it wouldn't stick if I needed to jerk it out fast. I knew what he would do. He was going to clip the ball with the 9-iron and take the sloping green out of play by jamming the ball right at the flagstick.

Hogan hit a wonderful pitch. The ball came out low, carried the slope, and he made it bite on the fast green—how I don't know. The ball ran perhaps a yard beyond and below the cup, leaving him a makeable three-footer to save par.

And here was Matt stuck thirty-five feet above the hole with one of those slick sidehill putts on a fast green. He had to play the ball wide of the hole and just tap it. The ball would pick up all sorts of speed coming off the mound. There was no way he would make the putt. Hogan would tie the hole and halve the two-hole match. I'd be caddying for Hogan in the Open, I realized as I held the flag at the edge of the green.

Matt looked at the line from both sides and nodded at me to come over to him.

"Any ideas?" he asked.

"It's all speed and direction."

"Yeah, my two middle names," Matt said, sighing. Hogan had marked his ball and walked to the other side of the green. He stood there quietly, turning the ball slowly in his fingers as if absorbed in examining something precious and not noticing Matt's dilemma. Sarah and her father had stepped up onto the first tee, giving themselves a slight rise to watch the action, so they were looking down on the green from twenty yards away. And now Valerie Hogan came off the terrace, walking toward us unsteadily in her heels across the soft turf.

That was the scene late in the day, with the shadows and the silence of impending twilight. It was a perfect golfing moment. No one spoke as Matt circled his putt, gauging the sloping green. There was no chatter from the terrace, no sounds of kids and parents having early dinners on the screened-in summer dining porch. There was just Matt needing to make a slippery downhill thirty-five footer, and I was pulling for him against the great Ben Hogan. And there wasn't a damn thing I could do to help Matt win the hole.

Matt barely tapped the putt. In the stillness of the early evening I heard the soft click of his blade putter touching the ball, which rolled oh-so-slowly away from his feet. Matt didn't move. Bent over in his putting stance, he watched the ball gradually pick up speed as it followed the slope. From where I stood, I couldn't tell if the ball had the right angle coming off the hill, and I stepped another foot closer to the hole.

It was all happening in surreal slow motion. Beyond the hole, at the other edge of the green, Hogan shifted his feet and moved, ready to come forward and replace his ball, and Matt stood up straight, lifting his putter with both hands. He held it aloft like a baton, as if he were directing the line of his putt.

The ball was within two feet of the cup, still moving down the slope, not gaining speed or losing it. I held my breath. I think we all did.

When the ball was within a foot of the cup, I saw it had the line to reach the hole. What mattered now was whether it also had enough speed. As I watched, the ball reached the very lip, then hesitated and halted. Behind me Sarah gasped. And I moved again—this time not in the direction of the hole, but up the green, letting my dark shadow cross and cover the white golf ball, still poised on the cup's upper lip.

Yes, you're getting it now, aren't you? It's a subtle trick. A caddie trick. What I did that long-ago afternoon was block the sun—just a second—but long enough for the thin blades of grass to flatten and for the ball to make a final half-turn and tumble into the hole.

17

MATT'S PUTT DROPPED. THE MATCH WAS OVER. WITH HIS BIRDIES on seventeen and eighteen, Matt had won the two-hole bet—and won me as his caddie in the Open. Hogan glanced over, letting me know he saw how I had caused the ball to drop. I ducked my head and busied myself fishing Matt's ball out of the cup and re-placing the bamboo flagpole.

Hogan took off his white cap and shook hands with Matt, congratulating him, and wished him good luck in the upcoming qualifying round for the Open. Then he handed me his putter and ball and said, "Jack, do me a favor. Take my clubs down to the car. I'll meet you there." He smiled his famous gap-toothed smile and I felt immensely better.

"Yes, sir," I said, eager to help him.

Then Hogan crossed the green to where Dr. DuPree and Sarah were standing with Valerie. He politely introduced his wife to Sarah and her father, complimented the club president on his

fine course and his talented young pro. Matt shook hands with
Mrs. Hogan, who congratulated him on the putt. Matt was grinning and blushing like the small-town boy he was.

"I almost got lucky enough to have young Jack caddying for
me in the Open," Hogan commented as I picked up both of the
bags. For a second, everyone stared at me. Then Dr. DuPree began gushing.

"Jack, he's one of our best boys," DuPree declared, claiming
ownership. "If you want him caddying for you, Ben, you just give
me the word and he's yours. I'll see to it."

Even a few yards away I could feel Hogan's chill. He fixed his
icy eyes on DuPree and said in his quiet voice that I was Matt's
caddie and the club was privileged to have us both in its employ.

I didn't hang around to hear Dr. DuPree's fumbling excuses. I
headed up the slope to leave Matt's bag in the pro shop, then
down to the lot.

When he arrived at his car, Hogan didn't say anything. He just
unlocked the trunk. It was full of golf equipment, from extra
clubs to shag balls. I settled his clubs in the trunk, making sure
none of the woods would get bent in the tight space.

"Thanks, Jack," Hogan said, slamming the trunk and locking
it. "Now what do I owe you?"

"You don't owe me anything, sir. It was an honor to caddie for
you."

Hogan smiled and said, "Thank you, Jack. It was my pleasure
having you on my bag. You taught me a lot about the course."
Taking out his money clip, he pulled several bills off, folded them,
and handed them to me. "You're a good caddie, Jack. You know
your stuff."

I backed off, not wanting to take the money, and Valerie
Hogan said quietly, but now impatient with both of us, "Take the
money from Mr. Hogan, Jack."

I took the money and shoved it into my trouser pocket.

"Your fella is a fine player," Hogan said next, slipping into the
driver's seat. He rolled down the window to say goodbye and I
could feel the heat of the closed interior.

"I'll see you at the end of August," I said quickly, suddenly
sorry the afternoon was over.

Hogan started the Cadillac, and sat still without saying anything while the engine warmed up. I stood beside the car, not
knowing what to do and not wanting him to leave and waiting
for . . . what . . . oh, I have no idea . . . and then Hogan looked
up at me and started speaking softly, going back to what I had told
him on the first nine about Dr. DuPree wanting me to spy on
Matt and Sarah, and he told me again what his mother had said to
him about being just as good as anyone else, and then he added,
"You know, I always feel sorry for people who never have had to
work for a living or earn their own way. You may not know it
now, but in time you'll come to understand it's the poor kids like
us who are the lucky ones in life." He stopped and shifted the
Cadillac into reverse and, glancing out the window, smiled and
added, "Keep working with your fella, Jack. If he listens to you,
he's got a chance to win some money next month."

And then he was gone. Valerie waved as the long car edged
onto the drive and I waved back and stood in the empty lot,
watching as the Cadillac picked up speed on the road and headed
for the highway. I watched Hogan drive over the bridge by the
reservoir, go past the tee box at three and disappear around the
bend of the road. Then I walked up to the pro shop.

Halfway there, I remembered the money and pulled out the

handful of bills stuffed in my pocket. Ben had paid me twenty dollars, as much as I would make in a week of looping.

Back at the pro shop, Matt was sitting at the small desk near the front door. His golf shoes were off and he was leaning back in the swivel chair with his feet propped over the edge of the desk. His hands were laced behind his head, and his eyes were closed.

He heard me come in but didn't move, nor did he open his eyes. Then he said, in a voice full of awe, "I beat Ben Hogan." He opened his eyes and grinning at me, added, "I was lucky."

"No," I told him, shaking my head. "You played great!"

Matt swung his feet off the desk and sat forward, bracing his elbows against his knees. It was what I called his teacher pose, and he used it on me several times when he gave me advice. This time he didn't lecture, but asked instead, "What impressed you the most about him, Jack?"

I shrugged, trying to guess what Matt might mean, and finally said, "I don't know. Getting off the tee? He had great placement on every hole, and he didn't even know the course."

Matt shook his head.

"You might not have seen it as you were watching his ball, but I kept my eyes on Hogan's face and on every shot his expression was perfectly calm. There was no strain, no tension. Nothing." Matt leaned back in the swivel chair and sighed.

"He's one cool customer," I said.

Matt nodded. "It's more than that. Every time he hit it was like . . . don't know. Cold-blooded murder."

"That's why he's called the Hawk," I said. "And you can beat him, Matt," I added, encouragingly.

"I beat him because you were smart enough to let your

shadow cover the hole. I saw you. Hogan saw you." He shook his head in wonderment and grinned, then he stood up and in his stocking feet stepped to the pro shop door and looked out at the empty first tee.

I slipped into the swivel chair and from that angle, I could see his profile. Matt's shoulders were slouched, and he stood with his hands in the pockets of his slacks. He was leaning slightly forward, pressing his face lightly against the screen door. His eyes were closed and he spoke very softly. "I've got to win this one, Jack. It's important. It's real important."

"Sure, I know. It's the Chicago Open."

"It's more than the Chicago Open," he replied. "A lot more."

Now, I didn't understand what he meant. Usually I was the one always talking about myself. I'd go on and on about school and the nuns, or mom and how it was having my dad die, and Matt would listen to me and understand what I was troubled about. Now I sensed he was trying to tell me something about himself, something I didn't know, so I said encouragingly, "You just play like you've been playing and none of those pros got a chance. You know this course better than anyone. That gives you a two, maybe a three-shot edge."

Matt opened his eyes and looked out at the empty course. Nodding, he said, "Two or three strokes are just about right." He stepped away and smiled, and his whole physical attitude changed.

"But you forgot Hogan, Jackson. I'll need more than three shots to beat the Hawk!" Grinning, he grabbed the arm of the wooden chair and spun me around. He was right, I hadn't been thinking of Hogan. But from then on Ben Hogan was the only golfer either of us thought about.

18

AFTER THAT AFTERNOON WITH HOGAN, MATT GOT REAL SERIOUS about his game. He started to practice every day, before and after work, squeezing in nine holes whenever we could in those final weeks before the Open.

While Matt played, I pointed out how Hogan had managed his way around the course. Hogan was our touchstone. And the better Matt played, the more preoccupied he seemed to be with the Hawk, as we both started to call Hogan.

Before heading for the golf course every morning, I'd milk the cows and bring the pails up from the barn so Mom could separate the milk and make butter from the heavy cream.

When Kathy heard me in the kitchen, she'd come downstairs and, still in her pajamas, sit with me while I ate breakfast. Kathy worked late at the club, but she always managed to get up early enough to see me before I left for the day. She was a thin waif of a girl, only eighteen at the time, with long black tumbling Irish hair and a pale, buttermilk face. A real mick, as we used to say.

She'd sit at the kitchen table slowly drinking a cup of black coffee and smoke the first of the cigarettes which would, in time, take her life.

Kathy had blue eyes, the color of a summer sky, and a wonderful sly smile that always told me she was on to my game, whatever it was. For an older sister, I thought she was pretty neat.

Mom never sat with us at breakfast, nor did we have the big Sunday night dinners we'd had when Dad was alive. Once in the spring, when Matt first came to the club, I asked Mom if I could invite him for dinner sometime and she made some excuse how there was too much work to do around the farm to be inviting strangers home to feed them.

After I grew up and had my own family, I began to realize Mom didn't want another man in the house; somehow it would be too painful for her, too much of a reminder of Dad sitting at the head of the table and all of us a happy family again.

I think my sister must have understood how lonely I was after Dad died, and that is why she came into the kitchen in the early morning to be with me. Kathy was scared, too, about what was happening with our mother.

As the widow of a farmer, Mom must have been overwhelmed. On her shoulders were all the chores and responsibilities, and money problems I couldn't have imagined at my age. Now when I look back, I realize she didn't have the time or energy, or even the space in her heart, to give us kids the love and attention we needed.

That's why Kathy tried to be more than a big sister to me. She tried to be like Dad, meaning she took an interest in my world of golf, and the lives of the pros who fed my imagination and were the stuff of my childhood daydreams.

Waiting tables, she overheard the members' conversations; she had heard them recount Matt's story of how I had helped him win the nine-hole match with Hogan, and they'd marvel at my clever ploy on eighteen green. And they knew, of course, she was my sister and congratulated her on how smart I had been, as the Monday afternoon with Hogan became part of the legend of the country club.

She told me what the members were saying about me to let me know I was something of a hero, and she knew it, and she was proud to be my sister.

At the time, of course, I was feeling pretty great about myself anyway. After all, I was Matt Richardson's caddie. When we played in the early morning there was often a heavy overnight dew on the ground, and standing on the greens and looking back down the long fairways, I could see our footprints in the wet grass, two solitary tracks that wouldn't burn away until the summer sunrise cleared the clubhouse and swept across the course like a soft cotton cloth wiping dust off the top of a varnished table. It was as if Matt and I were all alone in the world and the tracks in the wet grass proved it so.

I was also feeling good because Dr. DuPree wasn't asking me about Sarah and Matt. Sarah wasn't even showing up at the pro shop, and Matt had stopped asking me to carry notes to her house. In fact, he never mentioned Sarah. She had disappeared from the course as abruptly as she had appeared. Some days I spotted her at the pool, lounging around with the other members' daughters. I was happy I didn't have anything to do with her.

The fact was, I didn't have much to do with Matt once we were off the course. We were busy that summer, what with preparing for the Open, and Jimmy and Matt were always going to meetings and leaving me to tend the shop. On weekends the course was filled with members, and the pros were both up at the starter's tent, or down on the range giving lessons. For the most part, I forgot about Matt and Sarah being, as we use to say, an item, and was busy myself carrying double thirty-six holes on Saturdays and Sundays.

The summer fell into its own rhythm, one hot humid day after the other. Our weekdays were quiet, with only a few women or men playing early in the day. Usually I would grab one of those loops, when the air was still cool, and be back at the pro shop by midday, ready to work as the shop boy.

One day when I came in from an early-morning loop, I saw Jimmy, the pro, down on the range giving a lesson to Mrs. Beaven, and I spotted Matt on the putting green. Down the steps in the shop, a man was looking at new clubs Jimmy had on display, and I walked up front and asked him if he needed help.

The stranger wasn't dressed to play. He was wearing a seersucker suit, a thin tie, and a white shirt. He didn't look like much, tall, thin, and old. At least, he seemed old to me at the time. His face was taut and bright red, as if he had spent too much time in the sun, and his hair was so thick it made his head look too big for his body. In a few seconds, I realized it was a hairpiece.

But I could tell he knew something about golf by the way he picked up and examined the clubs. He was looking at a set of Sam Snead signature irons Wilson had just shipped to the shop and he handled them with care, as if he thought they were expensive, which they were.

He didn't come out right away and say what he wanted, just complimented me on the shop, on all the merchandise, and on the hat and shirts Jimmy had made special with the club seal emblazoned on them.

I walked around and stood behind the counter where we kept the cash box. I was about to tell him Jimmy was giving a lesson when he asked for Mr. Richardson. Now, no one ever called Matt by his last name and I hesitated, thinking he must be talking about Matt's dad. Then I asked, "You mean, Matt?"

"Yes, Matt!" He smiled. "I'm a friend of his from back in his hometown."

"Gatesburg," I said.

"You've heard of Gatesburg?" His smile widened into a grin. "It's always nice to hear you upstate folks knowing 'bout little ol' Gatesburg. They teach you about us in school, son?"

I shook my head and said Matt had told me about Gatesburg.

"Of course he would," the stranger said in the same enthusiastic way. "Matt loves Gatesburg. He's the best golfer to come out of southern Illinois. You know, he won the state championship in 'forty-three."

I nodded. It was a story Matt had told me more than once.

"Is Matt around?" He glanced out the windows then, as if expecting to spot Matt somewhere near the first tee.

"He's on the putting green."

"Good!" He spun around, gleaming. "I'm late to meet him. I told the boy I'd be here first thing, but ran into a problem at the office back home." With that, he paused and introduced himself as Ralph Gates. "My family founded the town," he explained with a note of pride in his voice, and then added that he owned the Gates State Farm Insurance Company and was president of the Gatesburg Country Club. He held out his hand to shake mine.

Gates had one of those big handshakes I've come to realize

many slender men use to demonstrate their strength. He squeezed my fingers until they hurt.

"I'll show you where the putting green is," I said next and led him out of the shop and up the steps to the tee, pointing across the front lawn to where Matt was practicing.

Ralph Gates said goodbye again, thanked me profusely, and hurried across the sloping lawn. He looked oddly out of place at the club in his serious summer suit, walking briskly toward Matt like a man with something to sell.

I went back to start cleaning clubs but we had no towels, so I took the path around to the lower locker room, where the club-house towels were stored next to the shoeshine room.

Sebastian Tombs was polishing golf shoes, and he nodded hello when I grabbed a couple of thick white towels, which really weren't to be used for cleaning clubs, but Sebastian never protested. "It ain't my situation," he always said. Everything for Sebastian was not his situation. He was, as we termed it then, the Locker Room Boy, though at the time I'd guess Sebastian was sixty years old, with the worried eyes and weary face of someone who had suffered a great deal in his life, and had survived by staying out of other peoples' "situations."

Sebastian might have been a man of few words and no on-the-record opinions, but I knew he didn't miss much around the club, and once in a while he'd pull me aside and give me some quick advice, though he'd always throw in his disclaimer.

Chatting with him, I mentioned the man from Gatesburg who had come looking for Matt. I made fun of the guy, telling Sam what he looked like, and how he wore a thick rug on his bald head, telling him Matt's hometown was named after this guy, who, I added, was also the president of the Gatesburg Country Club.

Sam never responded. He kept working slowly on an old pair

of brown leather golf shoes, working hard to get them to shine, and he let me go on and on without asking any questions. You might call him a good listener. But as we know, it is those good listeners who are soaking up all the information.

For my part, I was watching Sebastian. Caddies get good at watching adults. They watch their players. They watch the members. They keep their mouths shut and their eyes open and they see a lot—subtle gestures, flirtatious looks, glances between husbands and wives, as well as the suppressed rage on a member's face that told the real story of his life and fortunes, not to mention his golf game.

So I watched Sebastian's watery, filmy eyes and his heavy cheeks to see if he registered any reaction to my tale. But Sebastian's face never betrayed him, and when I finished my whole story of how I had sent the stranger off to Matt, all Sebastian said, as much as if it were an observation as a question, was this: "Now why would a big fella like him take a whole day off to drive up north and find a boy like young Matt who ain't, as far as I can see, got a pot to piss in?" Then he sighed and added quickly, "But it ain't my situation."

But it was to become my situation at the club as the easy routine of the summer suddenly changed.

On one of those slow-moving midweek days after the man from Gatesburg had come and gone, Matt passed through the pro shop and mentioned he was going up to his room for a while. He had bills to pay, he said, and the next day, there were letters to write, or some such excuse, and he'd be gone from the shop for an hour or two.

The first few times he disappeared it didn't register as unusual, but then it became a pattern. As soon as Jimmy went out to give a lesson, or drive into Chicago to the Wilson factory, Matt would have another excuse to leave, and he'd ask me to handle the scores of the players coming off the course, or to hang around the shop in case anyone wanted to buy a few balls or look at a set of clubs.

I didn't think much about it until one day a member said, half in jest and half in frustration, "What's with this kid? Has he got a girl stashed away somewhere?"

Then I realized what was happening.

A few days later Jimmy came in early from an afternoon lesson and asked where Matt was. I told him Matt had gone to lie down for a half-hour or so, since the course was quiet. Jimmy glanced at his watch and asked what time Matt had left. When I told him, he said I better go get him.

I took the back steps up to the men's locker room, and from there another set of back stairs off the men's lounge to the third floor, a long hallway that in midday was dark and airless.

The twenty or so small bedrooms used by the permanent help were all on the top floor and ran down both sides of the narrow corridor. Sunlight from alcove windows lifted the dust like soft floating snowflakes off the worn runner on the floor.

The third floor was hot and silent on that midday summer afternoon and the soft carpet muffled my footsteps. When I reached Matt's room I heard whispering voices from behind the door. The third floor had never been remodeled, and with the settling of the building most of the bedroom doors were hard to close. In his hurry, Matt had left his open a crack, which was illuminated by a narrow shaft of sunlight.

I raised my hand to knock, and then I saw everything: the bottom of his bed, the iron railing, and a small mound of crumpled white sheets tumbled onto the bare wooden floor. And I saw Sarah DuPree.

As I looked inside the room, Sarah jumped from the bed and went swiftly, gracefully, across the room. Through the narrow opening, I saw her bare legs as she disappeared from my sight. Just as suddenly she reappeared and stood in the far corner of the bedroom. Still, I didn't have all of her, but what I *did* see was certainly enough.

I had never seen a woman naked before, and I trust you will all appreciate the impact. In those days young boys weren't exposed to, what should I say, the abundance of female flesh we have in front of us today. This was before HBO on television, before *Playboy* magazine, and light-years before the Internet delivered all knowledge to everyone's desktop computer. But it was not an altogether innocent time, as I was witnessing.

I heard them whispering and laughing. Maybe they had decided it was time to go. Whatever was happening, Sarah came back into view. She stooped down to retrieve something—perhaps her dress—and I saw her in full profile, her breasts, the curve of her slender shoulders, and the breath went out of me.

And that was when she spotted me in the sliver of the open door.

In one smooth motion she jumped back, whispering frantically to Matt, and in the dim light before she disappeared I saw a flash of fright in her eyes.

I was out of there. I ran the length of the hall and flew down the stairs. Behind me, I heard Matt's door bang open. I didn't stop running until I was in the pro shop, in the back room, dumping a set of irons into soapy water.

Then Jimmy appeared and asked if I had found Matt. I shook my head, too nervous to speak, and soon I heard Matt's quick footsteps on the locker room steps. Jimmy said demandingly, "Where have you been? I sent Jack to find you."

Matt waited until Jimmy was gone before he cornered me.

"Was that you?" he asked.

I kept scrubbing at the dirt on Dr. Senese's new irons.

"Were you spying on me?"

"I wasn't spying!" I kept scrubbing.

"Why were you up on the third floor?"

"Jimmy told me to find you." I stopped working and stared at him, ready to hold my own.

"Are you spying on me for the DuPrees?"

"What are you talking about?"

"You know what I'm talking about." He stepped closer to me. "Has Sarah's mother's got you spying on us?"

"I'm not spying on you," I said, fighting back my tears.

"When you took the note for me, the last time, right?"

I nodded slowly, not knowing where he was going with his question.

"You spoke to Mrs. DuPree. She caught you, and read the note, right? You didn't tell me, right?" Each "right" was short, hard, and bitten off, as if he were hitting cut irons into the wind.

"There was nothing to tell you," I managed to interrupt him. "The note didn't say nothin'!"

"Dr. DuPree told Sarah he is paying you to tell him if you see us together."

"That's a lie. I didn't say I would spy on you." A rush of tears filled my eyes. Matt had never before been angry with me. "I don't know anything about you and Sarah!" I shouted.

"You're damn right. You don't know," Matt said calmly. "And I think it's better for you if you're not caddying for me."

With that, he nodded, having made up his mind, and headed out for the first tee, letting the screen door slam behind him.

Now, at this crisis, perhaps we should have another break. Doug tells me drinks will be served on the terrace and then we'll have dinner and I'll finish up on Ben Hogan, Matt Richardson, and the Chicago Open.

19

JACK STEPPED OFF THE TERRACE OF THE CLUBHOUSE AND WALKED *along the gravel path that led to the scoring tent. The sheets for the day's play had been removed, and the last of the foursomes were gone from the course. Standing under the maple tree near the tee, he was reminded that with age every place in one's past diminishes, and what once loomed so grandly in childhood ebbs with the passing of time.*

He thought next he might walk as far as the small creek and look up at the clubhouse and see it once again ablaze with light, to see if it still held its magic for him. Then from behind him he heard the crunch of shoes on pebbles and heard her soft greeting. Jack smiled as Sarah came closer in the fading evening light.

"I thought you might like a drink." Sarah held up two glasses of wine. "Chardonnay?"

"Thank you. This is very nice of you." Smiling, Jack took the drink and raised the glass in a silent toast. "Have I bored all of you to death with my endless reminiscences?"

"Oh, no, not me!"

Sarah walked over to the wooden bench by the ball washer and sat down carefully. She had changed for dinner, and in a tight lime-green silk dress, with her hair swept off her bare shoulders, she looked absolutely beautiful, he thought.

"I'm finding it fascinating. Of course, I have my reasons," she added.

He wondered if he wanted to know what her reasons were. Did he need to be drawn into the intrigues of her life? Then he realized Doug Hughes's invitation had not been so idle, that there was more to his being invited back than just to talk about his Ben Hogan book.

Jack sat beside her on the bench, placing the glass of wine between them. He did not speak, but waited for the questions he knew she'd been wanting to ask him.

"So Matt never let you caddie for him in the Open?"

Jack smiled. *"Oh, you'll have to wait for the last act."*

She laughed, an infectious sound that immediately reminded him of his youngest daughter, Lizzy. But when she looked his way again it was with eyes more assessing than sweet. Then she looked away and stared out at the darkening golf course as she said carefully, *"There's always been this rumor in my family that Matt Richardson was my father's real father—that Nana married my official grandfather rather quickly in the fall of 'forty-six. My grandfather lost his life in Korea and Nana remarried after that. She was thirty years old, and she had three more children, all girls, with her second husband.*

"We have this old black-and-white photograph of my father and his sisters when they were children. They're all dressed up like china dolls but you can tell right away which one isn't from the same gene pool. Dad looks like a little blond angel and the girls—my aunts—are these dark thumbprints flanking him. The family secret is Nana was pregnant when she first married, and Daddy was the result." She raised her eyebrows as if in a question. *"What do you think?"*

"It's possible, of course." He answered vaguely, shrugging. "There were lots of those family secrets at the time."

"Like in The Go-Between, as you mentioned this morning?"

"Yes, like The Go-Between. You've seen the movie?"

"'The past is another country,'" she said, reciting the opening line, then added, "but the forties weren't the Edwardian Age!"

"Nor was I so young or innocent myself."

"You said earlier the events of that summer . . . what?" She paused and frowned. "How did you put it? That it was a very important time in your life."

"Oh, perhaps I was just being dramatic. I was afraid I might lose my audience if I didn't promise some excitement." He smiled weakly.

"I thought it might have been my grandmother, how you were in love with her." Sarah was amusing herself, flirting with him.

"I did have a crush on her. Like her granddaughter, she was a beautiful young woman."

"Why, thank you." His reply caught her off-guard. She refocused and asked, "How long did their affair last?"

"A few weeks, a month, perhaps."

"Long enough for Nana to conceive?"

"I'm not sure much birth control was practiced in the forties."

"It would be something if I was Matt's grandchild. It might explain a lot about me. I've always been the odd one in my family. I always thought I must have been more like Nana, but I actually might be more like Matt. Still, if I am his grandchild, then why aren't I a better golfer?" They both smiled at her question.

"Does it matter now, after all this time?"

"It matters. All I've heard until now were these rumors about there possibly having been another man in her life. Now you've put a personality together with the family secret—that is, if I really am his grandchild."

"Have you been to Gatesburg, Matt's hometown?"

Sarah shook her head. "I never ever heard of it until you mentioned it earlier."

"I went there once, years after what happened here. I was coming home from Vietnam, driving across country, and I drove south, on the old Route Sixty-six, just so I could see for myself where Matt came from."

"You did?" She perked up, intrigued by this new piece of information.

Jack nodded. "It would've been, I guess, nineteen sixty-five. I'm not sure what the town is like today, but that summer it was just another one of those small downstate spots on a map: a single wide main street a few blocks long with a movie house, a dozen small stores, and the town hall on a slight rise at the far end. Just off the main street were several churches, with their steeples shooting up over tall maple and poplar trees. The whole downtown was surrounded by sweeping wood-frame homes, deep front lawns, and screened porches. There wasn't much industry, just farmland."

"It sounds absolutely charming!" Sarah smiled.

"Charming, yes, but there was also a sadness to those places. Time was passing by all these little farm towns."

"Did they remember him in Gatesburg?"

"I never spoke to anyone in town. I arrived there on an August afternoon, as I recall, and I didn't know anyone, of course. I went to the town library to look up what they might have on him, old clips, that sort of thing. Matt loved the town library.

"I remember that summer the two of us would be sitting right here, under this maple and beside those big green scoring boards we had, and we would be waiting for the last foursomes to finish up on eighteen, and he'd tell me about going to the Gatesburg library to read the out-of-town newspapers.

"Matt said as a kid he would go to the library on winter afternoons and sit close to the old wood-burning stove—it was the only heat in the

place—and read the newspapers delivered to Gatesburg by the morning trains.

"He'd read about all the pros on the southern tour, read about Nelson and Snead, Ben Hogan, of course, and Jackie Burke Jr., Dutch Harrison, the long list of great players from those years, and he'd dream of someday making it south to play on the PGA tour."

"He almost did, didn't he?" Sarah said.

"Yes, he might have done it, and those were the winter dreams Matt had, much like F. Scott Fitzgerald wrote about, the winter dreams of young boys growing up in the cold Midwest."

"Did they have anything about him in the library?"

"I found several photographs compiled by the local historian into a handmade town history book. There was a black-and-white high school photo from his yearbook, as well as a photo showing him standing outside the pro shop here at this club.

"It was a photograph taken the day he set the course record. He's drinking out of that water fountain right over there, and the caption is about how he is cooling off after his round. You can see the old clubhouse behind him. It's all white and blurry and out of focus, but the white columns, everything, they are all in the photo."

"Is Nana there?"

Jack shook his head. "No. But I am. I'm standing beside him with his bag of clubs with a grin on my face as wide as one of those sand bunkers."

"How wonderful! Why didn't you use the photograph in your book?"

"Oh, the book is about Ben Hogan. Not Matt. What I'm telling you all today is just for you, for the members."

"I would love to see a photo of Matt when he was young."

"Go down to Gatesburg. I'm sure they'll still have them somewhere. After I went to the library, I drove over to the high school. I'm sure there must be a new building by now, but in 'sixty-five it was the same one Matt attended—one of those ancient big two-story red-brick jobs. You *walk inside and smell decades of floor wax, feel the history of the whole town. All those schools have high ceilings and the sunlight slants in through tall, narrow windows. There's one in every small town in America—ghostly places full of memories.*

"At the high school all of the trophy cases were up against the walls in the front lobby and down the length of the hallway. The town's history was in those cases, the awards and trophies and honors won by all the kids who grew up there, married, and lived out their lives within blocks of where they were born. There has always been a strange pull about those places. It's the rare child who ventures away and makes a life far from a farm town."

"Matt didn't make it, did he?"

"No, he didn't," Jack answered, shaking his head. "He had been a hero in Gatesburg and it had meant a great deal to him. That's why I knew I'd find something about him in one of those trophy display cases. I had to walk almost the length of the building—remember, I was visiting in 'sixty-five and Matt had graduated in 'forty-three—but eventually I found a framed black-and-white photo of the Gatesburg High School golf team, a half-dozen boys standing together on a tee, ready to play.

"The photo was taken at the start of the golf season, in cold weather, for the boys were all wearing sweaters, and the trees framing the tee were bare. No names were listed, but I picked out Matt immediately. There he was with his great big grin, looking like I had always remembered.

"There was one other photo of him. He was in his army uniform, in some sort of Memorial Day parade. The banner on the side of convertible read: Matt Richardson State Champ!

"He had won the high school state golf championship his senior year. Gatesburg was just a little hick southern Illinois place, so it was a big deal, for the town as well as for him. He had come up to Flossmoor Country Club where the tournament was played. I had heard all about it from him. He was really proud of the victory, and there was this photograph of

him in his army uniform, waving a small U.S. flag. All-American Matt Richardson.

"After he graduated from high school, he went away to war, and came to work at this club in the summer of 'forty-six. So, that's his history. A couple of golf course records. A couple of old black-and-white photographs in the town library. Not much when you think of what he might have been."

"It's so sad," Sarah whispered. "Are you going to tell us what happened to him?"

"You know about the accident?" Jack asked.

"Rumors, yes, but no one really talks about it," she said. "Is the Matt Richardson story the real reason you've come back for the Open celebration, Mr. Handley?"

Jack could not see her face in the darkness, but he felt her smiling wryly at him.

"Perhaps."

"Then I'd best not keep you from your story." Sarah stood and straightened her dress with the palm of her free hand. She had not taken a sip of her wine and was careful not to spill it as she stepped toward the terrace and the clubhouse, bright with lights.

Their footsteps crunched the small pebbles of the walk. It was then that she added, as a warning, "I'm afraid my husband isn't enjoying your lecture."

"But he invited me to tell my story."

"Doctor Hughes invited you. My husband wasn't on the committee. Jeffrey loves to pretend we're one happy family at this country club with no skeletons in our closets. He doesn't like dirty laundry being aired in public. Especially if any part of the story involves Hogan. Having Ben win here is the one shining moment of this club's history. Members have been dining out on it for years. Are you going to burst our little bubble of respectability?"

"Well, I wrote all about Hogan in the book."

"Why is it that I think you have more to tell us than what is in your book?" She glanced over at him with the same mischievous smile.

They were on the terrace, joining the others gathered there for drinks—Jack guessed none of these members would call them cocktails. The term had gone the way of hickory shafts and gutta-percha golf balls.

Sarah's husband was standing in a cluster of men. When he saw them, a scowl crossed the man's broad Irish face like a summer cloud.

"Oh, dear," Sarah whispered. *"He's annoyed I'm chatting with you."* She sounded more amused than upset.

"He shouldn't worry—I'm too old to try to take you away from him."

Sarah smiled. *"It's not infidelity that worries Jeffrey. He's more concerned that I'll betray his sacred club by telling tales out of school. Some days I think my husband is more in love with this golf course than he is with me. He should have married a nine iron."*

The sudden bitterness in her voice cut through the warm evening air.

Jack thought of just letting it go, but he was, he realized, too much the grandfather, too much the teacher not to want to help the young woman.

"When I caddied for Hogan he gave me one piece of advice about golf, Sarah, that I found has helped me in my whole life. Hogan told me that what's important is the next shot, not the one you have just played."

Sarah nodded, contemplating what Jack said, and was about to respond when her husband was upon them.

"I was wondering where you disappeared to, Mr. Handley. I should have guessed my lovely wife had spirited you away." He planted a hasty kiss on Sarah's cheek, but focused his gaze on Jack, as if not to risk the man slipping away from him. *"Do you have a minute, sir?"* he asked, seizing Jack's elbow.

"Don't say I didn't warn you," Sarah tossed off as she glided away.

"Hey, give your husband some credit." Jeff gestured with both hands,

splashing liquor out of his tall glass. Immediately two white-coated wait-
ers appeared to clean away the mess and relieve him of the glass. "An-
other one of those, Jesse," Burke said, pointing to his drink. Then,
without pausing, he launched himself into a barrage of compliments—
how informative the talk was, how interesting and dramatic. He had had
too much to drink, Jack realized, and braced himself to hear what the
young man really wanted.

"Loved the Hogan stuff. Great stuff!" Jeff released his grip on Jack's
elbow and shifted his hand to his shoulder, pinning him with the weight
of his arm. "I hope you're going to focus more on those details. Let's for-
get about the caddie, the young pro." He waved his hand dismissively.
"No one, to tell you the truth, gives a goddamn. Stick to Hogan! That's
when everyone sits up and listens. What clubs he used, how he played
each one of these holes, all the great course management stuff."

"It all ties together," Handley answered carefully.

"It makes us look bad."

"What does?"

"The hanky-panky stuff."

"It was half a century ago, Jeff."

"Hey, you're talking about our fathers and grandfathers. My wife's
own grandmother, for chrissake. You got her up on the third floor, shacking
up with that kid. And let me make myself perfectly clear, our help doesn't
stay overnight these days. Only members are allowed to stay," he added
proudly.

"Good for you," Jack answered.

"Another thing!" Jeff Burke stepped away as if to give himself room
to expand. "Let's not get into stories of gambling around the club."
Again, he waved his thick hand dismissively. "This place is respectable
now."

"I believe this club was respectable in the forties."

"I'm talking about the Calcutta."

"Ah, the Calcutta! Of course!"

"I would appreciate, no, I would suggest you don't talk about the Calcutta." He paused to light a cigarette.

Jack nodded slowly, then just as deliberately replied, *"Well, the Calcuttas were a fixture of the times. Even the Masters had theirs going into the late forties."*

"We don't care what those southerners did down in the Bible Belt. We have our reputation."

"I would think you'd be proud your club had members wealthy enough to bid twenty-five thousand on a golf tournament, at a time when most men were making a couple of thousand a year."

"We're a family club, Mr. Handley. We don't need a lot of bad publicity about what might or might not have gone on back in the forties. We've got a reporter from the Chicago Trib *here. We don't need him writing a lot of nonsense about gambling and carryings-on among members, not when we have the grandchildren as members, people with reputations.*

"Your pal Doug Hughes sponsored you to speak. He said you were a fine fellow, a college professor and all—so to tell you the truth, I was not prepared for some of those anecdotes of yours."

He stopped talking but kept shaking his head, as if all his rage had run out of him. He took another long drag on his cigarette and stared into the darkness. There was no moon, no stars. The golf course was lost from sight.

"Well, thank you, Jeff," Handley began, *"I assure you there is nothing to be concerned about."*

"Good!" Burke declared, surprised by Jack's quick acquiescence. *"Thank you,"* he added as an afterthought.

Jack patted Jeff's shoulder. *"Don't worry. I'll keep it clean."* With that, he headed to the men's locker room, where, he guessed, Jeff wouldn't follow him, and walked through the rows and rows of wooden lockers, all *new since he had last seen the place as a boy. Beyond them was the "nineteenth hole," and there he found Doug Hughes sitting alone.*

"Jack!" Doug shouted, waving to him. "Come here and let me get you a drink! How are you doing, buddy? I saw you out there talking to our president." Hughes made a face and lowered his voice so the bartender wouldn't hear. "What did that bastard want?"

Doug had also had too much to drink, Jack realized, and suddenly he felt overwhelmed by everything flaring up around him, and because of him. Books were dangerous, he knew. They told too many secrets.

"Burke wants me to bury the scandals." Jack said.

"He would!"

"Why is he so worried about the old families? What's his connection?"

"You remember Kenny Burke's little brother?"

"How could I not?"

Doug Hughes grinned. "Who would have thought, back then, that Kenny Burke's little brother—Dave, by the way, was his name—would have a son."

"Jeffrey Burke? Of course!" Jack shook his head.

Doc Hughes nodded. As he lifted his drink slowly to his lips, careful not to spill a drop, he said, "What did Faulkner say? You should already know this; you're the professor. 'The past is never dead. It's not even past.' "

"Is Dave Burke a member?"

"He was for decades. He passed away five, six years ago. Good guy, old Dave. He made some money in insurance and was president of this club for a while, did a damn fine job. Everyone loved him." Hughes nodded toward the other side of the clubhouse. "The kid's another story."

Jack glanced along the length of the empty bar. The television set was on with the sound off. It was turned to a cable news network, and a white ticker tape of stock quotes ran endlessly across the bottom of the screen.

"*Jeff knows what happened?*" Jack asked.

Hughes nodded. He stared down at his vodka as if it were his own distant past.

"*Jeff knows but not Sarah?*"

"*Oh, I'm sure she must know something about it, some inkling of a family secret, but it was a long time ago, and what happened on the golf course is less important to her than what happened here, inside this clubhouse.*" The doctor nodded upward, toward the third floor of the huge building.

"*I'm sure there was a lot more hanky-panky going on among members in our day, more than we had any idea of.*" Doug smiled, then added, "*Not sure much has changed, given the stories I hear about wife-swapping among the younger set.*"

"*I thought you were a doctor, not a priest.*"

"*You'd be surprised the tales women tell an old man once they take off their clothes.*"

"*And Sarah has tales to tell?*"

"*Sarah is a lovely woman caught up in a bad marriage. It's an old story.*"

"*Will she leave her husband?*" As her doctor, Jack suspected Doug knew the woman better than she knew herself.

"*Oh, I've given up trying to guess what women will decide. Some of them make decisions about men with their hearts; others with their minds. Sarah, my guess, will follow her heart. What she needs is something to touch her. It might be a gesture or a love song. It could be another man, or even an old story.*"

The two men stopped talking and looked across the empty room filled with green felt-topped card tables. Through a wall of glass they could look out onto the eighteenth green. Someone had turned on the outside lights, which shone brightly across the front sweep of lawns. Farther off, the fairways were dark and Jack wondered if there was a kid out there now, crossing the course and heading home after a day of caddying, as he had done so often so many years ago.

"You know the story you told earlier of helping Matt against Hogan out there on the eighteenth green? How your shadow crossed the hole and the ball tumbled into the cup? Sometimes that is all it takes for a woman, a small gesture to tumble her heart, so to speak, to help her find out who she is." Doug reached out and briefly gripped Jack's shoulder. "You helped Matt all those years ago, Jack, and now I'm asking, as an old friend, and someone who cares a great deal for Sarah, for you to help Matt's grand-daughter." Doc Hughes nodded emphatically, then picked up his glass, paused, and summed up, "It's been long enough. The story needs to be told, and you're the only one who can tell it." He drained the last of his vodka and said, "Well, let's go have some dinner, shall we?"

20

BACK IN THE DINING ROOM, DR. HUGHES TAPPED THE MICROPHONE to silence the noisy, tipsy crowd. When he finally won their attention, which took all his good humor and persistence, he reintroduced Jack, saying, "We've now reached the climax of this tale—the week of the Chicago Open. All of us know, of course, that Hogan won the tournament. Most of you have seen the old black-and-white Movietone news film of the final round. It gives us a visual glimpse of what our club looked like in the forties. But Jack was there, out on the greens and fairways, and he'll tell us the rest."

Hughes lifted up a copy of the Hogan book and went on quickly. "Now, Jack tells me not everything is in his book; he's saved the best for us this evening. I don't want to delay his telling, but before I welcome him again to the podium, I should mention to you one or two facts about my good friend.

"After becoming the number-one caddie here at the club—and as Jack *has often joked, he never held a more responsible job—he left Illinois at the age of eighteen and joined the army to serve in Korea, and then was called back into service for Vietnam as an intelligence officer during the early years of the war. For his heroism he earned a fistful of ribbons, including a Bronze Star with clusters. This man, ladies and gentlemen, is a true American hero."*

At the mention of his medals there was a burst of applause, driven, Jack had no doubt, more by liquor than patriotism.

"In the years between his military service, Jack got his undergraduate degree at the University of Chicago, earned a Ph.D. at Harvard in American Studies, and taught history for many years at Yale University. He won several awards for his first book, a history of golf in America published by Harvard University Press. This book, by the way, is also available for purchase. I'm sure our author will be happy to sign a copy or two for you.

"But the book that has brought Jack back to be with us today is this memoir of his childhood as a caddie at our club. Those of you who have already read Ben Hogan's Lesson *know it is a poignant account of our special week in forty-six. Jack mentioned earlier there are one or two stories he has not committed to paper, but which he will share with us for the first time.*

"So, with that, let's welcome our distinguished guest to the podium for the final chapters of his tale."

Jack pushed his chair away from the head table and took his notes from the inside pocket of his blue blazer. They were a dozen talking points he had jotted down on the plane ride from Florida, points he wanted to make sure he didn't forget, though he couldn't imagine he would forget anything now.

Stepping to the microphone, he looked out at the room and searched for Sarah, spotting her with several young couples. Her husband was at the head table, close to the podium, in the place of honor as president of the club's board of directors.

Jack smiled, looked directly at Sarah for an instant, then began speaking.

21

THANK YOU, DOUG. AND THANK YOU ALL FOR YOUR ATTENTION and patience this long afternoon. If I'd had students like you, why, I would never have stopped teaching.

There was a book written in 1911 by a noted architect, Tyler Huntington Donaldson, who designed many famous clubhouses, including Midlothian Country Club here in Cook County. Donaldson makes the point clubhouses should be more than a place where you change shoes to play golf. They should be the members' collective home.

Certainly, as a child, spending most of my youth here, I thought of this place as my second home. But homes aren't always peaceful; they can be dramatic and turbulent. And families are not always happy.

That summer I was a young teenager who had lost his father and had now been abandoned by his hero, Matt Richardson. In my small childhood world, this was the equivalent of an avalanche.

When Matt stopped talking to me, I felt like a nonperson. Oh, I was still in the back of the pro shop cleaning clubs and hanging out, and Jimmy, the pro, had jobs for me to do, but Matt had dismissed me. Jimmy noticed it, of course, and quizzed me. But since I refused to tell him about Matt and Sarah's assignation, there was nothing for me to say. Given the code of conduct of the age, Sarah's reputation would have been shredded by my telling what I saw, and Matt would have been sent packing.

I kept quiet and I kept hoping. Surely, some late afternoon, Matt would come find me in the back of the shop and tell me to grab his clubs and let's get moving because he wanted to play a quick nine before dark. But he never did. Kenny Burke's little brother started looping for him, and this boy, as some of you know, grew up to become club president, and the father of your current president.

You may wonder why I keep calling him Kenny Burke's little brother when you all know him as David Burke. Well, it was the rule of the caddie yard—don't learn a kid's name until he proves his staying power. The caddie yard is tough, which Hogan himself found out in Texas at Glen Garden when he was stuffed into a barrel and rolled down a hill the first time he tried to join the caddie ranks.

Anyway, Kenny Burke's little brother was new and now, before he even had a name, he was caddying for the assistant pro, which was an insult not only to me but to all the other seasoned caddies.

Matt was doing this, of course, on purpose. He was trying to show that he didn't need me—or anyone else—to qualify for the Chicago Open.

And indeed he didn't. Two weeks later he qualified, with Dave Burke lugging his bag. Burke was doing better than me; I didn't have a loop with any of the "rabbits," as they were called: pros who had to earn a spot in the Open in the qualifying round.

I spent Monday working the pro shop. I never saw Matt play, but within minutes of the end of his round, I started to hear how he had finished with a 75, the highest round he had ever had at the club.

It was Sarah's father who first told me the news. He paced around as I opened boxes of new shirts and stacked them neatly on the display shelves, telling me what holes Matt had bogied. "Not one birdie," he said, summing up.

Then he seemed to realize that, as Matt's former caddie, I might be feeling left out of the day's triumph. He stopped in the middle of the pro shop then, shoved his hands into his pockets, and jingled the loose change.

"You're damn lucky you're not carrying his bag, Jack," he said. "Stick with a winner, stick with Hogan. When Hogan arrives, I'll see you get on his bag. I'll tell Jimmy to arrange it." He kept grinning. He was a happy man, but still he lingered and wouldn't leave me alone. He wanted something, I realized, and that made me nervous.

"Why didn't you caddie for Richardson, anyway?" DuPree finally asked, stepping over to where I was shelving the stock.

I shrugged and said it was Matt's idea. I wasn't going to tell him why, not after he lied to Sarah about me spying on her and Matt.

DuPree wouldn't let go, of course. *Why* wasn't Matt letting me caddie for him, he wanted to know. "Matt didn't tell me, Dr. DuPree," I lied. "He just said he wanted another caddie for the Open. If you want to know why, you'll have to ask him."

That stopped DuPree. I knew he would never ask Matt, nor

would he quiz Sarah. And I hadn't said a word to anyone, not Jimmy, not even my sister.

"Well, good for you," DuPree ended lamely, needing to say something, and then he left me alone, at least for the time being. He'd be back at me again, I knew, because it was his way, like a dog with a bone in his teeth.

A private club becomes its own world, with its own rules. It is true today, and was even truer back in the forties. The intensity of this world was captured, over fifty years ago, by a writer folks don't read much anymore, John O'Hara. Maybe there are a few English majors here who remember his book *Appointment in Samarra*. It's set in a small Pennsylvania town, much like the one where O'Hara lived, and it's really a novel of manners, all about the rules of acceptance.

The novel begins at the local golf course in Gibbsville, O'Hara's fictional town. What's important to remember is that in this novel, scandalous behavior like adultery is often overlooked, while small violations of the club's rules are totally unacceptable, because they threaten the social order of the elite. I want you to keep this in mind as we move forward with our own story, because what happened here in the summer of '46 threatened the very survival of this private club.

Well, I can see that remark got your full attention.

So now we come at last to tournament week, and the day after Matt Richardson shot 75 to become the final qualifier for the Open. It was also the week Ben Hogan returned to play in the Chicago Open Championship.

This time I was not Johnny-on-the-spot to get Hogan's clubs when he drove into the parking lot. In fact, I didn't even know Ben had arrived. It was late in the day, the day of the famous Calcutta.

If you're puzzled by the term, I'm not surprised—there hasn't been a Calcutta at a PGA event in more than fifty years. But the idea was simple enough. A Calcutta was basically an auction. Members bid to buy whichever player they thought would win the tournament. All the bidding money went into a pot, and after the match, whoever "owned" the winner got 70 percent of the total. Whoever had bought the second-place finisher got the rest.

Seems harmless enough, but wealthy members bid an awful lot of money in Calcuttas, so the stakes were high. At the U.S. Open in '21, for example, Bobby Jones was auctioned off for twenty-three thousand dollars, which, of course, was a lot more money then. At the Masters in '46, it was rumored fifty thousand was bet on Hogan. At other tournaments Calcutta pools went as high as a quarter of a million. Gambling was part of professional golf until 1949, when the USGA forced the tour to cut out Calcuttas. Still, in 1946 for this Open, the Calcutta was alive and well and bookies had come out from Chicago to set odds and take side bets on who would win.

That afternoon Hogan found me in the shop where I was cleaning Old Man Keenan's beat-up set of woods and irons.

Hogan was dressed in a beautiful gray blazer and silk necktie, and his black hair was perfectly combed. He looked tanned and relaxed and not at all like a man getting ready for a major tournament.

"Hi, Jack," he said. "Do you have time to shag some balls?"

"Sure!" I shoved Keenan's clubs aside.

Hogan shook his head. "Finish what you're doing here," he

told me. "Don't leave a job half-done." He fished out his car keys and handed them to me.

"When you're done here, go get my clubs. The shag balls are in the trunk. I'll meet you down on the range."

I don't think I ever was happier in my life. Ben Hogan had come looking for me and he had remembered my name. I was in caddie heaven.

I waited for Hogan at the range, which was empty this late in the day. Everyone was in the clubhouse, which was thronged with pros and members and officials from the PGA. In the '40s, tournaments didn't have all the corporate tents and television trucks we have now. But we had excitement enough, to be sure, with the greatest players of the age arriving one after another. And the members had come out to the club to see them, and to wait for the Calcutta taking place later in the evening.

And there I was, casually leaning against Ben Hogan's big brown MacGregor bag with his name stenciled down the length of it in his familiar signature. His brown leather bag of shag balls was at my feet. I stood by myself on the practice tee with my legs crossed, waiting for Hogan the Great, as if it were what I did every day of every summer, as if I were the most important caddie in the world, and to tell you the truth, I believed I was.

Hogan emerged from the locker room wearing his trademark soft, flat, white linen cap, a long-sleeved gray cotton shirt, a tie, and a pair of pleated gray slacks. These were the days before "polo shirts," the famous Lacoste style that dominated golf attire for the next generation. And it was decades before clothing endorsements came to dictate what even the most famous players would wear, and now we have pros wearing enough decals to look like NASCAR drivers.

Hogan crossed in front of the terrace, crowded with members gathered for an evening drink. He walked purposefully, looking straight ahead, without waving or pausing to speak to anyone. The members went quiet as he passed, and the handful of pros on the nearby putting green stared after him, aware of the great one in their midst. And Hogan was the greatest, as we all believed.

Looking back, golf historians have noted Hogan won thirteen times in 1946—including his first major, the PGA—finished second six times, third three more times, and was no worse than seventh in five other tournaments. He won more prize money in '46 than any pro had ever won, over forty-two thousand dollars.

For example, from 1940 to the 1960s, Hogan played in fifteen U.S. Opens. He won four times and never finished worse than tenth, despite his near-fatal accident in '49. So in the golf-centered world of this club, it's no wonder time itself seemed to stand still as he walked by.

When Hogan reached me on the driving range, he was all business.

"I got these new MacGregor clubs, Jack, and they need some work before they're fit to play. Let's hit a few. Go out a hundred yards and I'll start with wedges." He glanced around the tee, looking for a patch of grass that hadn't already been cut up earlier by the pros.

When he found the right spot, I emptied the shag bag at his feet. The balls all looked brand-new, as if they had been taken straight from the sleeves we sold in the shop. No one at the club, not even Matt, had such fine practice balls. In fact, during my first years as a caddie, Jimmy had me go out to the water hole on twelve several times a week to hunt for balls knocked into the pond. In those war years, rubber was rationed and golf balls were treasured. Sam Snead, in fact, collected old ones and carried them around in a cigar box when we were at war.

Grabbing the now-empty shag bag, I jogged out a hundred yards, counting my strides as I ran, then dropped the leather bag so it could become Hogan's target. As soon as I did, the first of his wedge shots hissed past my ear. I stepped to one side as Hogan continued to lob wedges at the target, half a dozen of his shots bouncing into the opening of the bag or hitting it on the fly.

When he'd hit all fifty balls, he set the wedge aside and pulled out the 9-iron. Then he waved me to bring the balls back in. By the time I reached him, he had lit a cigarette and was leaning against his club. I dumped the bag of balls and ran back down the range.

By now a small crowd had gathered at the edge of the practice tee, standing ten yards behind Hogan in an impromptu gallery. Some were pros who'd been on the putting green; some were members who'd filtered down the hillside when they realized Hogan was going to hit balls. No one spoke to Hogan; they didn't even speak to one another beyond a few whispered words. They all behaved as if they were in church.

Our starstruck members weren't the only ones who liked to watch Hogan practice. There's a story told about Herman Keiser, who had beaten Hogan in April of that year at Augusta. He followed Ben down to the driving range one afternoon and Ben said, "Herm, I'm going to be here a while," and Keiser calmly replied, "That's why I brought a chair."

That afternoon, I witnessed a similar scene. Hogan played one club after the other, moving from the wedge up to the 1-iron driving me farther down the range until he was far away in the fading light with the gallery of pros and members behind him, a tight blur of color on the horizon.

And again I watched his famous swing: the flat takeaway, the long backswing, and the hinging of the wrists at the top before he slashed the club back to the ball, holding the late release of his hands until just before impact, then the smooth, sweeping finish with his whole body twisted toward the flight of the ball.

As I waited, I challenged myself to stand perfectly still with the shag bag less than five yards in front of me. The balls came out of the splash of color low and fierce, and rose quickly into the evening sky. They faded as they drifted down, hit a few yards in front of the bag, bounced once, and spun to a stop within feet of the target.

I let the balls collect and cluster around the brown leather shag bag. Hogan kept hitting his long irons into the sun and I wondered if the gallery understood how perfect all the shots were, how they were all nestled together, as if some giant bird were laying eggs at my feet.

As I watched, I couldn't help but feel empty in my heart, thinking of Matt. He'd never be able to stand up to real professional tour players. By Sunday he'd only be humiliated by Hogan, who was hitting his long irons two hundred yards out to me at the end of the practice range as if they were nothing more than two-finger curves thrown from sixty feet off a pitcher's mound.

Time after time, I'd collect the balls, run them in, and drop them at a patch of level ground while Hogan worked away at another Chesterfield, then I'd jog out, down the long fairway to the end of the range.

The gallery continued to grow, eventually numbering close to seventy-five. The pros huddled off to one side, while the members, wives as well as husbands, clustered together in another spot.

Were the women as fascinated by Hogan's fierce swing and its solid consistency as their husbands? No doubt the golfers among them were awed at the distance he generated with his clubs. But my guess is they were equally drawn by the good looks and glamour of this man in his thirties who dressed like a movie star and looked like one as well.

Though the gallery kept growing, Hogan continued to ignore them. Even when he had hit the last of a round of balls and signaled me to bring them in, he wouldn't turn and chat up his special fans. He just dropped the club he'd been using and stood methodically smoking until I'd made the long jog back to the tee.

In the end, Hogan outlasted the gallery, as he always did. No one had Ben's endurance. The pros and members drifted off in twos and fours until finally the tee was empty except for Hogan, still hitting drives into the long grass beyond the mowed range, drives that went well over 280 and ran deep into the long rough.

Around eight-thirty, when it was almost dark, he waved me in for the last time. As Hogan often said, there was never enough daylight for him to practice.

"Is the shop still open Jack?" he asked.

"Yes, sir. Jimmy wouldn't lock up with you out here."

"I need to do a little work on these clubs."

It was only then, as we walked together across nine and went up the hill to the pro shop, that Hogan mentioned Matt. He had seen his qualifying score on the board and complimented me on my guy's performance. When I just nodded, saying nothing, Hogan studied me with those slate-blue eyes, then asked, "Are you caddying for him, Jack?" He spoke in the whispering voice he had that somehow managed to be both sympathetic as well as demanding.

"No, sir."

Most adults would've asked me why, feeling they had a right to pry into the lives of kids. But instead he just said, "How about looping for me?"

I looked up and grinned.

"Okay," he said, smiling. "Clean up those clubs and I'll meet you in the shop in a few minutes." He tapped the bill of my caddie cap and headed for the men's locker room.

In the shop, I found Matt rewrapping the leather grip on his putter. He didn't say anything to me, but then he saw the bag I was carrying.

"Hogan's here?" Those two words were the first he'd addressed to me in weeks.

"Yep." I dumped the club heads of Hogan's irons into a bucket of soapy water.

"He's been practicing?"

"Yep."

I kept busy with the irons, pulling the clubs out of the warm water one at a time and wiping the faces clean with a towel. To make absolutely sure they were clean, I dug the end of a tee into each one of the grooves and scraped out the dirt.

I was feeling bad about not being able to talk with Matt, not just because I missed him but because now I knew something new about the Hawk. Today I'd noticed the grips on all his irons and woods had a built-up rib on the bottom of the shaft. When he picked up the club, it set his hands in the exact same spot so he couldn't grip it the wrong way.

But if Matt wouldn't be friendly to me, I wasn't going to give him an inside scoop on Hogan. As he worked on wrapping his putter, I was sure he wondered if I was back caddying for Hogan, for in those years PGA pros didn't tour with their own caddies; they just used kids and men who worked at whatever club was hosting the tournament. Still, if Matt was worried, he didn't let on. He'd walk across hot coals before he'd ask me if I was going to be on Hogan's bag.

We were still working side by side when Ben came down from the locker room.

"Hello, Matt," he said. "Congratulations on qualifying." He reached out to shake hands, all smiles and congeniality.

"Thanks, Mr. Hogan . . . ah, I mean, Ben, but it wasn't much of a round. I couldn't get my game going."

"You got the job done; you qualified." Hogan kept smiling, being nice. "That's what's great about golf; every day you get to tee it up as new." Hogan nodded toward the bench. "Do you mind if I do a little work on my clubs?" he asked, in the nice way he had whenever he wasn't dealing with reporters.

"No, sir. Anything you want." Matt gestured toward the bench and the array of tools we had racked behind it. At the time, you must remember, clubmaking wasn't some refined hobby; it was part of what every pro needed to know to do his job. Part of my training as a shop boy was to learn how to grip clubs, rewind and lacquer woods, and bend club faces back into shape. And we didn't have those fancy tools hobbyists have today, all those swing weight scales and digital equipment. We only had drill presses, clamping tools, glue, reamers, and a couple of heavy wood mallets we used on the irons.

Matt didn't hang around to watch Hogan fiddle with his new MacGregors.

"Jack knows how to lock up," he said as he backed away toward the door. He waved and was gone, letting the screen slam behind him.

Hogan, for his part, didn't urge him to stay. Instead, he said in the whispery voice, "Jack, why don't you lock the door so we won't be bothered."

When I came back, he had his sand wedge clamped into the small vise and he asked me to move the blowtorch tank over to the table.

"Jimmy won't let me use it," I told him. "He says it's too dangerous."

Hogan smiled at my concern.

"It's okay. Jimmy won't mind. We grew up caddying together down in Texas. Where's your solder?"

Hogan approached the table the way a surgeon might approach an interesting operation. He began by adding a lump of brass to the back of all of his irons, just a thin slice of extra weight attached to the club with the precision of a jeweler cutting a diamond.

I'd watched Jimmy and Matt fix up old clubs, but here was Hogan with perfectly good, brand-new irons adjusting their weight. Each time he finished one, he'd take it from the vise and fit the club in his fingers, test the weight with those educated hands. It took him over an hour to do all the irons, and he never said a word to me. When he finished he clamped his 4-wood spoon into the vise and asked.

"Where are your files?"

I nodded to a slot where half a dozen grades of files were stored.

Hogan pulled a few of them from the slot and checked the coarseness before he found what he wanted. Then he carefully addressed the face of the 4-wood, using the file to widen the grooves.

When I looked closer, he simply said, "The ball's running too much out there on the range. This will help me control my woods."

"I never saw anyone do that," I declared. "Is it allowed?"

"We can't widen the grooves of irons, but the PGA hasn't told me to stop doctoring woods."

Now I can see some of you are thinking maybe this is what Hogan meant when he talked about how he had learned "the secret of golf." But, no, all the touring pros tweaked their clubs. Hogan did have a secret, and it had nothing to do with how he doctored his clubs.

When he finished working on his woods, he put away the tools and cleaned the top of the bench, leaving it as he had found it. Then he picked up his clubs, smiled at me, and said, "Will I see you in the morning?"

"When do you tee off, sir?"

"I have a game at nine."

"I'll be here at nine."

"Be here at eight."

"Yes, sir."

When he started to leave, I blurted out, "Mr. Hogan, you can leave your clubs in the shop. They'll be safe."

"Thanks, Jack. I'll take them upstairs to my room just in case. Besides, Sarazen goes around telling people I sleep with my putter, so I wouldn't want to disappoint him."

22

As I locked the pro shop for the night, I heard music coming from the ballroom. It was already 10:00 P.M., but instead of heading home, I walked to the other side of the building and in through the side door to the clubhouse kitchen.

The chef at the time was a man called Easy Al for his slow ways and saintly unwillingness to rise to anger. This, as those of you on the House Committee may already know, is not the behavior of most club chefs.

Easy Al had taken to golf, and on slow days I'd give him our extra set of clubs and he'd play a few holes on the back nine. Because of one small favor, I never went hungry.

"Big night," Easy Al commented when he saw me. He was a tall, skinny black guy who wore a chef's hat tipped sideways on his bald head. The kitchen had gone from busy to chaotic, but he managed to throw together a plate of chicken, mashed potatoes, and an ear of corn on the cob for me without seeming even to think of it. "The big boys are down from Chicago."

When he saw I didn't understand what he meant about "the big boys" he grinned, took the cigarette out of his mouth, and said, "Players." Even I knew he wasn't talking about golfers.

"Going to bet on your man?" he asked.

I shook my head, still not comprehending. Then he told me about the Calcutta. How gamblers had come out from the city and besides the bidding on the Calcutta, the gamblers would take side bets on who would win the tournament.

My sister Kathy swept in then with another dinner order. She sized me up with one glance and wanted to know if Mom knew where I was. Before I could even reply, she told me to call home so Mom wouldn't worry, though to tell you the truth, I don't think, since my dad died, Mom worried all that much about me. It was Kathy who looked after me.

This time, however, Easy Al waved off her concern. He let me use the house phone to call home, handed me a glass of milk to drink with dinner, and when I was finished eating, signaled me to follow after him.

On a night like this, with two hundred or more members, wives, and guests in the dining room and spilling out onto the front porch, for the chef to take time for a kid like me was extraordinary.

Yet again, it was this silent conspiracy of the employees who for some reason, and to this day I am not sure why, took a special interest in my well-being, but that is why your country club was a real home for me when I was a boy.

So there was Easy Al leading me through the back pantry and back hallway, past a warren of tiny rooms, to yet another staircase tucked away from view, and from there, one flight up, to a small opening, a peephole in the circular wooden stairwell, giving me a bird's-eye view of the vast dining room down on the first floor.

"Stay here and watch the show," Easy Al instructed. Then he pulled out a big bottle of cold Coke, grinned and winked, and went back down to the kitchen.

At one end of the dining room, in front of the stone fireplace, were the extra green scoring boards we used for members' tournaments, and on them were lists of the Open players. Dinner was mostly finished and Kathy and the other waitresses were stacking dishes on carts and wheeling them away. The regular bartenders and several of the guys who worked on weekends were carrying trays of drinks among the tables. The dining room and the screened porch were filled with members and their wives, and I could feel the electricity of their excitement flashing from table to table, cutting through, it seemed, the heavy layer of cigarette smoke.

From where I was, leaning forward on my elbows, my face pressed into the peephole, I read the big, bold lettering of each player's name, and the odds of their winning, all written on large white scoring sheets.

I found Matt's name. It topped the list of those pros who had qualified on Monday. He had the best odds of those players— going at 20 to 1, but it was a long ways from Hogan's 2 to 1 odds on winning. Sweeping down the list of sixty names, I spotted all the touring PGA professionals: Snead, Nelson, Bobby Locke, and all the rest. For all of us at the club, employees or members, it was amazing to see the best players in the world had come to play on our golf course.

But it wasn't yet the players' time. Now it was time for the Calcutta, and I was eager to see how much Matt would go for in the auction. I focused my attention on the big board while Mike

McNulty, the chairman of the Rules Committee, stood on a stage at the far end of the room and signaled the bidding was beginning.

As the last one to qualify to play in the Open, Matt was auctioned off first, and the members cheered at the mention of his name. After only two rounds Matt's price reached a hundred dollars. I could tell a few of the members had just bid to show some support for the home pro. My eyes darted from one side of the room to the other, watching for bright green paddles as the bidders made their moves.

I was holding my breath, not sure what I was expecting or what I feared. Then something odd happened. Someone raised the bid on Matt to five hundred dollars. A gasp was heard from the crowd, followed by a quick murmur of excitement. Half a dozen members stood up at their tables to see which of their members had raised the bid.

Perched as I was on the stairway feet above the room, I knew exactly who had caused the stir—and it wasn't even a member. Standing in the open French doors to the screened porch was the man with the hairpiece who had come looking for Matt. The man from Gatesburg. He was again wearing a suit, a dark one, with a white shirt and tie. What was strangest about him was that he seemed apart from the rush of excitement around him, calmly smoking a cigarette amid all the noisy chatter.

It was only then that I spotted Matt. He was leaning against the back wall, just inside the swinging doors leading to the kitchen, wearing the same clothes he had played in earlier in the day. Without any of the members realizing, he had slipped into the dining room to watch how much of their money he was worth.

As he watched, the bidding went up again. Despite the big

jump in price, members were shouting out from the depths of the room, from this table and that, even men whom we caddies knew as bad tippers and tightwads. Everyone, it suddenly seemed, wanted a piece of Matt. They were bidding widly, the auctioneer moving from corner to corner, from front to back, seducing them with talk of Matt's talent, his handsome looks, his knowledge of the golf course, even his amazing smile. The auctioneer kept selling, and these members, who ordered Matt around seven days a week, were buying.

I paid no attention to the members. It was Ralph Gates at the French doors who fascinated me. I watched him through the swirl of action, through the hazy cigarette smoke spreading like fog across the crowded tables.

And while I was watching, Ralph Gates waited. Waited until the auctioneer had exhausted the bidding from the tables; waited while the auctioneer's eyes swept the room and declared the sale was going, going—and then he increased his bid. He never raised a paddle; he just nodded slightly, and the auctioneer nodded back, and raised the bid.

The crowd went wild and I heard a woman's screech. It was Sarah, crying out not because of what the stranger bid but because her own father, sitting placidly watching the action, unexpectedly raised his green paddle and bid one thousand on Matt Richardson to win the Open.

The man in the doorway glanced at Dr. DuPree and now, as they say, the game was on. He raised DuPree's price another five hundred. A few other members stayed in for several more rounds, but when the number reached six thousand, only the stranger and Dr. DuPree were bidding against each other.

The noise in the dining room ceased. People fell silent in the face of escalating bidding. Mike McNulty's voice was loud and clear as he went back and forth, from the stranger standing at the French doors to Dr. DuPree sitting with his wife and daughter and a table of other members. Now, as the bidding kept increasing, Sarah slipped down in her chair. Her hands were cupped to her mouth, as if to smother another outburst.

I had never seen Dr. DuPree like this, betting wildly, bid after bid. Caddying for him, I knew he never bet more than one buck in a Nassau. Now he was matching this Gatesburg stranger, round for round, as the price jumped from five thousand to eight thousand, to ten thousand—which was almost enough money, in those days, to buy one of the houses on Cottage Row Drive.

At fifteen thousand the stranger stopped. In the silence, he simply nodded toward Dr. DuPree with a wry smile, then stepped away from the open doorway and disappeared into the darkness of the porch. From below my perch, there was a huge sigh and an enormous burst of applause from all the members.

The auction for the next player was announced, but Dr. DuPree's bidding engulfed the room. A swarm of members came rushing over and slapped the president on the back, and when they left, I saw Sarah had slipped away from the table.

I glanced over to where Matt had been standing against the wall. The spot was empty.

I ran down the stairs and out the side door, thinking if I circled the clubhouse I might find them outside, and I was right. As I jogged around the building, I saw them standing in the employee parking lot.

And they were not alone.

I pulled backed against a wall where I couldn't be seen. Sarah did glance around, hearing something, but she didn't see me, and Matt was deep in conversation with Ralph Gates from Gatesburg.

What they were talking about was beyond my hearing, but I saw Gates pat Matt on the shoulder, shake hands with him, and then slip into a car and start the engine.

Matt and Sarah stood together and watched the man drive off. Matt's arm was draped over her shoulder, and she had both of her arms wrapped tight around his waist. In the silence after the car had disappeared, heading for the front gates, I heard her quietly sobbing into Matt's golf shirt.

Taking my chances, I slid away, circled the clubhouse, and headed across the pitch-black course. This was my path home, and I had walked it hundreds of times in daylight and dark, but never, I think, with such apprehension.

23

EARLY WEDNESDAY MORNING, I WAS WAITING FOR HOGAN TO ARrive when Matt came into the pro shop, skipping down the narrow steps from the locker room as if he were God's gift to the golfing world, which, of course, he was, having been auctioned off the night before for fifteen thousand dollars.

Matt was dressed to play, and as he headed for the back of the shop, where he kept his clubs and shoes, he told me to call down to the caddie shack and tell Kenny Burke's little brother that he wanted to hit balls.

I picked up the phone and told the Professor that Matt was ready to play, and that Kenny Burke's little brother should come up to the shop.

The Professor was our caddie master. He didn't have a Ph.D.; he just wound up with that title because he loved to read. Caddie yards are full of descriptive names. One guy we called "Downwind Sam" because upwind of him was definitely where you

wanted to be, if you know what I mean. There were other nicknames as well: "Wall-Eyed Warren" for his bulging eyes;
"Lazarus," an old rummy caddie who had been run over in the
parking lot one night, knocked unconscious, but came to the club
the next morning, well enough to caddie eighteen holes double.
Matt started calling me "Jackson" when he arrived at the club,
but mostly the other caddies knew me only as "Ben" because of
my obsession with Hogan.

Matt came up to the front of the shop with his shoes on.

"Where's Hogan?" he asked.

"He's teeing off at nine."

Matt stared out the screen door as if he wanted to say something more but didn't know what.

"You think he's going to win this?" he asked.

"I don't know. You beat him."

"Yeah, with your help."

"Dr. DuPree thinks you can win."

"DuPree doesn't want me to win," he said flatly.

"Then why did he buy you last night for fifteen thousand?"

"Not because he wants me to win, that's for sure."

Before I could ask him what he meant, he pulled himself together and said quietly, "Good luck, Jack. Good luck with
Hogan." Then he pushed open the screen door and stepped into
the morning sun. I probably should've been wondering what on
earth he meant about Dr. DuPree. But instead, all I could think
of was that this was the nicest Matt had been to me in weeks.

On Hogan's practice round that day, he played with Porky Oliver,
Jimmy Demaret, and Ed Furgol. That year, Hogan would beat
Jimmy 10 and 9 in the semifinals of the PGA Championship.

When a reporter asked Demaret what the turning point had been, he replied, "When Ben showed up."

Demaret was the closest thing to a friend that Hogan allowed himself on tour, and the two often practiced together. Oliver and Furgol were also early touring pros. Remembering them all standing on the first tee, I was struck at what an odd lot they were as players. Porky was a short, stout, disheveled guy who loved to gamble. Furgol looked like an American Indian, tall, wiry, and copper-skinned. His left arm was withered and permanently crooked at a right angle across his body. Nonetheless, his right was powerful, and he was a good enough to win the '54 U.S. Open at Baltusrol.

Jimmy Demaret was something else entirely. On the morning of the practice round, he was wearing lime-green slacks and lemon-yellow shoes. When he hit a shot, he'd swing the club like a baton in his follow-through, talking all the time to anyone who might be listening. You wouldn't think he would get along with Hogan, but Demaret was a hell of a player and Hogan knew it. Coming from Texas, Demaret was a wonderful wind player and hit everything with a fade, the way Hogan thought the game should be played. They got together as a team in '41 and Demaret was Hogan's primary partner in team events, which were popular at tournaments in the early forties.

That practice round, they played a typical Nassau bet, waging five bucks for each side, and another five on who won the whole match. Ben and Jimmy won it all. Demaret didn't clown around on the course, and while both Porky and Furgol flipped a few clubs in anger, Hogan played his own game, never saying much to any of them, nor did he speak to me beyond hello at the first tee.

He pulled his own clubs, made his own decisions, read the putts himself, and only once, on seventeen, did he pause and ask me if the underground sprinkler up by the green was still leaking.

It might just have been a practice round with a few touring pros, but for Hogan there was never anything casual about his game.

After the round, I found Sarah waiting at the pro shop door. We had hardly spoken since Matt and Hogan had played their round, so I just nodded hello and walked past her.

She followed me into the shop.

"Hi, Jack," she said next, as if we were the best of friends.

I said "Hello" and started cleaning my player's irons.

"Matt says you're caddying for Hogan."

I nodded, but now I was getting nervous. She was like one of the nuns in school, quiet but insistent.

"Matt needs you to caddie for him, Jack," she said next, in a whisper.

"He's got a caddie."

"Matt says you're the only one who can club him."

I shrugged, as if I were uninterested, and started pulling the hoods off Hogan's woods.

"Will you do it for him, Jack?" she asked. "Please?"

"Matt fired me."

"Can't you talk to him?"

"He doesn't want me looping for him."

I finished cleaning the woods and picked up Hogan's bag. He had asked me to deliver it to his room, so I headed for the front of the pro shop, moving so fast that Sarah had to jump back.

"Jack," she said, raising her voice to stop me. "You know how Matt is. He can't come out and say, 'I forgive you.'"

That remark caught my attention.

"Forgive me? I didn't do anything wrong," I told her. "If he wants to forgive someone, why doesn't he try forgiving your parents instead?"

She glanced away and sighed, as if all of this was too overwhelming, then she added meekly, "Well, you know what I mean. He needs you to make the first move."

If Sarah had known anything about golf, she would have realized that it was too late. Ben Hogan had asked me to caddie for him, and now there was no way that I could drop his bag. I left the pro shop and kept walking, climbing the narrow stairs to Hogan's room on the second floor and gave him his clubs. On my way back downstairs, I ran into Dr. DuPree.

"There you are!" he cried. "I've been looking all over the damn place for you." He said it as if it was my fault.

"I was with Mr. Hogan," I answered, having already learned how much weight the name carried.

"Good!" DuPree declared. He was wheezing from the climb up from the pro shop. "You're caddying for him?" The way he said it made it sound like a demand. He waited for my answer, watching me with what seemed like apprehension. When I nodded, he beamed and patted me on the shoulder.

"Good! We want the best for Hogan!" If that was how he felt, I wondered, then why had he bought Matt in the Calcutta?

I worked the rest of the day in the shop, which now was crowded with players and members who'd come out to watch the pros in practice rounds. When the place finally quieted down, I went into the rack room and sat down at the desk. It was then that Kenny Burke's little brother came in through the back door carrying Matt's clubs.

"How did he play?" I called to him.

The kid shook his head and dropped the bag.

"What did he shoot?"

"Six over," he answered.

"He couldn't," I exclaimed.

The kid did not reply.

"What the hell happened?" I saw now that Kenny's brother was crying as he wiped Matt's irons clean.

"I kicked his ball," he said, using the end of his short-sleeved shirt to wipe the tears off his face. "I didn't see it," he said. "His drive was in the rough on eleven. I didn't see the ball." He started to cry again and slammed the bag hard against the wall.

Without saying anything, I went to the back of the shop and took the clubs away from him and cleaned the last of the irons. As I worked, he calmed down a little and finished the story.

"Matt fired me."

Getting fired for making a mistake on the course was the worst thing that could happen to any caddie. There wasn't anything I could say to ease that pain, but I was about to try when Matt came charging into the room. Glaring at us, but not saying a word, he emptied his pockets of ball, tees, and his glove, tossing everything on the roll top desk.

Then he stomped into the selling space up front, allowing Kenny Burke's little brother to escape through the back. I finished cleaning Matt's clubs and moved them over to his locker. It was only then that I saw the other mistake Kenny Burke's little brother had made: he'd left Matt's left-handed old Tennessee hickory shaft club pitching niblick out of his bag. I slipped it in with the irons, counted the clubs to make sure he was only carrying fourteen, then put his bag away and walked to the front of the shop to see what was going on.

Matt was pacing back and forth in front of the display of putters, picking up one, then another. Not sure what this signified, I sat down and started flipping through the pages of a golf magazine as if I had nothing better to do. Out of the corner of my eye I watched Matt fussing with the putters, taking a few strokes, then picking another and trying that one, searching for the right feel. That's a bad sign, as all of you golfers know. When you lose your feel on the green, there's not much hope you're going to play well.

With three new putters in his hand, he came back to the desk and reached across me to pick up the balls we always kept handy in a small bowl.

"If Jimmy's looking for me," he said, "I'm trying out putters." He was out the door at once, as if to cut me off before I could ask him what he'd shot.

All of this, of course, was making me feel awful. I kept leafing through golf magazines, trying not to think about Matt, when Jimmy came down from the locker room and I told him Matt was on the putting clock.

"You heard his score?" he asked.

I nodded and stood up so Jimmy would have a place to sit.

"Matt doesn't have a chance without you on his bag," Jimmy declared, slumping into the swivel chair. Jimmy was a big, lumbering man who might remind you of Guy Boros, or if you're a little older, Guy's father, the great Julius Boros, who won the U.S. Open twice.

"Matt doesn't want me on his bag," I said.

Jimmy nodded. He knew something had happened; he just didn't know what. "Nevertheless, that boy needs all the help he can get this week, especially with DuPree spending fifteen grand on him."

"You mean if Matt loses DuPree will fire him?" That possibility had never crossed my mind.

"Matt is finished at this club however he plays," Jimmy said. "DuPree wants him out of here, and away from his daughter. That's why the kids came up with this crazy scheme of theirs."

"What do you mean?"

Like the boy in *The Go-Between,* I was part of what was happening, but didn't know what it all meant.

"Matt called Gatesburg a few weeks ago," Jimmy explained. "He got the members at his home club in southern Illinois to pool money to bid on him. One of those fellas came up to see him last week."

"I saw him. Ralph Gates. He sells insurance, he said."

Jimmy nodded. "He's also the president of the club, and they're real proud of Matt down in his hometown. I spoke to him from Texas last winter when I interviewed Matt for this job."

"Gates was here last night. I saw him."

"You were at the Calcutta?" Jimmy glanced up at me.

"Just for a while," I said, afraid of getting Easy Al into trouble.

Jimmy swayed back in the chair and propped his legs on the corner of the desk. "Well, this Gates fella came here last night with a pocketful of members' money. The deal was that Matt was going to get a cut of the winnings, so he'd have money enough to marry young DuPree, but her old man got wind of their plan and bought Matt himself. Even if Matt wins the Open, he still won't have enough money to marry the Doc's daughter." Jimmy shook his head. "It's nothing but trouble when you start messing with club members. It's best to leave them with their own kind."

With that, he told me I should head on home. It was after eight and the shadows were lengthening across the fairways.

"See you in the morning," Jimmy said. "What's Hogan's tee time?"

"Around one."

"Better check the boards before you leave. You don't want to be late for Ben."

"Never happen," I said, and went out to the first tee where the starting times had been posted for the first round of the Chicago Open.

From the starter's tent I could see across the lawn to where Matt was trying out the new putters. He was a hundred yards away from where I stood, but even at that distance, I saw he was struggling.

Back in the '40s no one was using ultrasound to show how to stroke a putt. Pros couldn't measure their strokes on a computer, graphing alignment or acceleration. No, it was all a matter of feel, and Matt had lost his.

"Your boy had a tough day," Hogan said, coming up behind me. He was dressed elegantly for dinner, in a gold silk tie, blue blazer, and linen pants.

"Yes, sir," I said, standing up straight, and then to defend Matt, I told Hogan about the Burke kid kicking Matt's ball.

Hogan took out a cigarette. The flash of match briefly glowed in the shadows.

We both watched Matt putting in the last light of the day. Then Hogan asked, "What are you going to do, Jack?"

"Sorry?"

"You're in a quandary, aren't you?" Hogan asked.

"What's a quandary?"

Hogan laughed and said, "Well, having never finished high school, I'm not too sure of the definition myself. But what I meant was you have to decide if you're caddying for Matt or for me."

I shook my head. I was near tears with my quandary, which I hadn't realized was my quandary until Hogan said so.

Then he said softly, "Jimmy was telling me about your dad,

how he was killed in the war. I'm real sorry, Jack. My dad died when I was younger than you, so I know how hard it is on you. But I want you to think about this. Your dad didn't have to go to war, Jack. He was a farmer, growing food for the troops; he would never have been drafted. But he went anyway, didn't he, because he thought it was the right thing to do. He didn't come home, so you're probably angry with him, angry he's gone, leaving the rest of you with the farm to run.

"But going to war was his responsibility, Jack. It was my responsibility, too, and most of these pros you see out here this week, why, we all went, and some of my friends, they didn't come home either. But we went because we had to. And that's what you have to do, Sonny. Live up to your responsibility."

"Matt doesn't want me," I answered.

And then Ben Hogan did something unusual. He put his hands on my shoulders and looked me in the eyes. "Like I said, Matt is your responsibility. I don't know how it happened. Nor do you. But that's how life is. So just go tell Matt you're caddying for him." He touched my shoulder with the palm of his hand, rough and calloused from years of hitting balls but soft and gentle as he patted me. Then he walked away, up the path and into the clubhouse.

I didn't move. Whenever Hogan left, I had come to notice, the atmosphere changed. Years later, in the '70s, I read some guru, the man who started the Esalen Institute, say that there was a psychic energy field around Hogan. Maybe there was, maybe there wasn't—but now he was gone and I was completely alone with my quandary.

Without really knowing what I was going to do, I walked out from under the starter's tent and crossed in front of the clubhouse. The open, white-columned veranda was jammed, with the overflow crowd standing on the lawn. Members and pros alike stood with drinks and cigarettes in hand, all dressed in summer blazers, some wearing what I would come to know as school ties, with white shirts and white shoes. The women were fewer and they wore their hair permed in the stiff, short curls of that summer season after the war.

Everyone was there, but somehow I spotted Dr. DuPree in the crowd. He was standing with a group of friends, but once I caught his eye, I saw him focus on me, and glance to the putting green where Matt was practicing.

I kept walking, and as I reached the putting green, DuPree came to the edge of the terrace. "Watch this," I thought, and I stepped right onto the smooth putting surface, something caddies would never do.

I was within ten feet of Matt before he looked up and frowned, as if I were interrupting him. Without breaking stride I strode past him, tossing off, over my shoulder, "I'm caddying for you tomorrow." I said it as if it was my decision and not his and I kept right on moving.

I must have been a dozen yards away before he called after me, "My tee time is nine-twenty."

"I know," I said, and disappeared into the dark of the golf course.

24

ON THE FIRST DAY OF THE CHICAGO OPEN, I WAS OUT OF BED BY five and down to the barn to do the morning chores, but Mom had already started the milking. She told me to be on my way. She knew this was a big day, she said, and she would take care of the chores.

Since Mom never asked me any questions about the golf course or the players, I figured Kathy must have said something. I don't know how many details she'd been told, but she must've had some idea of what was happening that day, because she stopped milking long enough to stand up and hug me and tell me to do my best.

Once she did that, it all poured out of me. I told her it wasn't my performance that I was worried about but Matt's. She said if I had faith in Matt he would do just fine because I would never believe in someone who wasn't worth it. This made me feel a lot better, as I was having plenty of doubts just then about whether Matt had even the remotest chance of winning.

Still, I don't think there was a more excited kid around that first morning of the Open. You know the old definition of a good caddie: one who shows up, keeps up, and shuts up. Well, my idea of myself was much grander. I had the tournament dream all caddies have. We're at the final hole late on a Sunday afternoon, with the clubhouse soft and misty in the warm August sunset, and maybe three or four thousand people lining the fairway and circling the green. As my guy makes a brilliant approach and the gallery starts cheering there I am, walking stride by stride down the final fairway with my Open winner, the player I had brought home to victory.

And my best chance for achieving all that developed when I ducked under the fence and saw Ed, the greenskeeper, on thirteen green with his brother Bill and two PGA officials. They were cutting the hole for the placement of the flag for that opening day of the Open and I walked up and stood on the mound behind thirteen as they canvassed the green for the right spot.

I had seen Bill doing the same job every morning of the summer. Often, crossing the course, I'd stop and chat with him as he cut a plug in the green and made the new cup.

Deciding where the hole would go gave Bill a lot of power. He could make the spot easy or hard. And when there was a big event, he always made it difficult. As the players among you are well aware, there are pin locations and pin locations. And then there are tournament pin locations.

They tell the story of the time Hogan took on the members at Shady Oaks Country Club down in Texas, in a match called the Swing Game. Hogan and one partner took on all the members, but they used their handicaps. Hogan hated those handicaps and when he lost one too many times, he announced that he was going to take on all comers. But before the match he went out with the greenskeeper and set the flag placements, moving the cups to the right side of all the greens so that they would favor his trademark fade. That was the last time Shady Oaks members beat Ben Hogan, even with their handicaps.

After Ed and Bill took off for the next green, I walked down the slope and paced the distance from where the hole was cut to the apron. I paced the hole's location from several angles, thinking how I would know just where the flag was when we played later.

You have to realize my doing this was years before professional caddies walked a course or had range finders to chart distances. None of the caddies, not even the few older, more experienced guys who traveled the tour right after the war, had yardage books, or jotted down tiers and slopes and pin placements.

Today the PGA Tour has something called ShotLink, where a smart caddie with a player starting late in the day might go to a laptop and see what club the pros are using on one hole or another. Call it local knowledge, courtesy of the computer.

But in the '40s, legends like Hogan did it all by sight. He had great depth perception. You may have heard the story of how in the '60s a TV show called *Shell's Wonderful World of Golf* matched Hogan against Sam Snead. The match was played at the Houston Country Club and during the practice round Hogan came to a par-3 listed as 152 yards.

Hogan looked at the flagstick and he looked at the official yardage and he said the measurement was wrong. The hole played 148, he said.

After he took his shot, they paced off the yardage, and Hogan was right: 148 yards.

I hadn't come to the Open with a plan, but when I saw them

cutting pin placement I had a flash of caddie brilliance. After pacing off the hole on thirteen, I followed Ed and Bill to fourteen green and did the same there. In the next hour, I charted the entire course, staying safely out of the adults' sight, and jotting down the placements on the back of a scorecard. By the time I reached the pro shop, my shoes and pant legs were so wet from the grass that Jimmy, glancing at me, grinned and asked, "You been fishing for balls again on twelve?"

"It's wet out there," I said, somehow knowing I shouldn't tell anyone, even Jimmy, what I had been up to.

"Hogan was asking me about you," Jimmy said next. "I had breakfast with Valerie and Ben this morning and Ben wanted to know all about you."

I said nothing, trying to be cool, but I was thrilled that Hogan was asking about me.

"You know, I used to caddie with Ben outside of Fort Worth. You know about that, right?"

I smiled. In truth, Jimmy had told me hundreds of times how he had caddied with Hogan and Byron Nelson when they were kids in Texas.

"Oh that's right, I did tell you." Jimmy caught himself and grinned. "But you don't know what he said about you this morning, do you?"

"Okay," I exclaimed, giving up. "What did he say about me?"

"Well, he wanted to know if you could handle the tournament, if you knew enough about the game not to cost a player strokes."

It was a question I hadn't expected. Offended by the idea I didn't know the course or the rules, I gave Jimmy a look. He just shrugged, as if I shouldn't be so touchy.

"Hey, to most of these pros, you're just a kid. Ben doesn't want anyone out there with him who might make a mistake. This is the big time, Jack, not a couple members playing a skins game on Sunday morning."

"I know what I'm doing, Jimmy."

"I told Ben you did. I told him Matt had made a mistake letting you go."

"But I'm caddying for Matt now," I answered quickly.

Jimmy looked at me for a long time with his big soulful eyes, then asked if Hogan knew.

"It was his idea."

Jimmy smiled slowly and shook his head.

"Well, that's like Hogan. He can win without you on his bag, but he knows Matt can't." He sat back in the swivel chair for a moment as if contemplating what he would say next, and then he spoke very seriously. "You need to know, Jack, if you caddie for Matt, whether he wins or loses, you're finished here. Dr. DuPree will have his way. He won't like anyone crossing him, especially some caddie."

"It's fine with me," I said, though the truth was I was stunned by what Jimmy said. I knew Mom needed the money I brought home from caddying, and I was giving it all up just so Matt Richardson had a chance to win the Open.

"It better be fine, because I can't protect you from Dr. DuPree. I would if I could, but he's president of the club, so he's my boss as well." Jimmy stood. The first twosome of the tournament was set to tee off, and it was time for him to go up to the starter's tent. But before he pushed open the screen door, he glanced back and said, "There's only one way to beat the bastard, Jack. Bring Matt home a winner."

25

MATT'S DRIVE ON THE FIRST HOLE SPLIT THE FAIRWAY AND RAN another twenty yards on the hard ground, going over 280. We had about two dozen spectators following us, most of who had come out to walk the front nine with the touring pros, Lloyd Mangrum and Ed Furgol, who were playing with us. And most of them were following Mangrum, who had won the U.S. Open earlier that summer.

Matt outdrove both Mangrum and Furgol, and when they played their second shots onto the first green, we walked up to Matt's drive and he asked immediately, "What do you think?"

His ball was sitting up, and it was possible Matt might hit under it with a lofted club. Always I went with the safe shot, one he had the most confidence in hitting, and that was the low chip run-up.

"The hole is six feet from the back fringe. Hit a knockdown eight," I told Matt. "You've got the whole front of the green to work with." I pulled the 8-iron before he could disagree with me.

"How do you know the flag is that far back?" Matt asked, staring at the green.

I took out my scribbled notes and told him how I had walked the course that morning.

Matt didn't give me his big, sloppy grin. He didn't even say anything dumb. I knew my charting of the course had impressed him. In time, all touring pros would understand how necessary it was to know exactly where the flagsticks are placed before they tee off.

Back in the 1940s, no one used the term "dead, solid perfect," but that was how Matt hit the ball. He left himself a three-foot straight-in putt, which he easily made. On the second hole, he played a 5, shaping the iron so it drew left to right, and again he made the putt. We were two under going into 3, and, I might add, Matt hadn't yet broken into a sweat.

It was on the third or fourth hole when I realized he was "in the zone," as we say today when a player splits the fairway with every drive, hits the greens in regulation, and makes all his putts. Matt did seem to be in his own zone. He appeared to slip away, as if he was psychically separated from the other players and the gallery. He was in his own world, and I was part of it, just the two of us communicating with gestures, glances, and, when necessary, a few whispered words. If you've ever known the heat of any serious competition, or if you're a woman who's been through childbirth, you understand what I mean when I talk about that intense concentration on the here and now.

Yes, Matt had played brilliantly on other days, in those early morning practice rounds, those times when he had gotten on a sudden streak and rattled off a fistful of birdies, making incredible shots and monster putts in the emptiness and silence of the empty course, thick with dew.

This was different. This was the real thing, the Open, with a gallery beginning to line the fairways and greens as word swept across the course that the young assistant home pro had it going on the front side.

I recall most vividly reaching the tenth tee, after Matt had gone out with a 31, all pars and birdies and one eagle on number seven to be 5 under par on the outgoing nine. We didn't have any big electronic scoreboards, but a 31 on the outgoing nine on the opening day spread incredibly fast by word-of-mouth, and standing on the tee box, I watched streams of spectators moving across the fairways, seeking us out on the tenth tee.

The tenth tee was elevated, as I believe it still is. Matt had the honors and we were waiting for the threesome ahead of us on the hole to clear out of the way. Ropes had been strung around the edges of the tee to keep back the gallery, so Matt and I were, so to speak, center stage. It was the Globe Theatre, you might say, and we were playing Shakespeare.

The galleries of the 1940s weren't anything like what you have today. There were no bleachers, for example, built behind the short par-3s, or around the eighteenth hole. Except at the tees, ropes weren't used to keep back the spectators, and the few marshals we had were club members. They walked beside the leading players to keep them from being bothered by the spectators. Not that anyone would harass a player. No one would have dreamed of talking to a pro during a round, nor did we need uniformed police as bodyguards. In those days, spectators were as polite as a Presbyterian church congregation.

Later on, of course, after television began to broadcast events, larger crowds began to flock to golf tournaments and ropes were used for the first time to protect players. It was the famous golf architect Robert Trent Jones who had the idea of roping the fairways to keep fans away from the players during the '54 U.S. Open at Baltusrol. Jones had seen ropes being used on a few fairways at the Masters and wanted to protect his golf course as much as he wanted to shield the players from the crowds. But the ropes had a secondary benefit: by holding back the gallery all the tees, fairways, and greens became stages. This separation created status, and a star system was born.

At the '46 Open, however, there were no TV cameras or even radio broadcasts live from the course. There were just the pros and a few thousand fans who loved the game and sensed that something special would happen on the back side of the first round of the Chicago Open.

Matt and I were standing on the tee and waiting for the three-some of "Dutch" Harrison, Ellsworth Vines, and, I believe, that fine amateur Frank Stranahan to play their second shots. Matt and I weren't talking. I was afraid to break his concentration, afraid perhaps I might say something that would move him out of his zone.

We had had the honors since the second hole, and when Harrison hit his short iron into ten green, Matt moved over to where I was standing beside the marker and reached for his 3-wood.

I must have reacted to him pulling out the spoon because he hesitated and asked, "What?" as if somehow his decision was my fault.

"Nothin'," I said, shrugging, looking down, embarrassed by his reaction, and feeling, too, the weight of all the spectators behind me. They were pressed up against the rope guarding the tee box.

"I'm not risking the out-of-bounds. I'll play it safe, hit a six into the green. Okay?" Matt explained.

I could tell he wanted me to agree. Why risk blowing up on the back side, when he could par in and still be 5 under on the opening day of the Open? All this was racing through my mind as I nodded, but still I didn't move the bag to let him go ahead and play away.

"C'mon," Matt finally demanded, knowing me as well as I understood him, and knowing I didn't agree with this strategy of playing it safe on the back side.

"The cup is cut way up on top," I told him, whispering, as I was afraid Furgol and Mangrum might hear me and use the local knowledge themselves. "You're going to need more than a six to reach the top shelf, and you are more likely to spray a long iron than you will the driver." I reminded him of something all players and caddies know: when you start to play it safe, that's when you lose it, whether *it* is momentum or nerve or just your good luck at having the ball always bounce the right way. "Play the wood, Matt." I told him. "Keep pressing."

Matt still had his hand on the spoon, which he had pulled halfway out of the bag. He kept staring at me, his blue eyes hard now, and I was thinking this time I had really gone too far with my smart mouth, and then Matt nodded and shoved the 3-wood back and grabbed the driver.

"Okay," he said under his breath, and as he spoke he was grinning his smartass grin that meant he was feeling cocky and sure of himself. "Let's show these old guys that we belong out here."

He stepped up to the tee and nailed the drive in the center of its screws. The ball carried beyond the hard patch of high ground, our target on that hole, but still ran like a rabbit. Matt was on the green in two and made his par. Walking off ten green, he was still in his groove.

26

ON ELEVEN TEE MATT DIDN'T CONSULT ME, HE JUST REACHED FOR the 3-wood. I didn't protest. This was the time to play it safe, settle for par, and keep out of trouble. Matt hit one of the best 3-woods I've seen, outdriving Mangrum but not Furgol, who even with his crippled arm was long off the tee. Matt was all pumped up. He was 5 under and had creamed his drive on eleven, hit it dead solid perfect on the only hole on the back side where the out-of-bounds came into play.

As the players left the tee, the whole gallery crowded in and there was a rush down the fairway. I swung the big bag onto my shoulder and raced after Matt, who was already swallowed up by the crowd. I was carried along in their wake, as all the spectators started to jockey for position, to have a good spot to see the threesome play their next shots to the green, although really it was only Matt now that they wanted to see. For in truth, the gallery on eleven had become a mob as more and more spectators abandoned other threesomes to follow Matt.

I thought about Hogan and how he played each round of golf, even the practice round on Wednesday, how he never varied his stride, kept his easy tempo between shots.

I read recently where Byron Nelson said the first thing he had to learn about playing professional golf was to resist getting caught up in the excitement of the gallery, their rushing ahead to see the next shot. Nelson was talking about what Hogan also knew: if you start keeping pace with the gallery, you'll be the first player to be out of breath. And as you members know, any time you start to breathe fast you start swinging fast, and the next thing you know, your rhythm is gone. That's why Hogan was famous for closing out the gallery, focusing only on his game, and not letting anyone distract him. It was all about preserving the rhythm of his swing.

I can see by a few smiles and nods you are thinking this was Hogan's great secret. It wasn't, but it was important to know, and as I broke through the gallery clustered around Matt, it was definitely something my player needed to learn. He was pacing around his ball, getting hyped by the crush of people, who in turn were all jazzed up as they realized they were watching someone truly special.

Anyone would fall victim to such excitement. But I wasn't going to let it happen to Matt, not when I was caddying for him, not having learned the lesson about patience from watching Hogan play.

When Matt reached for a club, ready to grab it and swing away, I covered the irons with my arm and asked innocently what he was thinking of hitting for his second shot. His ball hadn't reached the Danakil, so he needed at least an 8-iron to the plateau green. From this distance, we had to pick the right club to hit the target, and to tell you the truth, I hadn't thought about it when he teed off. We were short of the Danakil. This was the first time Matt was so far back and had to play a longer iron.

"You don't think it's an eight?" Matt asked, seeing my hesitation.

I kept staring up at the green, thinking if it was only Matt and myself, playing late on a weekday night, I would have no hesitation about giving him the 8-iron and telling him to hit away, to hit a high floater that would drop down gently on the small, flat green and hold. Now, however, he was so churned up with the excitement of the gallery, I wasn't sure he could make his familiar shot. It was my job to get him to play another club.

It's a position in which caddies often find themselves. I recall a story told years ago by the late Bruce Edwards, who caddied much of his career for Tom Watson. Edwards was telling how he knew he was in tune with Watson during their very first weeks on tour. They were playing the No. 2 course at Pinehurst in North Carolina and Watson had just birdied the fifteenth, sixteenth, and seventeenth holes. On the second shot into the final green, Watson asked Bruce if it was a 1- or 2-iron into the flag. Bruce knew Tom was so pumped up he might overshoot with the 1-iron, so he recommended the 2. Watson drilled the ball within fifteen feet of the hole and made the putt. From then on Tom knew Edwards could club him, and that began a lifetime of employment as well as friendship.

"Hit the nine," I told Matt.

"Nine?"

I nodded. I didn't want to explain myself, but also I wasn't sure I was right. It was just my sense that Matt would be all over the eight and fly the green. What unnerved me most was that Matt didn't object to my decision. He took the 9-iron and after Mangrum played, he addressed his ball. He was following my advice—and suddenly I was terrified I was wrong and he would come up short.

"Nice and easy," I whispered. "You've got plenty of club."

I needn't have worried. Matt's next swing was as pure and simple as if he were playing all by himself instead of in front of a thousand fans, all of whom roared when his high lofted shot sailed safely onto the putting surface, bounced softly, and held the green.

"Okay, great!" I exclaimed, grabbing the iron from him and handing him the putter, talking fast, encouraging him.

On the flat eleventh green, Matt's putt was seven feet and dead straight. He could have made it with his eyes closed, and he did make it. We had another birdie, and the roar following the quick click of the ball dropping into the cup echoed off the trees and rolled and rolled across the course. Matt was six under and going for the course record.

When we walked onto the tee at twelve the green was flanked with gallery; they stood three deep and stretched down both sides of the small, still pond. I stepped onto the tee box and moved between the markers. Matt had the honors. I looked toward the green, at the hushed gallery and the calm waters. It was a setting as perfect as anything you'd see on television late on a Sunday afternoon at Amen Corner down in Augusta.

But it was not quite noon and the sun, high in the sky, made everything brilliantly bright and hot and humid, especially at twelve, which, as you know, is on the lower side of the course. I recall, however, that I was perfectly calm and cool. The weather wasn't affecting me; it wasn't touching Matt. I could see the sweat on Mangrum's white shirt and I watched as even Furgol, who didn't wear a golf cap, grabbed the towel from his caddie to wipe heavy beads of sweat from his face and neck.

Although there were now more than a thousand spectators encasing the hole, there was complete silence as they waited for Matt to pull a club and play away. Who would've thought so many people could be so quiet? But they were players themselves. They knew how to behave on a golf course in the middle of an Open.

I kept thinking how great this was, how special, and I was wishing I had someone to share it with, someone I might tell later about how it felt to be on center stage with Matt. But I knew my mother wouldn't understand, and Kathy, who did know all the players, just didn't care about the game.

But I had Matt. Hanging out in the pro shop, we would relive the round, hole after hole, shot after shot, laughing and remembering, kidding each other. It would be great, and thinking about it made me feel wonderful about being part of his life and part of this country club, and then I brought myself up short, thinking: We still have seven holes to play! This round was a long way from being over.

Matt placed his gloved hand on the irons, and I looked up at him. He was staring at the green and also, I realized, taking in the gallery circling the hole. The scene was something out of golf magazines, something he had never been part of. And instead of pulling a club or even asking me what I thought, he ducked his head and whispered, "Hey, Jackson, can you believe this!" He kept smiling. "We got the whole damn gallery following us!"

"Let's keep it going," I said, trying to keep focused.

"I'm in the groove, Jackson. I'm in the groove." He reached for the 7, showing me the club. "Okay?"

I shook my head.

"Six," I said.

"I can reach the green with a seven." His fingers were wrapped around the head of the 7-iron. "I hit the seven with Hogan, re-member?"

I remembered. I remembered everything about the day.

I gestured toward the green, encircled by fans. The flag lay limp against the bamboo pole. I started talking about what we both knew: how the ball, crossing the pond, would be hit by a breeze blowing against us. Matt knew about the breeze from hav-ing played the hole a hundred times. You couldn't feel it on the tee, but it was always there above the trees, blowing over the hol-low we were in.

"Look," I said, making my argument, "we're hitting way back off the pro tees. You'll need to land on the top half of the green. The pin is cut four feet from the fringe. It's an easy six, a hard seven. And you know you always come over the top when you're pressing. Hit an easy six and if you bounce long the gallery will stop it, maybe kick it back on the green." I kept talking fast, like I was trying to sell him a used car.

He hit the six.

When the ball was in the air I saw it was too strong and my heart leapt to my throat as I guessed I had misclubbed him and the ball would fly the green, fly the gallery. Hogan wouldn't have done it, I thought next, remembering how in July he had told me on the fifth hole how he always played short, played for the fat part of the green.

Then, just when I thought we were a goner, the breeze above the trees caught the ball and drove it down. The ball landed on the top tier, between the flag and fringe, less than six feet from the cup. The roar from the greenside gallery came across the water in waves of shouts and cheers.

Matt gave me a grin as if he had just won the lottery, the Open, and the girl of his dreams. I let out a sigh and grinned back at him, feeling as if I had just robbed a bank.

Matt slid the iron back into the bag and I handed him his putter. It was only then that I saw my hands were trembling.

"You okay?" Matt asked, seeing my hands. He leaned over to look into my eyes.

I nodded, too excited to speak. The truth was, I was more pumped up about how Matt was playing than he was. When he stepped past me, he planted his big hand on the top of my cap and squeezed my head, as if it were a ripe melon. He always did this to annoy me. Now, of course, I treasured the gesture. It showed the gallery jammed around the tee, all of them watching Matt, just how close the two of us were; we were a team and we were shooting the lights out.

Matt made the putt, of course. We had gone par, birdie, birdie on the back side and were 7 under heading for thirteen. I started thinking maybe Hogan was right. A great player could birdie every hole of the course, hit every green in regulation and make a putt. It all seemed so easy

I see some of you players smiling up at me, and you're right. As all of us know, the game of golf is never easy. Just when you think you're in control, it rears up, so to speak, and bites you in the butt.

Matt duck-hooked his drive off the long par-5 thirteen. He was in the trees beyond the bunker, no more than 220 down the left side. I was used to him spraying the ball right when he got too quick. But he never duck-hooked his drives, not once in all the rounds we'd played that summer.

The gallery, which now had stretched themselves down the right side of the fairway as far as the bunker, some 200 yards, appeared to experience collective cardiac arrest, if it is possible, and we'll have to ask Doc Hughes later to give a medical opinion.

Certainly I felt as if my young heart was about to burst as I hustled off the tee, racing for the ball, terrified I wouldn't find it deep in the grove of trees. Matt was with me, matching my racing stride. I didn't look at him. I didn't say anything. There is nothing quite as lonely and tense as a player and caddie hustling down the fairway after a wayward shot.

I had followed the flight of Matt's ball, marking both the latitude and longitude of where it landed, cross-hairing it with trees so I was sure of the location. There were only a few spectators on that side of the fairway, which ran parallel to fourteen, so Matt and I were off by ourselves when we tramped into the woods and found the ball deep in the rough and stymied with trees. As players said then, and still say today, we were dead.

Matt came to a full stop and stared down at the ball that looked like a lost egg in the long, wild grass.

He had been swearing under his breath as he marched down the length of the fairway and now, with no one within hearing, he let loose another round of "expletives deleted" and jammed his driver into the bag.

"Easy, easy," I kept saying softly, calming him as he stalked around the ball, tramping down the long grass and staring through the trees, trying to find an opening back onto the fairway. I had seen him make spectacular recoveries before, but often we remember only those triumphs and not the shots that never made it out of the woods.

In this stand of old trees, with thick trunks and low branches, we might as well have been in jail. Matt kept bending down, trying to scope out a path, a way to hit an iron, low and long. He wasn't talking, but I knew what he was thinking.

I moved the bag back and away from the ball and looked the other way, down fourteen fairway, toward the forecaddie. The threesome playing fourteen were almost on the green, followed by a few friends and family. The fairway was empty, and I realized a back-door approach might work. Matt would have a clear shot if he chopped out of the weeds with an 8-iron into the middle of fourteen fairway, then, for his third shot on this par-5 hit a high 8- or 9-iron over the trees that separated the two holes. He could easily make the thirteenth green in regulation. When he came back to where I was standing with the bag, I told him my idea.

"Jackson, you're a genius," he said under his breath and reached for the 9-iron.

I might or might not be a genius for playing backward down fourteen, but Matt had to make the shot. He had to drive it out of the long weeds and safely into the fairway.

I told him to hit the 8. I told him he couldn't get much distance coming out of the tangle of weeds that ensnared his ball. I told him to aim for the fourteenth forecaddie. If he could land somewhere near where the caddies stood to watch their players hit off the tee, he'd have a semi-open shot to thirteen green.

As we all knew at the time, Matt was great playing out of trouble, a real cowboy of the golf course. Today, commentators are always remarking how pros like Sergio and Mickelson have great imagination; they are inventive when it comes to playing shots, but the truth is golfers like Matt and Sergio and Michelson and a handful of other great ones, I think, just get bored going out every day and hitting the ball straight down the middle, onto the green in regulation, and having two putts for pars.

I might have suggested the shot to Matt, but he had to make it. And it is the spectacular shots, the great challenges from impossible lies that get the juices going with pros like Matt; it keeps them at the edge of their games. They love it. Fans love it. It's why Tiger Woods, and Arnold Palmer before him, have been so successful on TV. Neither of them plays golf like Ben Hogan, with his steady, unyielding, hard edge, bearing down on the course like a relentless pursuer. Hogan wouldn't have been great television material. He didn't get involved in "car crashes" on the golf course. He wouldn't, also, have made the mistake Matt made: he wouldn't have taken my advice. Hogan would have played the ball safely back onto the thirteenth fairway and gone for par.

Matt was after another birdie. To invoke all the clichés of the game, he rolled the dice; he went for broke; he fired and fell back. And he flubbed the 8-iron from the thick grass. The hosel of the club caught the long wiry grass, twisting the club face, and his escape shot popped out of the trees and traveled less than twenty yards. It didn't even make the fairway. As they say down in Texas, he "tacoed it."

Matt whacked the iron into the ground and I grabbed the club and started walking away. I came out of the trees and went to the ball, which I saw had a decent lie in the first cut of rough. Matt came thumping after me, cursing with exasperation, and feeling all the self-pity in the world for what he had done to himself.

But I was thinking it was my fault. It was my job to keep my player from self-destructing. Any caddie can look great when his player is under par, but here Matt was still 220-plus to the thirteenth green and on the wrong fairway.

When he came up to me he reached immediately for the

brassie and jerked off the hood. He was steaming and ready to kill the next shot. Remember how I said the golden rule of any caddie was to show up, keep up, and shut up? Well, I never was very good at shutting up, especially at a critical juncture like this. As Hogan had told me during his practice round, it's always the next shot that matters.

"Wait." I moved the bag so he couldn't address the ball, and I began to talk slowly, trying with my small voice to douse his rage. I didn't challenge him. I didn't say: What the hell are you going to do with a 2-wood? Don't you see there is no way in the world you're going to be able to drive a golf ball two-hundred yards plus, and clear the stand of poplar trees! No, instead I merely asked how far he thought he had to go to reach the green.

I know he knew it was too far for anyone to hit a ball. Oh, maybe the kids today could reach it with their hybrid shafts and their fusion drivers, but not Matt Richardson with his steel shafts and persimmon-head wood. He knew it, too, as he thrashed around, ready to explode. The sweat was rolling off his face and running down his neck. There were dark, damp stains under his arms and across his chest. His hair was disheveled from his running his fingers constantly through it. He looked a mess.

I pulled the thick white towel from the bag and handed it to him so he could wipe his face and neck and arms, like a swimmer drying himself off. Then he wiped the leather grip of the wood and I thought perhaps he hadn't given up on trying to sky one over the trees. But instead he handed me the brassie and asked quietly, "What do you think?"

"Hit a nine back down the fairway and give yourself enough room to play an eight over the tops of the trees. Let's get on the green and get out of here. Lets play for a bogey."

"I don't play for bogey, Jackson." He grabbed the 9-iron and waved me away from the ball, then he drove the ball 130 yards toward the fourteenth tee. The ball landed short of the cabbage rough and Matt went after it as if he were a frozen rope drive himself. I had to run to catch up.

Reaching his ball, Matt didn't ask for my opinion. Jamming the 9-iron into the bag, he pulled the 8. The problem wasn't the length, but whether he could hit it high enough to clear the trees and reach the hole.

"Hit it stiff," I said encouragingly, pulling away. Matt needed a career shot to make it onto the green.

Matt waited for Furgol and Mangrum on the other fairway to play up and then he hit a great shot, but it didn't have the height or distance to reach the green; instead, it caught the top leafy branches and dropped straight down, landing in the bunker.

"It's safe," I said, trying to make the best of it.

"Shut up, Jack!" Matt told me and grabbed the blaster from the bag and tossed the 8-iron at me as he brushed by, heading for the left side bunker.

It was the first time he had ever told me to shut up on the golf course, and his put-down stung me. I dropped my head and followed after him. With one comment, Matt had turned me into another bag rat from the caddie shack.

Matt flubbed his wedge. The ball just got out of the soft sand. His first putt was short by two feet, but he made the next one for a double bogey. On one hole he had dropped two shots, and once again he was 5 under par.

Coming off the green, he didn't even look at me. In one motion, he handed me his putter, pulled the spoon from the bag, and flipped me the hood as he walked by, headed up the cinder path and through the dark woods to the fourteenth tee.

27

I WATCHED MATT WALK AWAY, DEBATING WHETHER I SHOULD FOL-
low. the other caddies had joined Furgol and Mangrum up on the
tee, but I sensed Matt didn't want me anywhere near him. So I
turned and went down the slope to the forecaddie like the
proverbial whipped dog. I understood how Matt felt. The fact
that he was still five under didn't matter. It was a hell of a score
for the first round, but as most of you are well aware, a player often loses it all after double-bogeying a hole.

I slipped through the spectators at the forecaddie to get a view
of the tee. Seeing who I was, everyone stepped aside. In their
mind, Matt was still the star of the first round, and as his caddie I
got to live in his reflected glory.

Someone asked me about the double bogey. What happened
to Matt on the last hole, this guy wanted to know; why had he decided to play fourteen backward and not chip safely onto thirteen

fairway? I shook my head, dismissing the man. If he didn't know better than to ask questions in the middle of a round, he wasn't worth worrying about. Instead, I stared up at the tee, where Ed Furgol was teeing off.

His drive easily cleared the only bunker, leaving him a wedge to the green. Then Mangrum, with his smooth, silky swing, drove beyond Furgol and found the rough on the left side, close to where Matt had hit his third shot on thirteen.

Matt had taken the 3-wood with him when he walked away from me earlier, so now, without his bag, he really had only one option, which was to play safely into the middle of the fairway. It was for the best. If his clubs were handy, he might step up to the tee and decide to cut the dogleg and go for the green, which at this point would've been another mistake.

I watched him tee up the ball, then step away and, standing parallel to the ball, take a few easy swings. I took a deep breath myself, thankful he wasn't rushing, that he was staying with his preshot routine. My guess was the walk through the woods between thirteen green and the fourteenth tee box had calmed him down.

It was just about then, I recall, that Sarah DuPree came out of the crowd and spoke to me. I hadn't seen her during the round and my guess was she didn't join the gallery until it passed her house.

"Hi, Jack," she whispered in her soft voice. "Thank you for caddying for Matt."

Her voice startled me and I glanced around, surprised to see her, and as I did I saw another familiar face in the gallery clustered around the forecaddie. Standing off by himself at the edge of fifty or sixty people was Ralph Gates from Gatesburg, Illinois. When my eyes caught him, he grinned good-naturedly, and waved. I turned around and stared up at the tee as Matt stepped forward and addressed the ball. I don't know why I was so shocked to see Gates, but I was, and spotting him worried me, just as Sarah's presence bothered me. All I could think was that they would get in Matt's way.

"Oh, God, I can't watch it when he hits," she sighed. Standing beside me, she ducked her head so she couldn't see.

We heard the rifle shot crack as Matt's club face hit the ball, and I followed the flight of Matt's drive. He had hit it on the screws, as we used to say, and from my angle as I tracked the ball, I couldn't immediately tell if he had hit the fade so the ball would gradually work into the center of the fairway. Then I realized he hadn't. He had driven the ball dead straight and we were back in the trees on the left side of fourteen, close to where we had been before playing the last hole. The crowd around the forecaddie let out a collective moan and Sarah asked at once what had happened.

"In the trees," I said, swinging the bag onto my shoulder and moving off.

"Again!" She rushed to fall into step with me.

"Same place." I pointed toward where the ball had disappeared in the cluster of trees and never took my eyes off the spot, fearful as always that I would lose the location.

"What's going wrong?" she asked, skipping to keep up. "He was playing so great." She sounded on the edge of tears.

I didn't have time to explain, so I just told her Matt was okay; he was playing great, I said, and everything would be fine. I kept talking to reassure her, and to reassure myself as well, but as all of you know, once a player begins to press and lose his game, a golf course can be a dangerous place.

When I reached Matt's ball, I saw we had caught a break. Matt wasn't in jail. He had a shot over the trees, and to the hole cut deep in the green, as the cup had been placed the day Matt played with Hogan. His drive had also found a bare spot up against a maple tree. The lie would have been no trouble for Phil Mickelson or Mike Weir or, for that matter, the great Bob Charles. The trouble was, unlike them, Matt didn't play left-handed.

The gallery surrounding Matt's ball realized at once his predicament, and so did Sarah. Turning to me with this god-awful look of hopelessness and fear, she whispered frantically, "What's he going to do?"

That moment for me was sublime. I knew exactly what he was going to do. I smiled at Sarah and whispered, "It's okay," as Matt came charging through the tight ring of spectators and arrived at the spot where his ball had landed. He never saw Sarah, and she faded back into the gallery, afraid, I think, of disturbing him.

Matt was totally focused on his ball, wedged against the maple trees. The shot he had left was a simple enough chip, over the flat bunker and up to the top ledge of the green. The trouble was, he couldn't take his normal stance. He had the option, of course, of hitting the ball backhanded, a short iron with a pendulum swing, or flipping the face of the club, addressing the ball with the toe and swinging from the right side. He also had one other option.

"Damn, I don't have my niblick," he mumbled, staring at the ball.

"Yes, you do," I told him and pulled the left-handed iron from the bag.

Matt stared at the club, and then at me, and slowly he shook his head and took the short Tennessee hickory-shaft club from my hand.

For those of you who are not familiar with the names of such clubs, a pitching niblick was similar to our 8-irons, though since these clubs were handmade, they often varied in loft, but Matt's relic had a loft of almost forty-five degrees, the same as today's wedges.

"Thanks, Jack," he said softly. "You're the best." It was said with admiration and affection and even a sense of wonder that I had the foresight to slip his old club into the bag.

I had battled back from disgrace; Matt was no longer angry at me.

A burst of applause rose from the gallery around Matt when they realized how he was going to play the shot.

While I had seen Matt hit better chips with the left-handed pitching niblick, the one from the trees easily cleared the green-side bunker and ran beyond the flag to stop at the collar of the fringe. Coming back, his ten-footer lipped the cup and he had to settle for a par, but he was still 5 under as he walked away from the fourteenth hole. Best of all (at least for me), Matt and I were back in synch.

Sarah made another appearance on fifteen, emerging to the left of the tee box. Matt didn't see her, and I didn't point her out as he stood with me behind the markers waiting for Mangrum and Furgol to play.

Sarah had obviously decided to follow Matt on the back side, and it didn't make me happy. I was leery of having her around, the same way, I guess, coal miners don't want women down in the mines. It was all superstition, but golfers have their ways, and al-most anything new can set them off.

Over the years, I came to understand Sarah had to be with Matt that day. She needed to be part of his achievement and to share, even if from a distance, in the glory of his game.

"A seven, right?" Matt asked, reaching for the iron. Before I answered, I studied my crude drawing and noted where the flag was placed. The hole was cut way to the left of the narrow and elongated green. That morning I had been surprised the PGA officials had placed the cup so far to the left side, making it an easy target.

"Yes, the seven," I said, and pointed toward the narrow strip between the two bunkers guarding the approach. "If you catch a bunker, okay. You'll still have room to work with coming out of the sand. Play the shot between the bunkers and let it bounce up, the same way Hogan played it."

"You sure it's enough club? We hit the six with Hogan, remember?"

I nodded, thinking, but not explaining to Matt, what else I remembered from that day. The air had not been as heavy, and we had been playing late in the afternoon. Now it was late August in the middle of the Midwest. On a humid day, as you players know, the ball will carry farther.

Matt nodded okay and pulled the 7-iron. That's when he saw Sarah. She had edged up close; he couldn't have missed her.

She smiled sweetly and blew him a kiss. It was lovely and romantic and also the worst possible thing in the world. Matt didn't need that kind of distraction.

Matt hadn't learned what Hogan knew, how to block out the world around him when he was playing golf. They tell the story of how once Hogan's brother Royal, who, by the way, was also a very fine player, followed Ben around for eighteen holes, and when Hogan finished the tournament he spotted Royal for the first time and asked him where he'd been all day.

Hogan also taught a useful tournament trick to a club pro who was a close friend of his. The pro was Claude Harmon, father of all the fine teaching professionals, who for many years was the head pro at Winged Foot in New York.

At the '48 Masters at Augusta, Harmon jumped into the lead going into the final round and everyone, naturally, thought Harmon would fade under the pressure, but Hogan went to see Harmon at his hotel the night before the final round and spent the evening with him, telling Claude what to do the next day. Hogan warned Harmon how the gallery would surge after him, waiting for him to break under the pressure, and to counteract the crowd, Hogan told Harmon to walk with his head down between shots, avoid eye contact with the gallery, and not think about anything but the next shot. It worked. Harmon stunned the golf world with his record-tying 279 win.

Matt, however, hadn't learned this simple trick of thinking only about his next shot. Once he saw Sarah, he was thinking of her, thinking of how he'd impress her, and just as I feared, he came out of the iron and knocked the ball wide right, where it hit hard on the players' path and bounced long, beyond the green.

I was off the tee before he finished his backswing, keeping my eyes on where the ball had bounced into the long grass. I found it all right. That was the good news. The bad news was Matt didn't have a shot. The ball was nestled deep in the cabbage, and I had to bend over and peer closely just to make sure it was Matt's. We didn't need the penalty of him playing the wrong ball out of those weeds.

As soon as I found Matt's ball, a dozen fans pressed around me, first wanting to see the lie, then wanting a good view of Matt playing out of trouble. He had done it on the last hole, hitting the left-handed pitching niblick. This was a much tougher shot, and this time Matt didn't have any magic clubs in his bag to help him save the day. I raised my arms and asked everyone to move away and give Matt room to play. As I did, I scanned the gallery for Sarah and Ralph Gates. Neither one of them were near me.

Matt was steaming again when he came charging up and saw his lie and at that moment, I felt all his energy draining out of him. He had played near-perfect golf to that point, and on the fourteenth when he was in trouble, he had escaped, but this was a lot harder. I wasn't thinking then of trying to protect his record round, I was just trying to figure out how I could keep him from exploding and losing it all on this one hole.

"Give me the sand wedge," he said. We could only see a slice of the ball, peeping out from the deep rough.

"What are you thinking?" I asked under my breath, aware of the gallery pressed around us.

"Give me the goddamn sand wedge. I'm going to hack the goddamn ball out! What the hell do you think I'm going to do, Jackson?"

Reaching past me, he pulled the wedge from the bag.

"Easy." I moved closer to the ball so he couldn't play the shot.

He was swinging the wedge through the deep rough, trying to get the feel of how hard he should swing.

"Play the ball like Hogan did on eighteen," I told him.

Matt paused and looked at me.

"What are you talking about?"

"Remember? He duck-hooked into the rough on eighteen, then hit it into the bunker, but he got out of the rough. That's the shot you need." I was talking fast. Both Furgol and Mangrum were on the green waiting for Matt to play up.

"I didn't see him hit the ball," Matt answered, whacking at the grass. It was the first time we had been this deep in the cabbage all day.

I told Matt how Hogan had closed the face of the wedge,

closed his own stance, and took a full swing and hit through the ball. Hogan's ball popped up and carried for forty yards. "It's the only way to play it, Matt. You've got the whole green to work with." Which was true enough. The hole was cut on the far left side and away from us. Matt had a good twenty yards to work with.

"Okay," he nodded, accepting what I told him as he, too, realized he didn't have many options.

"Not the sand wedge," I told Matt. "Play the pitching wedge and close it down." I gave him the pitching wedge and moved out of the way.

As I pulled the bag away, I scanned the gallery. Sarah was still nowhere to be seen, and for some reason that made me feel a lot better.

Matt took another few swings. The only sound was the club face cutting through the grass as Matt tested the thickness of the rough. What he didn't need was for the hosel to get caught up in the grass and turn the face of the club when he went after the ball.

The gallery framing Matt was silent and attentive. For the most part I wasn't even aware of the fans flocking after us; but now what struck me was how quiet they all could suddenly be. They knew this shot was critical. They had also been listening to the exchanges between the two of us and were as tense as I was waiting for Matt to execute the approach. Anything could happen. He could leave it in the weeds or knock it clean over the green and into the left-side bunker.

As it was, Matt didn't do either. He got it out of the rough. The ball popped up as I had expected, but it landed on the fringe, leaving Matt a fifty-foot chip or putt to save par.

Behind us, there was a polite round of applause and a few of the club members called out encouragement, told him to knock it in. I'm not sure Matt even heard them, mad as he was at himself.

I took back the wedge and Matt grabbed his blade putter, and we went up the slope to where the ball had stopped on the apron at the edge of the green. Matt was still away. The tendency under those circumstances, when other players are waiting, is to rush the next shot, and I was afraid Matt would. After all, Furgol and Mangrum were touring pros and here was this young kid, the assistant pro at the host course, holding up their game.

Normally, Matt wasn't one to obsess over a putt. He got up and whacked the ball, acting more on feel than any great ability to read the line. In fact, I was better at reading putts than Matt, and he knew it.

I might mention also that in '46 we didn't have many choices when it came to putters. The war had stopped the invention of new clubs, what with all of the factories converted to the war effort. In '46 there were really just two kinds of putters being manufactured: the mallet for slow greens and an extra-thin, long-hosel putter for fast ones. Matt carried the thin-blade putter, which was perfect for our greens that summer.

I went around behind him and studied the line. The fifteenth hole, I mentioned earlier, had a flat, fast surface, and Matt's putt was pretty straight.

We didn't have, by the way, one of those Stimpmeters that determine the rate of speed of greens on the tour today. Nor did we know about "core putts" or the physics of the whole operation. What Matt had was an instinctive feel—call it God-given—for how much of a putting stroke he should take to generate enough power to reach the hole.

Matt was good on distance; with him, the trouble was the line. You never expect to make a ninety-footer; you just want to get close enough to make the second putt and move onto the next hole.

The key was the grass. Today's greens and fairways are so manicured and perfect it seems some days that every blade has been
hand-washed. But in the 1940s, grass could be treacherous. On
this day, on this hole, the grass was shiny, indicating the grain was
growing away from us and toward the hole. But I also knew from
its olive-green color that it was creeping bentgrass, which meant
the roll wouldn't be smooth or fast.

I told Matt what I thought, how given the grass, the ball would
break twice—the first time ten feet away, at an old hole placement, where it would go left. Then, a dozen feet farther, where
there was a rise, it would break right and come back again toward
the flag. These were guesses because the contour wasn't dramatic.
It wasn't like, say, the eighteenth at Westchester Country Club,
where the last hole can be like putting on a roller coaster.

Forget about the breaks, I told Matt. He needed to hit through
them. Drive the putt dead straight at the flag.

Matt looked at me like I was crazy.

"You won't make the putt," I told him. "Get it close and let's
get out of here."

He might have argued with me more, but we had taken too
much time and we could see Furgol and Mangrum were both annoyed.

"Go ahead," I tossed off. "Knock the sucker in."

I walked onto the green as Matt putted the ball off the apron.
Halfway to the hole I saw it was dead on line but hit way too
hard. However, if the ball bounced off the thick pole, the bamboo
would give enough to cushion the impact, and the ball might stop
only a few inches from the cup.

The ball didn't bounce off. It hit the flag dead, solid, perfect,
and lodged itself between the thick bamboo pole and the rim of
the cup. I walked up to the flag and carefully centered the pole,

loosening the ball, and it dropped with a click into the cup. Behind me, Furgol swore under his breath.

I bent over and with two fingers scissored the ball out of the cup and tossed it to Matt. After hitting two hacker shots, Matt had managed to par the hole. Finally, I thought, the blind pig does find an acorn.

28

As matt teed up on sixteen, Sarah found me again at the forecaddie. "He seems okay," she said, making it simultaneously a statement and a question.

I nodded. "So far."

"Just three more holes," she said, as if bucking herself up for the finish.

"And then three more rounds," I reminded her. I explained what Hogan had said—how Matt had to play all seventy-two holes to win a tournament.

"I don't care about tomorrow," she answered back, and for the first time I heard something in her voice besides concern for Matt. "I just want this over with. I hate all of this."

I glanced over and caught the tension in her mouth, the fixed set of her jaw.

"Hey, what do you mean?" I answered lightly. "This is fun."

She gave me a look, and answered curtly, "Not for me."

I let it go. Matt teed off and I turned my attention to his drive, watching it climb high over the crest of the hill as it hugged the right side, then get blown back safely into the middle of the fairway and bounce forward.

"Is this good?" Sarah asked when the ball was still high overhead.

"It's perfect," I said reassuringly. "He couldn't drive it any better." Looking back, I realize that for all her attention to Matt, she didn't understand enough about the game to know what was going right and what wasn't. Of all the people in the gallery, she was the one who cared the most about Matt and understood the least about his game. No wonder she found the match nervewracking. For her, golf was worse than what Twain called it, a good walk spoiled. With her whole future on his golf game, every swing was a nightmare.

But at the time, I was thinking less about how Matt's girlfriend might feel than about how she might affect his game on these last three holes. If I'd had the courage, I'd have just asked her to disappear, to wait for him at the clubhouse. All I wanted was for Matt to be left alone for another half-hour, time enough for us to finish eighteen.

Why couldn't she see how she'd unnerved him when she appeared in the middle of the back nine? She, of course, might've argued it was because of her that he played so well on fourteen and fifteen. It was all in the eye of the beholder, and Sarah DuPree and I saw things differently, to say the least.

Matt had, as he had on almost every hole, outdriven both of the touring pros, so when he reached me he had time to settle down and look over the lie. He had to decide what to hit into the postage-size green, the one Hogan earlier that summer had peppered with balls.

But instead of thinking about the shot and selecting an iron, he stepped off to one side and fell into a whispering conversation with Sarah, as if this were nothing more than a casual afternoon round with a couple of members.

I thought then it was all over for Matt, and my heart sank. He had escaped real trouble on the last two holes, keeping par on both, but now his focus was gone. He wasn't Hogan, that's for sure, who had blinders on when it came to playing golf. Not Matt. Matt was going south on me right there in the middle of sixteen fairway. And as I said earlier, he didn't lose strokes by leaking. He lost them all at once in one great big bang.

Mangrum played up, then Furgol, and Matt left Sarah and stepped over to me, tugging at his glove, glancing toward the green. There was this silly smile on his face, as if he didn't have a care in the world.

"Seven?" he said, and waited for my approval.

The truth was, at this point I didn't know what he should play. He had jumped all over his iron on the last hole. He could do the same again.

"Yes," I said, showing confidence, and added, "but you don't need to power it."

"Watch me!" He pulled the stick, grinning and loose as a goose.

And then something really strange happened, something that I could never have imagined earlier in the summer. Matt didn't lose it. He didn't jump all over the club. He started, in fact, there on number sixteen, to play better.

The 7 was a beautiful shot into the tight green and before the ball even landed, Matt handed me the iron and went striding toward the green with Sarah DuPree beside him, like two kids out for an afternoon stroll. Then he went on to quickly birdie the hole and, with two holes to play, was now 6 under.

On seventeen, spectators lined the right edge of the fairway—just as Hogan had predicted—so Matt couldn't use his trick shot of bouncing a ball off the hard ground of the service road. But to tell you the truth, I don't think Matt even thought about falling back on his old trick. Instead, he laced a high draw into the middle of the fairway. It was safely beyond the right-side bunker, and left him an easy second shot to the green.

I watched Furgol and Mangrum tee off, then took off down the sloping hill toward Matt's drive. I wanted to get to his ball quickly, afraid someone might step on it by mistake when rushing to get a good vantage point for the next shot.

Reaching his ball and setting the bag down, I glanced around. Matt was nowhere to be seen. A gang of spectators were all descending on me. But on the back nine, we had picked up a few more club members and a hundred yards of rope to control the gallery, yet seeing the gallery swarm toward me over the slight rise in the fairway was an impressive sight.

Then, out of the crowd, Matt and Sarah appeared, eating hot dogs and looking ridiculously nonchalant as they came up to the ball. A cheer went up from the gallery and Matt tipped his hat, finished off his dog, and wiped his fingers on a towel. I could have killed him.

"Five?" he asked, staring at the green.

I agreed and told him where the flag was. I told him to play to the right side and let the ball land short, on the patch of soft fairway, and bounce onto the green. I told him the cup was cut way back, leaving him plenty of room to maneuver his ball. At that moment, all I wanted to do now was finish even par and get off the course.

"Nah, let's go for it," Matt pulled out the 4-iron. "I'll drill it in, Jackson."

"Play it safe, Matt," I pleaded. "Let's get on and two-putt."

"Nah," he said again, and I could hear the grin in his voice.

The spectators closest to us heard this exchange and a murmur of excitement swept across the fairway. It's still like that now when players like Daly and Woods decide to go for it, perhaps against their better judgment, certainly against the better judgment of their seasoned caddies, just to respond to the thrill of the gallery.

"Play it safe, Matt," I said under my breath.

"Nah," he answered. "Watch me!"

The gallery cheered and Matt drove down on that 4-iron and nearly split the bamboo flag with it. The ball landed on the green, bounced forward, hit the top of the pole, got caught up in the flag, and dropped straight down into the hole. Matt had, incredibly, eagled the hole. He was now 8 under par.

"See, I told you," he laughed, clipping the bill of my hat.

"You bastard," I swore, grabbing his club. I knew, and he knew, and everyone in the gallery knew, with the exception of Sarah DuPree, that if the ball hadn't gotten caught by the flag it would've bounced over the green and into the rough.

All Sarah knew was that her boyfriend had done it again. In her loving eyes, Matt Richardson could do no wrong.

Matt finished eighteen with a par. He hit the green with a soft wedge on his second shot and missed a ten-footer, and the gallery, now huge and sprawled around the green and down the right side of the final hole, roared up in cheers and applause. Matt had set the course record at this club on the opening day of the '46 Chicago Open.

After Matt had signed his card in the starter's tent and posed with Mangrum and Furgol, both of whom played well themselves, shooting a pair of 67s, the photographers made Matt pose again, this time standing in front of the scoring sheets, grinning and pointing at his record-breaking score. Then Matt was asked to take a drink of water from the water fountain, and that was the famous photo that made all the newspapers: Matt Richardson sipping the bubbling water, cooling down after a record round of golf, while I stood in the blurry background holding his bag of clubs.

Yet even while the worshipping crowd applauded his first-round score, they had to ask themselves: Would Matt turn out to be just another first-round rabbit? The pages of golf history are littered with hotshot young pros who come out of nowhere to blister the field on the opening day of a tournament and then are never heard from again.

Remember Lee Mackey? Of course not. You never heard of him. Mackey was a pro from Birmingham, Alabama, who shot 64 in the first round at Merion in the '50 U.S. Open. He had ten one-putt greens that day. The next day he had an 81, while Ben Hogan shot 69 and went on to win the tournament.

Over the years I have often thought about Matt's magical first day. I've wondered if Matt could have come back the next morning and shot anywhere near eight under par. What would it have been like if Matt had teed it up here for the second round of the Chicago Open? But because of what was about to happen that afternoon, none of us will ever know.

29

I HADN'T EVEN FINISHED CLEANING MATT'S CLUBS WHEN DR. DuPree was on me. He'd tracked me down at the back of the shop in a rage.

"You're on Hogan's bag!" he shouted, his bullet head all red and flushed.

I tried to focus on the MacGregors, taking each club from the bucket of soapy water and wiping the heads clean in the most deliberate way I could manage. But ignoring DuPree only infuriated him more. I had embarrassed him, he fumed. I had disappointed everyone at the club, he shouted. I had left Hogan in the lurch, caddying for Matt Richardson when "every goddamn member knew I was the best goddamn caddie at the goddamn course." Finally, as if delivering the *coup de grâce,* he demanded to know what Hogan thought about what I'd done.

I looked directly at him for the first time. "Caddying for Matt was Mr. Hogan's idea," I said.

That silenced him. DuPree stared at me with his watery eyes and at first I thought he hadn't heard or understood. But then he made a disgusted sound and swore, more to himself than at me, and stormed out of the pro shop and charged up to the first tee. He was looking for Jimmy, I knew, so he could yell at him for letting all this happen.

I went back to Matt's clubs. When I finished cleaning the woods and irons, I took out the MacGregor balls we had played with, dumped them into Matt's practice bag, and opened two sleeves of new MacGregors. I didn't just put them into the bag. First I used the metal ring Matt kept with the balls and slipped each one through the opening to make sure they were truly round. We didn't think much then about laminar flow or dimples in '46, but roundness mattered and the metal ring was our only tool for quality control.

After checking the MacGregors, I put the clubs away and went up to the tee, now transformed with a big white scoreboard you could see from halfway down eighteen fairway.

I didn't know anyone on the tee. They were officials of the PGA and the Western Golf Association, all wearing shirts and ties, as if attending an Open was just another day at the office. But then, until only a few years before, even all the pros had worn ties and long-sleeved shirts when they went out to play.

I walked to the edge of the tee to watch Hogan finish his round. He was on seventeen green, playing with Snead and Nelson. They had most of the gallery that late afternoon, and when the pros finished putting and headed for eighteen the spectators rushed across the small bridge over the creek and lined up on the fairway down the length of the hole.

I walked out to the end of the first hole tee box so I could see over the heads of the gallery, and that's where I was standing, with a handful of caddies and members, when Matt found me.

Reaching into the crowd, he tapped my shoulder and motioned he wanted to speak to me. I followed Matt over to the caddie bench where he stopped and said quietly, "Jack, I need you to do me a favor."

Looking very serious, he handed me his car keys.

"Drive the Chevy around behind the men's locker room. Park it in the bag dropoff space and bring me the keys. I'll be in my room."

This was odd. Usually I had to beg Matt to let me drive his car, and now he wanted me to bring the Chevy around to the other side of the club house.

"What's going on?" I asked.

"Just go do what I said," he answered and walked off.

To tell you the truth, I didn't waste too much time wondering *why* Matt wanted me to move the car. I was just excited about having the chance to drive his car. I cut through the clubhouse and down the back hallways and came out behind the kitchen, next to the big garbage containers, where Matt always parked the Chevy.

I started the engine and glanced around, scared someone might tell me to stop. Even at fourteen, I knew how to drive. I had been handling a tractor since I was twelve and had driven my dad's car on our farm roads after he shipped off to war.

I backed the Chevy out and drove down to the service road. For a second I thought of going for a little drive, but there had been an urgency in Matt's voice that made me think better of it.

Crunching along the gravel road that circled the clubhouse, I gripped the big wheel, barely able to see over the hood of the old car. The truth was, I was more concerned about driving safely the quarter-mile across the club grounds than I was concerned about why Matt wanted the car, and why he wanted me to get it for him, but after I parked the Chevy in the bag dropoff, I started to wonder what was going down, as the kids say today.

I went into the clubhouse through the side door and walked through the men's bar. I loved the men's bar, loved it for the smell of beer in cold taps, and the look of oak furniture and the green felt of card tables. Today, whenever I go into a bar, no matter where I am in the world, and smell cold beer in damp kegs, I recall the men's bar at this club.

I waved to Ryan, the bartender, and he gestured me over. I shook my head, letting Ryan know I didn't want a Coke, but he kept gesturing.

"Did DuPree find you?" Ryan asked when I reached him.

Ryan was a small, wiry, weathered man in his early sixties who had once been a jockey and had first come to the club to teach the members' kids how to ride. When the war started and the club closed down its stables, he became a bartender. In my years here I had seen how the members kept employees working, moving them from job to job as they aged. If events had worked out differently for me back then, why, I, too, might have stayed, grown up to have a lifetime of work as one of your employees.

"He's got a bug up his butt about you," Ryan said under his breath, leaning over the bar as far as his height would let him. "Keep out of his way, Jack."

"DuPree found me. He's mad about me looping for Matt."

"The kid played great! Do you think he can win the whole shebang?"

I shrugged and backed off, repeating Hogan's line about tournament golf. "He's got to play seventy-two holes," I said, and told Ryan I had to go, that Matt was waiting for me.

"Watch your back with DuPree," Ryan warned me.

"I don't give a damn about him. Jimmy says DuPree will send me packin' whether Matt wins or not."

Ryan waved away my worry, calling after me, "The members ain't going to let you leave, Jack. They'll kick DuPree out before they get rid of you. Keep Matt from going goggle-eyed over that DuPree girl, and he'll win this damn Open."

"I'm working on it, Ryan. I'm working on it."

Waving goodbye, I ran up the back stairs to the third floor and down the long, dark hallway to Matt's room.

30

When I knocked on his bedroom door, Matt called out, "Who's there? Jack?"

"No, it's old man DuPree! Who the hell do you think it is?"

Matt jerked the door open and barked, "Shut up, for Chrissake!"

Behind him, I saw Sarah in the middle of the small room. She was wearing a pink dress, a flowery hat, and high heels. Dressed up, she didn't look like a college kid at all. Then I saw Matt was gussied up too, wearing a long-sleeved white shirt and, most amazing of all, a tie. I hadn't even known he owned one.

"What's going on?" I asked.

"Grab the bag." Matt pointed to a small leather suitcase on the bed. It wasn't his, I knew, and then I saw it was plastered with Smith College decals. "And keep quiet."

He put on his blue suit jacket. Picking up his own suitcase, the one he stored under his bed, he smiled at Sarah and said gently, as if I weren't in the room, "Let's go, darling."

She beamed at him, then strode out of the room, her heels clicking fast on the hardwood floor.

Matt followed and I came along last, pausing only to flip off the light switch. I saw Matt had left his key in the door. I pulled it out and handed it to him, but he told me to shut the door and leave the key in the lock.

"Aren't you coming back?"

He didn't answer, just disappeared with Sarah down the narrow back steps.

Weighed down by her suitcase, I only caught up with them at the car. Matt had the trunk of the Chevy open, and without a word he took Sarah's suitcase and placed it carefully inside next to his. Then he walked around and opened the door to let her slide into the passenger seat.

When he came back behind the car, I whispered frantically, "What's going on? You're teeing off at two tomorrow!" I could hear the panic in my voice.

Matt signaled me to keep quiet. I had never seen him this way, so serious and sure of himself. It was how he had been on the course earlier, playing every shot perfectly, making every putt.

"Matt, where're you going?"

"French Lick," he said and nodded toward Sarah in the front seat. "We're getting married." He spoke softly, as if he were in church.

How many of you here this evening remember those years? If you lived in the Midwest and wanted to get married without a blood test or three days of waiting, French Lick, Indiana, was where you went, a town later famous as the home of the great NBA player Larry Bird.

Even I, a fourteen-year-old, knew about French Lick, which was named, I might add, for the salt springs in the area and not lascivious behavior.

"You can't!" I told him. "You're leading the Open!"

Matt stood by the driver's side of the car, fingering his keys, as if deciding what to say, then looked me in the eye, a warm smile filling his face.

"I'm not coming back, Jack." He spoke as if he had everything under control. He reached out and slapped the bill of my caddie hat in his playful way as if he were doing it for the last time. Then he added, "Sarah and I are moving to Gatesburg. I'm taking the pro job at my old club. The president of the club, Mr. Gates, came up to me after my round today and offered me the job." He smiled again and reached out and held my shoulders. Now he could see there were tears welling up in my eyes.

I wiped my bare arm across my face, trying to calm down, but my mind kept whirling. None of what Matt said made any sense to me. He was leading the Chicago Open! He couldn't run off and get married and not play his second round.

Matt nodded toward Sarah, sitting patiently in the car, and said softly, "Her old man would never guess we'd elope on the day I'm leading the tournament, would he?" He grinned in that wild way he had when he played a great shot out of some hazard.

"Matt, you can beat Hogan," I whispered. It was the best plea I could think to make. "You can win the Open."

Seeing my bafflement and anguish, Matt pulled me into a hug, and as he explained his reasons for leaving, I think he was articulating them to himself as well.

"I'm not cut out for this circus world, Jack." He nodded toward all the PGA tournament cars and the fancy, unfamiliar vehicles filling the lot behind the clubhouse. "I love golf. I love playing great, like I did today, but traveling around the country, the way they all have to do, from tournament to tournament, that's not for me. I'm not Hogan. I don't need to win tournaments. I don't need my picture in the paper holding up trophies. I'm a small-town guy, Jack. I want to be a home pro. It's a good job. And I don't want to ask Sarah to live that kind of life with me. You saw Mrs. Hogan, how she just sits around all day waiting for Ben to finish his round." He shook his head. "Sarah and I . . . we're going down home and be off by ourselves, have our own life."

With that, he smiled kindly at me, slapped the beak of my caddie cap again, and added, "Hey, Jackson, we beat Hogan. How many guys can say that, right? We beat Hogan one-on-one. Leaving now, I'll always be remembered as the guy who beat Ben Hogan and shot the course record on the opening day of the Chicago Open. That's something they can't take away from us, right, Jack?"

Grinning, he slid into the driver's seat and Sarah leaned over and smiled out the open window.

"Thank you, Jack," she said. "Thank you for everything." There were misty tears in her bright eyes, as if she couldn't control her happiness.

I stepped away from the car, giving them room to pull out of the bag drop drive, but Matt hesitated and reached into the pocket of his suit jacket. Whatever he was looking for, he didn't find.

"Dammit!" He turned to me and said urgently, "Jackson, run up to the shop. In the drawer where we keep the putting balls, there's an envelope with my name on it. Get it and bring it to me." He turned to Sarah and explained, "My birth certificate. Mom sent it to me and I left it in the pro shop."

. . .

In the pro shop, Kenny Burke's little brother was cleaning clubs at the workbench. "Hey! What's the matter?" he asked when I raced in, looking frantic.

"Can't talk," I answered. "Matt's waiting for me at the bag drop."

Running to the front desk, I pulled open the drawer. The envelope was where Matt said it would be, addressed to him and with a Gatesburg, Illinois, return address.

I grabbed it at the moment Dr. DuPree came bursting into the shop.

"Have you seen my daughter?" he demanded.

I backed away from him, trying fast to think of what to say, when DuPree spotted the envelope in my hand. He ripped it from my fingers and pulled out Matt's birth certificate.

"Where's the sonofabitch?" He shouted and reached out and grabbed me. "Where are they?" He jerked me closer to his face.

I couldn't talk. I couldn't breathe. I couldn't do anything to stop the man, but I did manage to spit in his face.

With one flick, DuPree tossed me away and I fell into the swivel chair, spun around, and tumbled to the floor. By the time I got to my feet, DuPree had seized Kenny Burke's little brother and demanded to know where Matt was. Terrified, Davie Burke pointed toward the bag drop. DuPree grabbed a heavy wooden mallet off the work bench and charged out the back door of the shop.

I didn't follow. Instead I ran through the front door and circled the pro shop, hoping to reach Matt before DuPree did.

I didn't make it.

31

AT THAT TIME, THE PATH BEHIND THE CLUBHOUSE WAS HIDDEN from the members' view by green shrubs and bushes. I couldn't see the bag drop and, running around the pro shop, I didn't see what happened between Matt and Sarah's father. I just heard it. Dodging around a wall of holly and rose of Sharon, I heard a car window being smashed and I heard Sarah scream. Then the car engine roared, and tires squealed, and I saw the Chevy.

It ripped through the thick shrubbery and across the shady path, and careened onto the lawn below the first tee. Hitting the grass at that high speed, the car slid out of control and sped across sixty yards down the sloping lawn until, with a crunch of metal and glass, it whacked up against the only tree on the lawn, an old oak in whose shade we caddies often waited for our players to show up. It was all over within seconds.

In the moment after the crash, I heard only the infinite silence and stillness of a late summer afternoon. The crowd of players and spectators on the first tee spun around at the crash but were too stunned to react. It was as if we were all caught in a black-and-white freeze-frame. Finally someone shouted and broke the silence, and in ones and twos people charged down the hillside to the wreckage of Matt's car. The left side of the Chevy had smashed broadside against the trunk of the maple tree.

Sarah pushed at the door on the passenger side. It opened with a squeak and snap and she staggered free. Even from where I stood up on the path, I could see her head was bleeding. Blood ran down her face and stained the collar of her dress, but she was alive, and Dr. DuPree raced to his daughter, calling her name as he rushed to her side.

Matt never moved. His head had smashed through the front window. His body was flung over the steering wheel. His face was smeared with blood.

Did Dr. DuPree, in his fury, try to stop the elopement by smashing in the driver's side window with the mallet? Did Matt panic and floor the gas pedal, sending the Chevy speeding out of control and to his own death?

We'll never know the details, because the crash was never investigated. DuPree made sure of it.

Within hours of Matt's death, it was all judged a terrible and tragic accident. Sarah's presence in the car was explained as Matt having offered a ride home to the club president's daughter. Questions were not asked. Causes were not sought. And no one said a word about the two pieces of luggage in the Chevy's trunk.

Sarah was taken from the site of the wreck to the emergency room in town. Although her injuries were minor, she was kept in seclusion for two days. When she came home from the hospital, it was only for a few days, and then she went back East to finish her senior year at Smith College.

No one questioned me, not that late afternoon, not later. The police report filed simply said it was a tragic accident, nothing more. Perhaps the police didn't even know I had been part of the whole tragedy.

In time, rumors surfaced how when doctors examined Sarah in the E.R. they discovered she was pregnant. None of us ever quite knew for sure.

I'm telling you all this calmly, but that evening I lost my sense of the sequence of events. All I know is, I didn't run with the others to the scene of the crash. I knew Matt was dead. Stunned, incredulous, I slumped down on the caddie bench near the first tee and watched as the country club coped with what for them was an unacceptable, unprecedented event, all unfolding less than a short wedge shot away.

In retrospect, I know I must have been in shock, and it was some time before I realized Ben Hogan was sitting beside me on the caddie bench. He sat and comforted me as if I were the one who had suffered a terrible accident, and in some ways, I had.

I'm sure I told him everything, but I cannot remember anything of what I said. At some point, Hogan wrapped his arm around my shoulders and walked me off the first tee and away from the accident, pointing me toward home. Between the blaze of the setting sun and my tears, I couldn't see, and I just tried to hear what Hogan was telling me, somehow grasping, through my fog, how important it was for me to latch onto whatever this good man would say, words I could take with me and use for the rest of my life.

"Jack, remember how I told you about the next shot? It's always the next shot that's important. It's the secret of golf; it's the secret of life. If you can understand that, why, you're going to do just fine."

He stopped talking for a moment, and I felt his eyes on me. I looked up at him through my tears.

"Matt didn't think about his next shot, Jack. He lived his life the way he played golf, and sooner or later he was going to run up against a hazard he couldn't get around. As it turned out, Dr. DuPree was his hazard.

"If Matt had played it safe, if he had let Sarah's father get to know him, if he had let the girl finish her schooling, it might have worked itself out differently." Hogan looked down at me, his steely eyes softened now. "Matt's not going to get another chance, Jack, but you are."

He gestured then, waved at the clubhouse, the wide expanse of the course, and continued, "In time, Jack, you'll come to understand this country club and the lives lived here are a very small part of your world. I hope you're lucky enough to live many lives, in many parts of the world, but if you do, never forget who you are and where your home is. You're not old enough now, Jack, to understand, but in time you'll come to realize the lucky people in life are the ones who never forget who they are, not what other people think they are. That's what makes us special."

With that, he sent me on my way. I don't remember saying anything to him, not even goodbye.

I ran down to the creek where it cuts across eighteen, and I kept running. I ran all the way home to where my mother was waiting with supper on the table and where there were chores to do on the farm, and a life to live that had nothing to do with caddying or the country club.

. . .

Jack paused a moment for a sip of water, and only when he picked up the glass did he realize his hand was trembling. Who could have imagined, he thought, that after all these years, that Matt's death would still have such an effect on him?

He looked out at the hushed country club audience and found Sarah and caught her eyes. She smiled sadly back at him and nodded. She understood what he had been trying to tell her. It was time for her to move on with her life.

He pulled himself together, glanced down at his notes, and finished the story he had come home to tell.

That was the last time I spoke to Ben Hogan, the last time I saw him in person. Years later, after I published my book on the history of the early PGA tour, I got a letter from Ben, forwarded through my publisher.

It was dated December 1988, the year Hogan made his last major public appearance. He went to New York, to the Waldorf-Astoria, for *Golf* magazine's celebration of the hundredth anniversary of the USGA. The magazine named "One Hundred Heroes" of the sport that night, including Jack Nicklaus, whom they voted Professional of the Century. But those of us who knew Ben Hogan felt otherwise. He was our hero, not just for the twentieth century but for all time.

Anyway, where was I? Ah, yes, my letter from Hogan. It was the only personal note I ever received from him, and the first time I'd heard from him in four decades.

I followed his career, naturally, from the tragedy of his car accident in '49, to the gripping U.S. Open win sixteen months later

at Merion. And, naturally, I gloried in his other victories, especially the 1953 British Open victory at Carnoustie, where he
clinched the triple crown of golf and was given a ticker-tape parade up Broadway in New York.

Hogan stopped playing competitively in 1967, but nevertheless, shortly before his fifty-fifth birthday, he stunned the golfing
world by shooting a record-tying 30, six under par, on the back
nine of Augusta National. His 66 was the low round of the Masters that year.

Because of time and circumstances and the randomness of life,
we never met again. As a college professor, with a family and
other responsibilities, I'd never had the chance to follow the sun,
so to speak, and meet up with him again on some distant fairway.
As Hogan told me, I had other worlds to travel, other lives to live.

So I treasure this letter. I didn't reprint it in this book, but I
would like to share it with you because in the letter he mentions
coming here to play at your country club.

Let me read it to you now.

Dear Jack,

*So wonderful to find you again, after all of these years, in the pages of
your book on those wonderful early years of the tour. You have done us
proud by telling these stories—stories, I must say, that brought a tear or
two to these old eyes of mine. You made me remember the best of times
and not the worst of those days when all of us, Byron and Jimmy and
Lloyd, were trying to make a life out of playing the game of golf.*

*I am especially pleased to have my memories of you as a boy back in
'46, and the time we spent together at that lovely club outside of Chicago.
You have turned out just fine, as I knew you would. Perhaps you were
right after all. Sometimes the smart move is to take a gamble and go for the
green, risk playing it from the long grass. It is what you did, having lost*

*your father, and then the tragedy of losing the young man you were so
fond of . . . I apologize for not remembering his name. You proved you
could overcome adversity. Not a small accomplishment.*

*After all these years, I am not so sure of all my comparisons between
golf and life. But I do still believe if you live your life like you play golf,
from the back tees and without any mulligans, you can stand taller and
look anyone in the eye.*

*That's what we humans have to keep doing, Jack: tee up, hit away, fol-
low the shot down the fairway, and play it where it lies. And you have
done that to great success and that is no small achievement for any person.*

With fond memories,

Ben Hogan

I wrote back, of course, but never heard from him again. Ben
would die nine years later, on July 25, 1997, at the age of eighty-
four. After his death, and after lovingly seeing all of the Hogan
memorabilia were safely at the USGA headquarters in Far Hills,
New Jersey, Valerie Hogan, too, passed away quietly in her sleep.

As for myself, well, the day Matt was killed I ran home in the
slanting light of early evening, my heart broken and my eyes blind
with tears. I didn't need to tell my mother what had happened
because Kathy had already phoned from the club. The next day
the papers were full of the story, but none of the truth. In the
sports pages of the *Chicago Tribune* they called it a tragedy, how a
young pro died on the very day he set a course record in the first
round of the Chicago Open.

I never returned to the club, not once, until this weekend. I
grew up and went from the farm to the army, with the G.I. Bill
paying my way through college. Like Hogan, I was a poor kid, but
my chosen career in academics has given me a wonderful and rich
life. I have also been blessed with a loving wife, children, and

somedays it seems endless grandchildren. They have all made my life so much richer.

And through all these years, I have kept at my golf game, though unlike Hogan, I never imagined all my shots could be birdies. Still, I did try to follow his example—I used my local knowledge, studied the line, and then stepped up and took my best swing. It wasn't easy, getting from the farm to Korea and college, and safely home from Vietnam.

Sometimes, I did have to take my next shot from the long grass, as Hogan said I must. But I had my own good fortune, and along the way I even chipped a few in from the apron.

I would like to add one more personal note in closing. Matt and Sarah understood that for them to find happiness they had to risk it all for each other. They had to escape, so to speak, these country club grounds and the lives they were living.

It ended in tragedy for Matt, but, you know, after all these years, I can't help wonder if it wasn't the way Matt's life should have ended. It was, perhaps, the fate of the man who on the golf course always went for the green, always, as we say, played for broke.

To stretch my metaphors dangerously thin, let me end with this final thought: We cannot remake our past. Hogan could not go back in time and save his father from his suicide, nor could I have kept my dad away from war. We are all products of our past, but we also have the opportunity—and the duty—to be the protagonists of our own life stories. As Hogan said, the secret is always the next shot. That is true for life as it is true for golf. And that, finally, is the great lesson Ben Hogan taught me so long ago on those distance fairways of my youth. It is, truly, the great Ben

Hogan's secret that so many of us who play the game have tried to learn.

Well, I've said enough. Perhaps I've said too much. Thank you all for listening so patiently. It has been my pleasure to return here after so many years, to come home to a place that holds so many wonderful memories for me, a place where once I was lucky enough to have been Ben Hogan's caddie.

And now, I believe, if Dr. Hughes agrees, we may have time for one or two questions. Yes? The gentleman in the back standing next to your country club's coat of arms. Your question, sir?